MURDER
ON THE
EIFFEL TOWER

MURDER

ON THE

EIFFEL TOWER

CLAUDE IZNER

Translated by Isabel Reid

ST. MARTIN'S MINOTAUR ❧ NEW YORK

This is a work of fiction. All of the characters, organizations, and events portrayed in this novel are either products of the author's imagination or are used fictitiously.

www.minotaurbooks.com

Library of Congress Cataloging-in-Publication Data

Izner, Claude.
    [Mystère rue des Saints-Pères. English]
    Murder on the Eiffel Tower : a Victor Legris mystery / Claude Izner ; translated by Isabel Reid.
        p. cm.
    ISBN-13: 978-0-312-38374-9
    ISBN-10: 0-312-38374-6
    I. Reid, Isabel. II. Title.

PQ2709.Z64 M913 2008
843'.92—dc22

                2008020343

First published in France as *Mystère rue des Saints-Pères* by Éditions 10/18, Département d'Univers Poche

First St. Martin's Minotaur Edition: September 2008

10 9 8 7 6 5 4 3 2 1

Paris dresse sa tour
ainsi qu'une grande giraffe inquiète
sa tour
qui, le soir venu,
craint les fantômes.

Paris raises its tower
like a big, anxious giraffe
its tower
which, come night-time,
is frightened of ghosts.

PIERRE MAC ORLAN (*Tel était Paris*)

For Étia and Maurice
Jaime and Bernard
Jonathan and David
Rachel

MURDER ON THE EIFFEL TOWER

Claude Izner

Claude Izner is the pen-name of two sisters, Liliane Korb and Laurence Lefèvre. Both booksellers on the banks of the Seine, they are experts on nineteenth-century Paris.

PROLOGUE

12 May 1889

Storm clouds raced over the barren plain between the fortifications and the goods station at Les Batignolles, where the scrubby grass smelled unpleasantly of sewers. Rag-and-bone men, grouped around carts filled with household rubbish, were using their gaffs to level the mounds of detritus, raising eddies of dust. A train approached from far in the distance, gradually getting bigger and bigger.

A gang of children came running down the hillocks, shrieking: 'There he is! Buffalo Bill is coming!'

Jean Méring straightened up and, hands on hips, leant backwards to relieve his aching joints. It had been a good haul: a three-legged chair, a rocking horse that had lost its stuffing, an old umbrella, a soldier's epaulette and a piece of wash-basin rimmed with gold. He turned towards Henri Capus, a lean old man with a faded beard.

'I'm going to see the Redskins. Are you coming?' he said, adjusting the wicker basket on his shoulders.

He picked up his chair, passed the Cook Agency vehicles and joined the crowd of onlookers gathered around the station, a mixture of workmen, petit bourgeois, and high society people who had come in carriages.

With a great hiss of steam, a locomotive followed by an

endless convoy of coaches pulled up beside the platform. A covered wagon stopped in front of Jean Méring. Inside, panic-stricken horses were stamping wildly, and tossing their manes. Sunburned men in cowboy hats and Indians with painted faces and feather headdresses leant out of the doors. Everyone was jostling to catch a glimpse. Jean Méring slapped the nape of his neck: an insect sting. Immediately he faltered, slid sideways, staggered, and then stumbled against a woman, who pushed him away, thinking he was drunk. His legs buckled and, as he lost his grip on the chair, he sank to the ground, dragged down by the weight of his basket. He tried to raise his head but already he was too weak. He could faintly hear Henri Capus's voice.

'What's the matter, my friend? Hold on, I'll help you. Where does it hurt?'

With a tremendous effort Méring managed to gasp: 'A . . . bee . . .'

His eyes were watering and his sight was becoming blurred. Amazingly, in the space of just a few minutes, his whole body had become as limp as an old rag. He could no longer feel his limbs, his lungs were straining for air. In his last moments of lucid thought he knew that he was about to die. He made a final effort to cling to life, then let go, slipping into the abyss, down . . . down . . . down . . . The last thing he saw was a dandelion flower, which was blooming between the paving stones, as yellow as the sun.

LE FIGARO, 13 MAY 1889 (page 4)

CURIOUS DEATH OF A RAG-AND-BONE MAN

A rag-and-bone man from Rue de la Parcheminerie has died from a bee-sting. The accident occurred yesterday morning at Batignolles station as Buffalo Bill and his troupe arrived in Paris. Bystanders tried in vain to revive the victim. The enquiry has revealed that the dead man was Jean Méring, 42, a former Communard who had been deported to New Caledonia but returned to Paris after the amnesty of 1880.

The man crumpled the newspaper into a ball and tossed it into the waste-bin.

CHAPTER ONE

Wednesday 22 June

WEARING a tight new corset that creaked with every step, Eugénie Patinot walked down Avenue des Peupliers. She felt weary at the prospect of what already promised to be an exhausting day. Endlessly pestered by the children, she had reluctantly left the cool of the veranda. If outwardly she gave an impression of dignified composure, inside she was in turmoil: tightness in her chest, stomach cramps, a dull pain in her hip and, on top of everything, palpitations.

'Don't run, Marie-Amélie. Hector, stop whistling, it's vulgar.'

'We're going to miss the bus, Aunt! Hector and I are going to sit upstairs. Have you definitely got the tickets?'

Eugénie stopped and opened her reticule to make sure that she did have the tickets, which her brother-in-law had bought several days earlier.

'Hurry up, Aunt,' urged Marie-Amélie.

Eugénie glared. The child really knew how to annoy her. A capricious little boy, Hector was hardly any better. Only Gontran, the eldest, was tolerable, as long as he kept quiet.

There were about ten passengers waiting at the omnibus station on Rue d'Auteuil. Eugénie recognised Louise Vergne, the housemaid from the Le Massons. She was carrying a large basket of linen to the laundry, probably the one on Rue Mirabeau, and was quite unselfconsciously wiping her pale face with a handkerchief as big as a sheet. There was no way of avoiding her. Eugénie stifled her irritation. The woman was only a servant but always spoke to her as an equal, with overfamiliarity, and yet Eugénie had never dared point out this impropriety.

'Ah, Madame Patinot, how hot it is for June! I feel I might melt away.'

'That would be no bad thing,' muttered Eugénie.

'Are you going far, Madame Patinot?'

'To the Expo. These three little devils begged my sister to go.'

'Poor dear, the things you have to do. Aren't you frightened? All those foreigners . . .'

'I want to see Buffalo Bill's circus at Neuilly. There are real Redskins who shoot real arrows!'

'That's enough, Hector! Oh that's good, he's wearing odd socks – a white one, and a grey one.'

'It's coming, Aunt, it's coming!'

Omnibus A, drawn by three stolid horses, stopped by the pavement. Marie-Amélie ran upstairs.

'I can see your drawers,' shrieked Hector, following her up.

'I don't care! From up here everything's beautiful,' retorted the little girl.

Sitting next to Gontran, who was glued to her side, Eugénie reflected on the fact that the worst moments of one's life were those spent on public transport. She hated travelling; it made her feel lost and alone, like a dead leaf floating at the mercy of the tiniest breeze.

'Is that a new outfit you've bought yourself?' asked Louise Vergne.

The treachery of the question was not lost on Eugénie. 'It's a present from my sister,' she replied curtly, smoothing the silk of the flame-coloured dress into which she was tightly packed.

She omitted to mention that her sister had already worn the dress for two seasons, but added softly: 'Mind you don't miss your stop, my dear.'

Having silenced the tiresome woman, Eugénie opened her purse and counted her money, pleased that they had taken the omnibus rather than a carriage. The saving would give her a little more to put by. It was worth the sacrifice.

Louise Vergne rose haughtily like an offended duchess. 'If I were you, I would hide your bag. They say that all of London's pickpockets have emigrated to the Champ-de-Mars,' was her parting remark as she got off.

Immediately Gontran piped up, 'Did you know that they had to manufacture eighteen thousand pieces in the workshops of Levallois-Perret, and that it took two hundred workmen to assemble them on the site? People predicted that it would collapse after two hundred and eighty metres but it didn't.'

Here we go, thought Eugénie. 'What are you talking about?'

'Why, the Tower, of course!'

'Sit up straight and wipe your nose.'

'If you wanted to transport it somewhere else on wheels you would need ten thousand horses,' Gontran continued, rubbing his nose.

Hector and Marie-Amélie came bounding down from the top deck. 'We're here, look!'

Pointing straight up into the sky on the other side of the Seine, Gustave Eiffel's bronze-coloured tower was reminiscent of a giant streetlamp topped with gold. Panic-stricken, Eugénie searched for a pretext to get out of climbing it. When she couldn't think of one, she laid a hand on her pounding heart. *If I survive this I shall say fifty Paternosters at Notre-Dame d'Auteuil.*

The bus drew up in front of the enormous Trocadero Palace, flanked by minarets. Down below, beyond the grey ribbon of the river filled with boats, the fifty hectares of the Universal Exposition were spread before them.

Tightly clutching her bag, her eyes fixed on the children, Eugénie began her descent into hell. She charged down Colline de Chaillot, passing the fruits of the world display, the tortured bonsai of the Japanese garden, and the dark entrance of 'Journey to the Centre of the Earth' without a second glance. Though the whalebones of her corset chafed her ribs and her feet begged for mercy, she did not slacken her pace. She just wanted to get this over and done with as soon as possible and get back on terra firma . . .

Finally, she held out her tickets and pushed the children under the canopy of the Pont d'Iéna. 'Listen to me carefully,' she said slowly and deliberately. 'If you stray from me by so much as a centimetre – do you hear me? a centimetre – we're going home.'

Then she plunged headlong into the fray. A huge crowd was jostling around the multicoloured kiosks, forming a human tide of French people and foreigners of all races. The minstrels of

Leicester Square, with their soot-blackened faces, led the way along the left bank, to the rhythm of banjos.

With pounding heart, and overwhelmed by the noise, Eugénie clung to Gontran, who was unmoved by the hubbub. The Exposition seemed to come at them from all sides. Jostled between the street vendors, the Annamese rickshaw-pullers and Egyptian donkey-drivers, they finally succeeded in joining the queue in front of the southern pillar of the Tower.

Moving reluctantly along in the queue, Eugénie looked enviously at the elegant young people comfortably installed in special rolling chairs, pushed by employees in peaked caps. *That's what I need . . .*

'Aunt, look!'

She looked up and saw a forest of crossbars and small beams, in the midst of which a lift slid up and down. At once she was seized with a desire to flee as fast and far as her exhausted legs would carry her.

She dimly heard Gontran's monotonous voice: 'Three hundred and one metres . . . leading straight up to the second floor . . . four lifts. Otis, Combaluzier . . .'

Otis, Combaluzier. Something about those strange names suddenly reminded her of the projectile vehicle, in that book by Jules Verne whose title escaped her.

'Those preferring to walk up the one thousand seven hundred and ten steps will take an hour to do so . . .'

She remembered now: it was *From the Earth to the Moon*! What if the cables snapped . . . ?

'Aunt, I want a balloon! A helium balloon! A blue one! Give me a sou, Aunt, a sou!'

A clout on the ear more like!

She regained her self-control. A poor relation, given a roof over her head out of pure charity, could not afford to give free rein to her feelings. Regretfully she held out a sou to Hector.

Gontran was still reciting impassively from the Exhibition Guide. '. . . on average, eleven thousand visitors a day, and the Tower can accommodate ten thousand people at any one time . . .'

He stopped abruptly, sensing the icy glare of the man just ahead of them, an immaculately dressed middle-aged man of Japanese origin. He stared at Gontran unblinkingly until he lowered his eyes, then slowly turned away, satisfied.

Turning towards the ticket window, Eugénie was so overcome by panic that she was unable to string two words together.

Marie-Amélie pushed her aside and, standing on tiptoes, bellowed: 'Four tickets for the second platform, please.'

'Why the second? The first platform is high enough,' stammered Eugénie.

'We must sign the Golden Book in the *Figaro* Pavilion, have you forgotten? Papa insisted – he wants to read our names in the newspaper. Pay the lady, Aunt.'

Propelled to the back of the lift, close behind a Japanese man whose face bore an expression of childish delight, Eugénie collapsed onto a wooden bench and commended her soul to God. She could not stop thinking about an advertisement glimpsed in the *Journal des Modes* that declared: 'Do you lack iron? Are you anaemic? Chlorotic? Bravais tincture restores the blood and combats fatigue.'

'Bravais, Bravais, Bravais,' she chanted to herself.

There was a sudden jolt. Her heart in her mouth, she saw the red mesh of a birdcage passing by. She had just time to think, *Mon Dieu*, what am I doing here?, when the lift came to a stop on the second floor, one hundred and sixteen metres above the ground.

Leaning against the railing on the first floor of the Tower, Victor Legris was keeping an eye on the coming and going of the lifts. His business associate had suggested they meet between the Flemish restaurant and the Anglo-American bar. The gallery was crammed and the atmosphere was electric with the nervous laughter of women, the animated conversation of men. Those returning for a second visit looked blasé. The lifts stopped, discharged their cargo and set off again. A motley throng stretched back along the stairs. Victor loosened his cravat and undid his top shirt button. The sun was beating down and he was thirsty. Hat in hand, he wandered as far as the souvenir shop.

A blue balloon brushed past his nose and a piercing voice cried out: 'He was a cowboy, I tell you! He signed the Golden Book behind us. He comes from New York!'

Victor observed the two boys and the little girl whose face was pressed up against the shop window.

'Everything's so beautiful! The brooch with the Eiffel Tower on top, and the fans and the embroidered handkerchiefs . . .'

'Why do you never believe me?' yelled the little boy with the balloon. 'I'm sure he's part of Buffalo Bill's troupe!'

'That's enough about Buffalo Bill – why don't you look at the view instead?' The older boy pointed towards the horizon. 'Do you realise we can see Chartres from here? It's a hundred and twenty kilometres away. And there are the towers of Notre-Dame and there, those of Saint-Sulpice. Then there's the dome of the Panthéon, the Val-de-Grâce. It's amazing, like being giants in *Gulliver's Travels*!'

'What are those things that look like enormous boiled eggs?'

'That's the Observatory. And further away over there is Montmartre, where they're building the Basilica.'

'It looks like a piece of pumice stone,' muttered the younger boy. 'Gontran, if I let my balloon go will it float all the way to America?'

I would love to be their age and have their enthusiasm, thought Victor. Even if they live fifty years more, they'll never know greater excitement than this.

He caught sight of his reflection in the shop window: a slim man of medium height, thirtyish, with a harassed expression and a thick moustache.

Is that really me? Why do I look so disillusioned?

He went up to the railing and glanced down on the hordes of people milling around the Palace of Fine Arts, hurrying up Rue du Caire, storming the little Decauville train and massing in front of the vast Machinery Hall. Suddenly he felt that the atmosphere had become hostile.

'Aunt, look after my balloon.'

Glued to her seat like a barnacle to a rock, Eugénie Patinot was determined not to move. Without a word of protest she let Hector knot the string of the balloon around her wrist. The garlands and flags of the Flemish restaurant fluttered in a light breeze and made her vertigo worse. She recalled a few lines of a song:

> *Le doux vertige de l'amour*
> *Souffle parfois sur nos vieux jours . . .*

She felt suddenly sick.

'Marie-Amélie, stay with me.'

'That's not fair! The boys are—'

'Do as you're told.'

She was worn out after that interminable wait on the second platform with all the people wanting to sign the Golden Book, pushing and shoving. Her cheeks were flushed and her hands trembled – where would she find the courage to bear the lift ride for a third time? Clumsily, she tucked a lock of grey hair back under her hat. Someone sat down beside her, rose again, stumbled, and leant heavily on her shoulder without apologising. She let out a little cry – something had stung her on the base of the neck. A bee? Yes, definitely a bee! She waved her arms in fright and jumped to her feet, then lost her balance as her legs refused to hold her. She managed to sit back down on the bench. A feeling of great heaviness began to spread through her limbs and she had difficulty breathing. She leant back against the gallery partition. If only she could go to sleep, and forget her fear and tiredness . . . Just before she lost consciousness she remembered something the priest had said to her after the death of her child: 'Life here on earth is only a sort of prelude, it is written in the Bible, and the Bible is the Word of God.' She saw Marie-Amélie run away, disappearing into the crowd, but she didn't have the strength to call her back as a weight was pressing down on her chest. Before her watering eyes the crowd drifted heedlessly in a circle that seemed to close in on her, nearer and nearer . . .

Victor was fanning himself with his hat at the entrance to the Anglo-American bar as he tried to spot his friend Marius Bonnet amongst the mosaic of dark frock coats and light-coloured dresses. Someone tapped him on the shoulder and he turned towards a small plump man of about forty, who was hiding his advancing baldness under a Panama hat worn at an angle.

'I say, Marius, what's got into you? Why did you choose a place like this to meet? In honour of what? I didn't understand your message at all.'

'Oh, don't complain: the world seen from up here seems quite ridiculous and that fortifies the soul. Where's your business associate?'

'He's coming. So, tell me, what's this all about?'

'We're celebrating the fiftieth issue of my newspaper. The first edition came out on the fourth of May, on the eve of the centenary celebrations of the opening of the Estates General at Versailles. Personally, I'm happy to make do with a three-hundred-metre tower, and I wanted you to join the party.'

'So you're no longer a reporter for *Le Temps*?'

'I've given up working at *Le Temps*. A great deal has

happened since I last visited your bookshop! Have you forgotten our discussion?'

'I must admit that I didn't really take your plans seriously.'

'Well, old chap, you're going to be surprised. And if I have gone ahead, it's partly because of your business associate.'

'Kenji?'

'Yes, Monsieur Mori really cut me to the quick when he mocked my indecisiveness. So I took the plunge; you see before you the director and editor-in-chief of *Le Passe-partout*, a daily newspaper with a great future. Besides, I want to make you a very interesting proposition.'

Victor considered Marius's chubby face doubtfully. He had met him some years earlier at the house of the painter Meissonier, and had been very taken with the voluble and enthusiastic southerner. Marius was a witty conversationalist, peppered his speech with literary quotations, and charmed both men and women with his apparent candour, but he also had a razor-sharp tongue and never hesitated to voice what others thought wiser to keep to themselves.

'Come, I'm going to introduce you to our team. There are only a few of us. We're a long way off rivalling the eighty thousand copies sold by *Le Figaro* but being small doesn't stop you being great – think of Alexander.'

They pushed their way through the crowd to a table where two men and two women sat sipping drinks.

'Children, let me introduce Victor Legris, my learned bookseller friend whom I've often spoken about. His collaboration will be invaluable to us. Victor, this is Eudoxie Allard, our peerless secretary, accountant, co-ordinator and general factotum.'

Eudoxie Allard, a languorous, heavy-lidded brunette, looked him up and down and, judging him to be of only limited and strictly professional interest, gave him a noncommittal smile.

'That chap dressed like a dandy is Antonin Clusel. He's an expert at unearthing information,' Marius went on. 'Besides, you've already met him; he's been to your bookshop with me. He's very persistent: once he's on the trail of something he never gives up.'

Victor saw an affable young man with flaxen hair, whose nose bent slightly to the left. Beside him was a large disillusioned-looking fellow with protuberant eyes, who was contemplating his glass.

'To his right, Isidore Gouvier, police deserter. He can gain access to the most secret information. Finally, Mademoiselle Tasha Kherson, a compatriot of Turgenev's and our illustrator and caricaturist.'

Victor shook everyone's hands but only remembered the illustrator's first name, Tasha, with her red hair pulled back in a chignon under a little hat decorated with marguerites, and her pretty unmade-up face. She looked at him with friendly interest, and a wave of warmth spread through him. He made a real effort to follow what Marius was saying, but was distracted by the slightest movement of the young woman.

Tasha was surreptitiously watching him. She had a vague feeling that she knew him. He gave the impression of being on the defensive, withdrawn, yet neither his voice nor his manner betrayed any shyness. Where had she seen that profile before?

'Ah, at last, here's Monsieur Kenji Mori!' Marius exclaimed.

Victor rose from his chair and suddenly Tasha remembered where she had seen him: he reminded her of a subject in a Le Nain painting.

'Over here, Monsieur Mori!'

The new arrival came over, very much at ease, and bowed while Marius made the introductions once more. When it came to the turn of Eudoxie and Tasha, Kenji Mori doffed his bowler hat and kissed their hands.

There was a moment's silence. Marius asked him if he liked champagne. Kenji Mori replied that although the sparkling drink could never compare to sake, he would be delighted to have a glass. Impressed by the virile allure of this polite, refined Asian man, Eudoxie speedily revised her preconceptions of him. The others seemed to be expecting something from Kenji Mori. He had unwittingly upset the equilibrium of the group.

'My friend Victor's business associate is Japanese,' announced Marius triumphantly.

Victor noticed Tasha's almost imperceptible smile. Their eyes met and she saw his expression change. He finds me attractive, she thought. She would have liked to sketch his face: *he has an interesting, sensual mouth . . .*

Leaning towards Kenji Mori, Eudoxie asked: 'Have you visited the Japanese Pavilion?'

'I'm not interested in Japanese knick-knacks manufactured in bulk and intended for bazaars,' he replied without departing from his customary affability.

'Yet there are some beautiful pieces on display,' said Tasha, 'especially the prints . . .'

'In the West, few people who are not experts understand that kind of pictorial art. For them they are nothing more than pretty, exotic images with which to decorate the Henri the Second-style drawing rooms. You clutter your homes with such a profusion of objects that in the end you don't notice any of them.'

Tasha protested vehemently. 'You're wrong! Why tar everyone with the same brush? I was lucky enough to see the exhibition of Japanese prints organised by the Van Gogh brothers. *The Great Wave* by Hokusai made a real impression on me.'

Isidore Gouvier suddenly intervened. 'Talking about making an impression – up here one might almost be on the bridge of a transatlantic liner,' he remarked in a sinister tone. 'All we need is a really good ground swell to topple this red pylon you've made me climb.'

They laughed.

'Don't criticise Monsieur Eiffel's Tower. It's the technical apotheosis of our century,' declared Kenji Mori. 'It's amazing to think its seven thousand tonnes of iron weigh no more heavily on the ground than a ten-metre-high wall.'

'Especially if that wall were as long as the Great Wall of China,' retorted Tasha.

There was a silence. Victor studied the pretty redhead. Twenty-two, twenty-three years old at most. She had a self-confidence that was very provocative. He felt his heart quicken, then regain its normal rhythm.

Antonin Clusel got up, muttering: 'I'm going to the gallery for a cigarette.'

Marius cleared his throat. 'Children, a toast to a prosperous future for *Le Passe-partout* and our new literary columnist, Victor Legris.'

'Not so fast. You can't trap me like that. I'll have to think about it first,' laughed Victor.

'*Boss*! It's an emergency!'

Everyone turned to look at Antonin Clusel.

'What is it?'

'There's a woman outside. She's dead.'

Marius leaped up. 'To work, children. Tasha, I want sketches, right away. Eudoxie, hurry back to the office – we'll have to prepare a special edition. Quickly! Isidore, off you go to police headquarters and try to find out the exact cause of death. Antonin, you come with me.'

He turned to his guests. 'Monsieur Mori, Victor, I do apologise, but news waits for nobody. Think about my proposition!' he called before dashing outside.

The lift operating on the southern pillar had been halted on their floor. Marius Bonnet, Antonin Clusel and Tasha Kherson elbowed their way through the barrage of onlookers and reached the bench where the body of a woman in a red dress lay. She was open-mouthed and her skin was livid. Her dilated pupils were staring at a blue balloon, which floated on the end of a string tied to her wrist. Driven by force of habit, Tasha took a sketchbook out of her bag and quickly did a rough drawing of the scene: the dead woman, her hat, which had fallen on the ground, and the sorrowful and yet inquisitive expressions of the people tightly packed around her.

'Did anyone see anything?' asked Marius.

'Are you from the police?'

'I'm a journalist.'

'I was there!' shouted a pleasant-looking woman. 'What terrible luck — to pay forty sous just to end up dead! It's expensive, Monsieur, two francs to get to the first floor of this Tower, which is scarcely higher than the top of Notre-Dame. When you add the price of entry to the Exposition, that makes a hundred sous, a day's work, just to end up like this . . .'

'Your name?' Marius was equipped with a notebook.

'Simone Langlois, seamstress. I noticed that lady as I went by. She looked as if she was suffering; I get vertigo too. I thought it couldn't be that serious, and in any case she had her children with her.'

'Her children?'

'Yes, the two boys and the girl, over there. The youngest had given her his balloon. I went into the souvenir shop, just to have a look. It's lovely but expensive.'

'Is that them?' Marius indicated three children huddled together.

Simone Langlois nodded. 'When I came out again, the woman was asleep. Her little girl was shaking her and whining: "Let's go now, I'm hungry, I want a toffee apple." The woman's head was flopping from side to side . . .'

The seamstress punctuated her speech with theatrical gestures, clearly excited to be the centre of attention.

'I went up to her, in case she was really ill. I hardly touched her and she keeled over like a rag doll. I think I actually screamed. Some gentlemen ran over and picked her up. When I saw her face I thought I would faint.'

Antonin Clusel had crouched down to the children's level. The little girl was quietly whimpering.

'I want Mama . . . Mama!'

'Where do you live?'

'Avenue des Peupliers, in Auteuil . . . She was stung by a bee.'

'A bee? Are you sure?'

'Yes, I'm sure. She went, "Ow!", and said, "I've been stung by a bee."'

'What's your name?'

'Marie-Amélie de Nanteuil. I want to go home.'

'Are they your brother and sister?' Antonin asked the older of the two boys.

'Yes, Monsieur.'

'We're going to notify your father.'

'No, he works at the Ministry; it's Mama you should tell.'

Antonin looked at the body in bewilderment. Marius came to the rescue.

'So that lady's not your mother? Is she your governess?'

'She's our Aunt Eugénie, she lives with us.'

'Eugénie de Nanteuil?'

'Eugénie Patinot, she's . . . she *was* my mother's sister,' mumbled Gontran, whose eyes were filling with tears.

'Out of the way, please! Let's have some space!'

There was a ripple of movement and exclamations. A police inspector followed by two stretcher-bearers squeezed through the crowd.

'I've got their address, Boss,' murmured Antonin, who had just questioned Hector.

'Jump in a cab and go and find out what you can from the family, the servants, even the dog! I want to know everything about the victim, her past, where she spent her time, the colour of her skirts. I want enough copy for an article as long as your arm! This time *Le Matin* will not have the scoop on a story! Let's go!'

Leaning on the terrace of the Anglo-American bar, Victor and Kenji watched as, down below, the stretcher-bearers removed the body of a woman in red.

'I fear we'll have to walk down,' remarked Kenji, startling Victor who, pressed against the guardrail, was totally absorbed in his contemplation of the impertinent Russian redhead as she argued with Marius Bonnet.

'Come on, let's go while there aren't too many people on the stairs,' he added impatiently. 'I'm not disappointed that the meeting was cut short; that illustrator has no manners and your journalist friend is a charlatan. Are you really going to write a literary column for him?'

'I have no idea,' replied Victor distractedly. 'Do you mind if I stay here a moment?'

'On the Tower? Have you been seduced by the architecture?'

'No, no, at the Exposition. There's a photographic section in the Palace of Liberal Arts and I'd like to see the newest camera models.'

They passed the French restaurant and started down the stairs. In front of them, a father was teaching his offspring about the method of climbing the Tower extolled by Gustave Eiffel.

'Slowly, children, with your hands on the rail. That's right. Now swing your body from side to side, take your time.'

'Excuse us, excuse us,' said Kenji, adding under his breath to Victor: 'Some people are quite mad! They go up on their knees, or on stilts, or backwards.'

As they reached ground level, policemen were pushing aside onlookers in order to clear a way for the stretcher-bearers, who were coming out of the lift. Victor could just discern fingers sticking out from under a sheet thrown over the body.

'I'm going back to the bookshop,' said Kenji. 'I don't like to leave Joseph to his own devices for too long. Do you know what his nickname for the Comtesse de Salignac is? The battle-axe! One of our most important customers!'

'The one who swears by Zénaïde Fleuriot?'

They crossed the French garden, which was laid out around the base of the Tower, interspersed with waterfalls and copses. Victor glanced up. What looked like an inverted exclamation mark was drifting towards the Machinery Hall: it was the blue balloon.

'Kenji, wait, have you forgotten?'

'Forgotten what?'

'The date – it's the twenty-second of June. Here you are, this is for you.'

With an air of mystery he held out a little parcel. Surprised, Kenji untied the golden string, to find, wrapped in tissue paper, a fob-watch.

'My mother gave it to me,' Victor went on. 'It belonged to my father and now it's yours. Happy birthday.'

'I was hoping you would forget about my birthday,' said Kenji, laughing. 'I'm fifty, you know!'

He turned away, looking at the watch, unable to speak. Finally he whispered, 'Thank you.'

He slipped the watch into his waistcoat and hurried off, not noticing that a piece of paper had fallen out of his pocket.

'I say, Kenji, you've dropped . . .'

But he was long gone. Victor smiled. It was typical of Kenji. Whenever he felt moved, he preferred to make an exit. Victor bent down to pick up the small-format newspaper printed over four pages.

LE FIGARO

UNIVERSAL EXPOSITION 1889

SPECIAL EDITION PRINTED ON THE EIFFEL TOWER

This edition has been presented to Monsieur Kenji Mori as a souvenir of his visit to the *Figaro* Pavilion on the second platform of the Eiffel Tower 115.73 metres above the Champ-de-Mars.

Paris, 22 June 1889

Victor couldn't help smiling. So that's why Kenji had been late arriving at the Anglo-American bar. He carefully put away the newspaper, which he would leave discreetly at Kenji's; there was no need for him to know that Victor had uncovered his little secret.

He turned off towards the Central American Pavilion, and skirted around the exotic plantations of Bolivia and Chile. A thin Englishwoman, a member of the Temperance Union, gripped his arm and demanded he buy one of her brochures condemning alcohol as the poison of heretics. He had barely extricated himself from this when a sandwich man gave him a handbill, announcing 'the big parade of Colonel Cody, the celebrated Buffalo Bill'. Irritated by all these useless bits of paper, he crossed the sumptuous foyer of the Palace of Liberal Arts and immersed himself in the labyrinth of halls, looking for George Eastman's famous camera.

'You press the button and Kodak does the rest, what a clever advertisement,' he was muttering to himself as he came down the stairs, when he suddenly found himself in a chamber of horrors, packed with scalpels, lancets, trocars, forceps, and acoustic wigs. *Quick, find the exit.* He hurried past, head down to avoid the graphic illustrations of the dangers of morphine addiction. When he saw a way out, he headed straight for it, only to end up surrounded by anatomical mouldings of frightening precision. He rushed towards the central rotunda, then suddenly stopped, having just spotted the Russian illustrator from *Le Passe-partout*, clutching a sketchbook in her lace-gloved hand. His pulse quickened. How vivacious she looked in her pearl-grey skirt and fitted jacket! He felt this slight woman wanted to gobble up life whilst capturing it with her pencil.

'I'm lost,' he admitted to her.

'So am I. I was hoping to see the model of the great temple at Ava dedicated to Buddha and I found myself in the prosthetics section instead. Have you seen it?' she laughed.

'What? Buddha?'

'No, the two-headed foetus! Let's get out of here!'

'Ice cream! Ice cream! Lovely vanilla ice cream!'

'Can I buy you one?' he asked her. 'To calm our nerves.'

'I have work to do and . . . I'd like to see Rue du Caire.'

'In that case you'll need a large ice cream. It's very hot in the land of the pyramids.'

Along Avenue de Suffren were a Chinese pavilion, a Romanian restaurant and an *isba*. They crossed the Moroccan quarter and immediately found themselves in the heart of the Egyptian bazaar.

'This is a rather haphazard way of travelling round the globe,' said Victor, who was not the least distracted from his interest in Tasha by the hustle and bustle around them.

She barely reached his shoulder and sometimes had to quicken her step to keep up with him. They wandered amongst the little donkeys grouped on the *moucharaby*. Stopping in front of a display of Egyptian cigarettes, Tasha took out her sketchbook and pencil. Looking over her shoulder, Victor saw the outline of a body on a bench with three tense-looking children standing next to it.

'What's that?' he asked, his eye drawn to the curve of her cheek.

She closed her sketchbook quickly with a look of concern.

'That woman, on the Tower . . . dying like that in the middle of all the festivities . . . I've got to go.'

'Can I leave you anywhere? I'm going home as well.'

'Where is your shop?'

'Eighteen Rue des Saints-Pères. You can't miss it, the sign says: "Elzévir, New and Antiquarian Books".'

'I'm going in the opposite direction, to Rue Notre-Dame-de-Lorette.'

'That's ideal, I have a meeting on Boulevard Haussmann,' he said quickly.

She looked at him with amusement and, after pretending to hesitate for a moment, accepted his offer.

He hailed a cab on Avenue de Saffron. Sitting side by side, they remained silent. Victor felt embarrassed. This girl was so unlike the other women he knew! You almost had to drag the words out of her mouth.

'How long have you been in Paris?'

'Almost two years.'

'I love your lilting accent. It has a touch of the Midi about it.'

She turned towards him and paused, giving her a pretext to study his profile, before replying in an intentionally exaggerated accent: 'Oh, you're from Odessa, Mademoiselle, they say in Moscow, while in Paris they say: she's from Marseille!'

Victor looked baffled, but then quickly caught on.

'Odessa, the Crimea, Little Russia, port on the Black Sea, cosmopolitan city hailed by Pushkin. The Duc de Richelieu, descendant of the famous cardinal, was governor at the beginning of the century. There is a statue of him there, if I'm not mistaken?'

'No, you're right. He sits on a throne in Roman dress at the top of a hundred and ninety-two steps, which join the port to the upper town. Marius is right, you are a mine of information, Monsieur Legris,' she declared with a straight face.

'Be kind to us scholars: all I do is read the travel writing I come across,' he said modestly. 'You yourself have mastered perfectly the subtleties of the language of Molière. Did you have a French governess?'

She burst out laughing.

'My mother is the daughter of French merchants and my father the son of German settlers. I learnt to juggle both languages from birth.'

'Have you worked for Marius long?'

'Three months. I managed to convince him that I was a gifted caricaturist.'

'Would you like to show me?' he asked, handing her the Buffalo Bill flier.

'With pleasure. I don't like him.'

With a few swift pencil lines she transformed the dashing Colonel Cody into a cartoon picador riding an old nag and pointing a rifle and bayonet at a bison begging for mercy.

'You've completely ruined it!' he exclaimed in dismay.

As he didn't seem to want to take back the flier, she stowed it in her bag saying: 'I enjoyed that, I really don't like that murderer. Do you know that in 1862 there were roughly nine thousand bison between the Missouri and the Rocky Mountains? They've all disappeared. There were also nearly two hundred thousand Sioux Indians, and those who are still alive have been parked in reservations.'

'Perhaps it's stupid of me,' said Victor, keen to change the subject, 'but I don't understand the attraction of illustrations in novels. It doubles the size of the book.'

'A good illustration can sometimes say more than an entire chapter. At the moment I'm illustrating a French adaptation of Shakespeare's tragedies. I am looking for models for the witches of *Macbeth*, and the surgical exhibition didn't inspire me much!' she laughed.

'You should take a look at Goya's *Los Caprichos*.'

'Do you have them?'

'A first edition, a superb quarto, eighty plates, with no discoloration,' he murmured, looking at her intently.

He had just noticed the roundness of her breasts beneath her white bodice. She moved away from him slightly.

'It belongs to my friend Kenji,' he went on, sitting back.

'The Japanese gentleman with the trenchant opinions?'

'Oh, indulge him. The current fashion for Japanese curios gets on his nerves.'

'You seem very fond of him.'

'He raised me. I lost my father when I was eight. We were living in London. Without Kenji's devotion, my mother would never have survived – she had no head for business.'

'How long ago was that?'

Was she trying to guess his age?

'Twenty-one years.'

'I scc . . .'

She fell silent again.

'When will you come by the bookshop?' he asked, trying to sound casual.

'I'll have to see – I have a very busy schedule.'

He frowned. Was there a man? Several, possibly. You could never tell with a woman like this.

'You have many demands on your time,' he said, feigning a sudden interest in the wooden cobbles of Boulevard des Capucines.

'Yes, I have to sell my skills to survive.'

The remark startled Victor.

'You can rarely live on what satisfies the spirit. *Le Passepartout* and illustrating books are what pay for my meals and rent.'

'And what is it that satisfies your spirit?'

'Painting. I learnt intaglio engraving and aquatint from my father at a very young age, and my mother taught me watercolour painting and drawing. They ran an art school and were real artists. My father painted and . . .' She shook her head. 'Let's leave the past buried in the past. In my eyes the only thing that matters is creativity. I don't know if I have any talent, I don't know if what I do may touch other people, but I can no more stop painting than an alcoholic can stop drinking. That is what counts for me; the end result is secondary.'

'Of course,' agreed Victor, who wasn't sure that he quite understood.

Odette wearied him with her holidays to Houlgate, her latest outfits, her society gossip. He suddenly felt upset to have such an insipid mistress. How different she was from this girl!

'And you?'

'Me?'

'Do you have a passion?'

'I like books and . . . photography. I bought an Acmé in London last winter. It's like a little dark room – people also call it a detective camera – and I . . . but I'm boring you.'

'No, no, I assure you, it's not because I'm a woman that I find technology impenetrable.'

'Right then, in that case I'll tell you about bromide plates, which will soon be overtaken by flexible celluloid film.'

Her consternation made him laugh.

'So you do understand.'

'I don't understand at all.'

Perhaps he had annoyed her. He wished he hadn't said anything.

'Like yours, my hobby comes with a certain amount of theory, but once you've mastered the basic principles—'

'It's not a hobby,' she cut him off abruptly.

'I beg your pardon?'

'Painting. It's not a hobby. When I paint I feel alive in every part of my being. It's not like . . . crocheting a doily!'

She drew back, leaning against the window. He could have hit himself.

'Are you angry? Please excuse me, I've been stupid.'

With a huge effort she turned towards him and gave him a forced smile.

'I'm a little tired at the moment, on edge.'

Stuck in a traffic jam on Boulevard de Clichy, the cab had not moved for a while.

'I'm going to get out here. We're very near my house. Goodbye,' was her parting remark as she opened the cab door.

'Wait!'

He couldn't stop her; she had already jumped onto the road. The driver of another cab cursed her and cracked his whip.

Victor hurriedly paid for their journey and followed Tasha, who was making quick progress up Rue Fontaine. *As long as she doesn't turn round* . . . She stopped on the edge of the pavement and he hid behind a Morris column. She set off again, crossed Rue Pigalle and went up Rue Notre-Dame-de-Lorette to number 60, where she pushed open the door of a heavy Haussmannian building.

His short-lived relief at finding out her address immediately gave way to a new worry: what if it was the home of one of her lovers? He would have to check by asking Marius. That meant he would have to see Marius, and no doubt accept his offer of writing a column.

Tomorrow, I'll go tomorrow, and if it really is where she lives, I shall send her flowers to apologise.

Apologise for what? Shouldn't she be the one to apologise? She hadn't even thanked him for the lift. He shrugged his shoulders. Women always had to be in the right!

As he wandered down Rue Le Peletier, imagining his next meeting with her, a newspaper vendor bumped into him, brandishing a special edition.

'Forty sous just to die! Buy *Le Passe-partout*! Mysterious death on the first floor of the three-hundred-metre Tower! Read the whole story for five centimes!'

CHAPTER TWO

Thursday 23 June

VICTOR went along Rue Croix-des-Petits-Champs. He had decided to have lunch in a brasserie on one of the Boulevards before making his mind up. He knew exactly what he would say: 'I was passing, so I thought I'd come and discuss your proposition.' At any rate it was his pretext for seeing Tasha again to make his peace with her. He had outlined the beginning of an article entitled 'French as It Is Written', sparing neither Balzac: 'A police commissioner silently replies, "She is not mad."' (*Cousin Bette*), nor Lamartine: 'The soles of my feet hurt from their desire to go out with you, Geneviève' (*Geneviève*), nor Vigny: 'That old servant in the employ of Marshal Effiat who had been dead for six months got ready to leave again' (*Cinq-Mars*).

He passed the headquarters of *L'Éclair* newspaper and turned into Galerie Véro-Dodat, looking for the sign of *Le Passe-partout*. Nothing. He turned on his heel, then, on the off chance, tried a metal gate that opened onto a row of courtyards. A song floated on the air, and there was a smell of honeysuckle and horsedung. He skirted a cart full of animal feed parked in front of a grain warehouse, passed some stables, and stopped a moment to watch two boys push a paper boat along the water in the gutter.

The editorial offices of *Le Passe-partout* were at the end of a blind alley: a dilapidated single-storey building wedged between a printing works and an engraver's workshop. He went in, and climbed up the spiral staircase, bumping into Eudoxie Allard and Isidore Gouvier, who were keeping watch behind a half-open door.

Isidore who was smoking a cigar, winked at Victor and joked, 'You've really got the little redhead's hackles up.'

'The redhead?' Victor asked.

Eudoxie turned and stared at him coldly. 'Can I help you?'

'May I see Monsieur Bonnet?'

'He has somebody with him,' she replied.

'And . . . Mademoiselle Tasha?'

'Absent. If you would like to wait . . .' She pointed to a low divan next to a pile of newspapers.

Disconcerted, Victor sat down, crossed his legs and picked up a copy of *Le Passe-partout*. Page one was almost entirely taken up with a satirical picture showing the Eiffel Tower chastely veiled in a flared underskirt. An enormous threatening bee circled its campanile, which wore a feathered hat. He could not resist a smile when he made out the artist's signature: 'Tasha K'.

He looked further down to find the main headline:

ACCIDENTAL DEATH OR MURDER?

We have the right to ask, having received the following anonymous message:

> *I won't spell it out*
> *But poor Eugénie Patinot*
> *Knew more than she ought.*

Are we dealing with a homicidal beekeeper who settles scores via an apian intermediary? Yesterday, towards the end of the day . . .

Victor started as loud shouting erupted suddenly from Marius's office.

'I'm warning you, Bonnet, one more article like this and—'

'Come now, Inspector, freedom of the press has existed for eight years, if I'm not mistaken.'

'Do you want to sabotage the Expo? The drawing on the front page is revolting.'

'That isn't what the public thinks. Do you know how many copies we sold this morning and how many we'll sell this evening, tomorrow and the day after that?'

'You've blown up out of all proportion a run-of-the-mill news story! What gives you the right to assert that the Patinot woman's death was suspicious?'

'I'm not asserting anything. I'm just posing the question.'

'Look here, Bonnet, you know as well as I do! The police are inundated with anonymous letters as soon as anybody kicks the bucket in unusual circumstances. Give me the message.'

'You have the one that was sent to *L'Éclair*, that should be enough, and in any case I don't know what I've done with it.'

The door opened suddenly, and out came a tall, furious-looking man. Isidore and Eudoxie raced back to their seats, and Victor stood up, slipping the newspaper into his pocket.

'Inspector!' called Marius from the doorway of his office. 'If this woman died of respiratory trouble, why has the investigation been entrusted to you? . . . Oh, Victor, I didn't know you were here. Did you hear us?'

'Vaguely. Who was that?'

'Inspector Lecacheur. Not a bad sort of fellow, but a bit dense. Have you read the latest news?'

'No.'

'The newspapers have received an anonymous letter leading one to suppose that it was murder, but the doctors have concluded that it was death from natural causes.'

'You mean that woman yesterday, on the Tower?'

'Yes. There are two possibilities: either these lines of doggerel are the work of some joker, or else someone did kill her. How? It's a mystery. The police probably know more than they're letting on. As to motives . . . was Eugénie Patinot, a pious and respectable widow, involved in blackmail? Was she witness to something she should not have seen?'

Marius pulled his waistcoat down over his stomach, bit off the end of his Havana cigar and spat it out.

'By putting Tasha's cartoon on the front page, I've alienated myself from all the "serious" press, who are forever trumpeting their claims of impartiality and so-called integrity! I'm running a huge risk, but I know I'm right. Follow me, I'll show you my new installation. Mind the staircase, it's riddled with woodworm. Have you given any thought to my proposition?'

'I'm in two minds. If I write what I really think, I'm worried I shall make trouble for you and irritate your readers.'

'Rubbish! Find an original way to put your ideas across and people will read you, that's the main thing. Follow my example and don't give it a second thought. You see, a newspaper is an ephemeral thing: printed articles end up at the fishmongers', the fried-potato sellers' or in public conveniences. What's published today is forgotten about tomorrow. We need fresh news every day to feed people's curiosity. What does the reader want for his five centimes? Everyday stories, dramas, scandals, superficial news, and murders.'

'That's quite sad.'

'You can't get away from it, old man, crime and sensationalist stuff are the kind of bread-and-butter news stories that make the cash registers ring.'

'You are very cynical!'

'I'm not, it's just what the public demands. Look, can you see the difference?' Marius was brandishing a copy of *Le Passepartout* and also one of *Le Gaulois*. 'On the one hand we have a daily without political ambition, on the other a mediocre newspaper stuffed with formal, solemn writing. Look, this article about General Boulanger, what's the purpose of that? The Republic no longer has to fear a *coup d'état* from him. The strong feelings towards him have evaporated. The French are fickle; they've replaced their blond prancing idol with a three-hundred-metre-high tower. You know, ordinary people could not care less about the parliamentary gazette, society events or financial reviews. They prefer an insipid saga that keeps them in suspense. I apply the only principle that pays: always please the greatest number of readers to achieve our sole aim of increasing circulation. As Flaubert said, "There are no fine subjects: Yvetot is as good as Constantinople!"'

He led Victor behind a partition where a man was running his fingers over the keyboard of a strange machine run on compressed air, which was spluttering out puffs of steam.

'This little marvel has cost me a fortune. It was invented by a German who emigrated to the United States, a genius called Ottmar Mergenthaler – remember that name. It's come directly to us from across the Atlantic. I'm the only person to own one in France.' He caressed the machine with the tenderness of a lover. 'Wonderful Linotype! Casting its own characters and creating lines of type ready for printing. Speed, old man, speed, that's what it's all about! I can bring out two or three editions a day! Soon I'll be based on the Boulevards. I'll expand my team, I've got big plans. From next week I'm launching a series of articles called "A Day at the Expo with . . .", personalities from the world of science, literature, the fine arts and fashion. The first one will be Savorgnan de Brazza – he has agreed to do it. In an age when immigration is a cause of discontent, it's interesting to recall that the man who gave us the Congo is an Italian who became a naturalised Frenchman after defending the Tricolour in 1870. Can I offer you a glass of something?'

'No, thank you. I have some book purchases to make.'

'Don't forget my literary column.'

'I'll think about it. Oh . . . I promised to lend a book to your illustrator, Sacha . . .'

'Tasha Kherson?'

'Yes. I wanted my assistant to deliver it to her, but I've mislaid her address.'

'Sixty, Rue Notre-Dame-de-Lorette. Watch out for the owner, a German woman in spectacles, and worse than any guard dog!'

Victor hastened to take his leave. He felt a lightness of spirit, just like a schoolboy who's managed to get off school. What flowers could he give her? Roses? Lilies? He jumped into a cab on Rue de Rivoli and closed his eyes, better to ponder the question.

A cab drew up on Rue des Saints-Pères, in front of the Hôpital de la Charité. A middle-aged man alighted in a dark frock coat and a top hat. He crossed the road, stopped for a few moments outside Debauve and Gallais, manufacturers of 'fine and hygienic' products, salivated over an advertisement singing the praises of carminative chocolate with angelica. He passed Rue Jacob, the breeding ground of such celebrated publishing houses as Firmin-Didot and Hetzel, and arrived at number 18, home to the Elzévir bookshop. In the shop windows, which were set in wood panelling of a greeny-bronze colour, novels by Maupassant, Huysmans, Paul Bourget and Jules Verne (whose latest title, *Two Years' Vacation*, was prominently displayed) were all arranged alongside antique bound editions.

Shading his eyes, the man scanned the inside of the shop, which seemed to be empty. In one corner he made out Kenji Mori, sitting at a small desk, writing. Surrounded by shelves covered in books, and piles of works that were waiting for a place to be found for them, he was copying out record cards with all the application of a schoolboy writing out lines. Occasionally he stopped to gaze at a bust of Molière, centrally positioned on a black marble mantelpiece. He then put his head back down and dipped his pen in an inkwell.

The man smiled, smoothed his pointed beard and pushed the door open. The sound of the door chime made Kenji Mori look up and an assistant appeared in grey overalls.

'Monsieur France!' they exclaimed together.

The man greeted them, and went up to a rectangular table with a green tablecloth on it. 'Where have the chairs gone?' he asked, with a look of amusement.

'I had them put away again,' grumbled Kenji Mori. 'Victor doesn't understand. People who just come here for a chat clutter up the place and annoy the real customers.'

'Does that include me?'

'You're quite a different matter. Joseph, get Monsieur France a chair from the back room!'

'Right away!' shouted the assistant.

Once the two men were seated side by side at the desk and Kenji had pushed his paperwork aside to lay out a selection of illustrated books for the benefit of his illustrious visitor, Joseph Pignot – known as Jojo – went back to his stool behind the counter. Every day after lunch he allowed himself a short break to do some reading. He was grateful to Monsieur Mori for letting him have this respite, because straight afterwards he would be busy until evening with the classification of books purchased on preceding days by Monsieur Legris, either at auction or from private vendors. He also had to serve customers, parcel up books, and sometimes deliver them to people's homes. When he had a large number of jobs to do, Monsieur Mori would talk about getting a second assistant, but Joseph insisted that he could handle everything, not wanting a rival in this kingdom of paper, which was his own private paradise.

The product of an illicit love between a fruit and vegetable vendor and a second-hand bookseller on Quai Voltaire, Joseph was a sickly child with a slightly hunched back, and his mother had given him an isolated upbringing, so that until well past the age of fifteen he had grown up on a diet of apples and novels. On an autumn day four years before, Madame Euphrosine Pignot had been delivering pears and figs to the Elzévir bookshop when Ernest Labarthe, the previous assistant, had collapsed over the table, felled by a stroke. Madame Pignot had helped the bookseller, Victor Legris (who had turned very pale), to lay out the dead man on the floor and took the liberty of slipping in a reference to her son's area of knowledge. The following week, Joseph was taken on.

The young man was an invaluable appointment. He had read everything, remembered everything, and could never be caught out with regard to the content of books and their date of publication, the size of their print run, the number of special editions and even the name of the printer. Beneath a mass of straw-coloured hair, which no amount of rain could turn curly, his huge, round, good-natured head was a vast repository of information. Moreover, he liked to say, his widely spaced rabbit-like front teeth brought him luck. Victor also recognised that since Jojo had been at the bookshop, sales figures had improved. Initially hostile to the boy, Kenji could not do without him now and, whilst always treating him a little harshly, actually adored him, and had only one criticism of him, which was that he did not always knot the string around the book parcels carefully enough.

Joseph returned to the book he was currently reading, *On the River* by Maupassant. But he could not concentrate on a word because he was too busy staring at the visitor sitting with Kenji.

He burned to tell him how much he admired his novels and literary criticism, but he did not dare. To calm himself he unfolded *L'Éclair*. A huge headline filled the top half of the front page:

THE DRAMA ON THE TOWER

CASE REMAINS A TOTAL MYSTERY

Yesterday afternoon, an enigmatic message arrived in the post at our editorial offices. It concerned the woman who died in the middle of the day on the first platform of the three-hundred-metre Tower at the Universal Exposition. We reproduce it here in its entirety:

I won't spell it out
But poor Eugénie Patinot
Knew more than she ought.

Joseph gave a little whistle. 'Monsieur Legris will like that.'

A majestic, aristocratic lady with greying hair entered the bookshop. Joseph folded up his paper and stood up. 'Madame la Comtesse . . .'

She gestured impatiently. 'Don't let me disturb you. I am going to rummage a little. I'm looking for some reading for my silly goose of a niece. Where do you keep Georges Ohnet?'

'Oh. Are you sure that's a good choice? His books are full of errors. A writer who can give a child born under the First Empire a level-crossing guard for a father . . .'

The Comtesse stared at Joseph through her lorgnette. 'Really? So what would you advise?'

'Do you know *The Crime of Sylvester Bonnard*?' he whispered, with a glance towards the desk.

'A crime? Oh, no, I will not yield to this new fashion. The newspapers are sufficiently full of appalling events. Did you hear about this business yesterday on the Eiffel Tower?'

'Yes, I was just . . .'

He stopped to admire the prettiest little redhead he had ever seen. She was inspecting the shop from the kerb, with a perplexed expression. The man in the topper said goodbye to Kenji and made for the door with a friendly wave to Joseph. Just as he was going out, the young red-headed woman decided to come in. He gallantly let her pass. The Comtesse immediately turned away from the assistant and made a beeline for Kenji, who, having spotted her, was attempting to take refuge in the rear of the shop.

'Monsieur Mori, what a pleasure to see you. I wanted to ask . . .'

Tasha approached the strange blond boy, who was devouring her with his eyes. He could almost be a mujik, she thought to herself. 'Tell me, that man who just left, wasn't it . . . ?'

'Monsieur Anatole France himself! How may I help?'

'I would like to speak to Monsieur Victor Legris.'

'I'm very sorry, he is not here. Can I be of assistance?'

'Monsieur Legris told me to come by, he has a book to show me. But never mind, I'll come back another day.'

'Wait, don't leave! I know this bookshop inside out. I'll find that book for you.'

'I've forgotten the title. They're Goya aquatints, bound in a volume.'

'Goya? Consider it done!'

Joseph slid a ladder on runners to the shelf containing art books and scuttled up it.

'I remember now. It's *Los Caprichos*,' said Tasha.

'There's no point turning everything upside-down, Joseph. We don't have them.'

Tasha turned to Kenji Mori, who was eyeing her coldly, having just seen the Comtesse out.

'Hello, how are you? Your business associate told me about this book yesterday. That's why . . .'

Kenji stood quite still, staring at her with a slightly quizzical look, as though he had forgotten their meeting the day before. The assistant was still noisily searching through the art books.

'Joseph, I'd rather you started wrapping up the books chosen by Monsieur France. They will need to go to him at five o'clock. On the way, you could leave *The Ironmaster* at the Comtesse de Salignac's home.'

'I know what. I'll go and look in the storeroom,' cried the boy.

'As I've told you, we do not . . .'

But Joseph had already dashed down to the basement. Kenji went back to his desk to go on compiling his catalogue. Tasha decided to wait for the assistant to return and went into the room where the Comtesse had joined Kenji a few moments earlier.

Also lined with books, this room was devoted to foreign travel. Tasha quickly looked along a row of Baedeker guides with their red spines, hardly paid any attention to the numerous volumes of the *Journal of Voyages, Discoveries and*

Modern Navigations, but was stopped in her tracks by a locked display cabinet, which contained some marvels: the *Second Voyage of Father Tachard to the Kingdom of Siam*, dated 1689, was open at a section showing an engraving of some strange bulbous plants. And very close to it gleamed the carefully waxed morocco binding of *An Account of the Pelew Islands*, which had come out in 1788, preceding the four quartos of *Cook's Third Voyage*. Other collections centred on Asia, notably the narration of an expedition into Tartary, Tibet and China in 1845, sat alongside geographical maps traced on vellum with coloured inks, and ethnographic curiosities, reminding Tasha of those she had recently admired at the Colonial Exhibition on the Esplanade des Invalides. Shell and agate bracelets framed quivers and blowpipes, themselves displayed above a series of small steel combs and metal rods with sharp points. Tasha took a step back to admire two long wooden shields decorated with etched designs. Someone coughed gently behind her.

'Um, Mademoiselle, I'm very sorry, Monsieur Mori was right, we do not have your *Caprichos*.'

'You mean Goya's,' Tasha remarked with a smile. 'Talking about caprice, would you indulge my whim to take a closer look at this work?' She indicated Damberger's *Voyage into the African Interior*.

Pink with embarrassment, Joseph pulled a key out of his pocket.

'As a rule I only open this for regular customers, but as you are so nice . . .' he whispered. It was the first time he had dared to compliment a young woman in this way: his hands were trembling. He put the book on a round table, and stepped back to let Tasha leaf through it.

'I can see that you're used to doing this, you don't bend the pages.'

'Joseph!'

'The boss is calling me. Yes, Boss?'

'Where have you hidden the order book?'

'I'm coming, Boss. Excuse me, Mademoiselle, I'll just be a moment.'

When he returned noiselessly, he stopped to look at the young woman leaning over the book. She straightened up and smiled at him.

'It is superb,' she said as she closed the volume. 'Tell me, what are these shields called?'

'Talawangs. They are from Borneo. Mr Mori attaches great value to them, as he brought them back himself.'

Tasha nibbled her thumbnail.

'You know,' Joseph said, lowering his voice and turning the key in the lock, 'he's not usually so disagreeable. I don't know what's wrong with him. Something must be worrying him.'

Tasha wanted to reply that she had come across Kenji's morose moods before, but she kept quiet. Back in the main bookshop, she shook hands with the boy, who turned puce, and thanked him profusely for his kindness.

'Monsieur,' she mumbled to Kenji's back. He turned in his chair and, without getting up, gave her a quick nod. Joseph hurried to open the door for Tasha and watched her as she walked off towards the Seine.

'Joseph, I'm going upstairs,' said Kenji.

He started up a narrow spiral staircase. On the first floor he turned right; on the left was Victor Legris's accommodation.

Kenji Mori's apartment was made up of two rooms and a bathroom laid out in a row. He worked in the first room and slept in the second. They had an odd mixture of Louis XIII-style and Japanese furnishings, separated as they were by a *fusuma*, a sliding partition, which consisted of a wooden frame containing a grid of slats with opaque paper glued in the spaces between them.

The sitting room was dominated by a walnut dresser with diamond marquetry, an oak table with turned legs, and a straight-backed armchair upholstered in floral tapestry material. The bedroom had a recess with a slightly raised floor covered with a mat on which lay a thick cotton blanket and a wooden pillow. The few items of decoration were all Japanese: Noh theatre masks, kakemonos, red lacquer dishes, and porcelain bowls for use in tea ceremonies.

Kenji was furious. Victor had seen that woman again after leaving her at the bottom of the Tower! Even worse, he had managed to interest her in the bookshop. And she had actually had the audacity to come!

He removed his jacket and slipped on a silk kimono. He sat down at the table, and his gaze fell upon *Le Figaro de la Tour*, which had been placed in front of the row of inkwells. Perplexed, he studied the newspaper: he did not recall putting it there. He shrugged his shoulders. He opened a drawer, and took out the timetable for the London and Dover Railway via Calais. He hesitated: did he want a daytime or overnight train? Eventually he marked the evening service with a red pen.

Getting up again, he went to the dresser and opened it to reveal a collection of books. He picked up a quarto edition and read the title with a smile: *Colección de estampas de asuntos caprichosos, inventadas y grabadas al aguafuerte por don Francisco de Goya y Lucientes, Madrid 1799.*

He went round the *fusuma* and kneeled down next to the recess, pulled back the mat and blanket, and after removing one of the slats from the base, wrapped *Los Caprichos* in some printed fabric and slid it to the end of the hiding place where he kept some personal papers. He put everything back in its place and returned to the sitting room. He selected three bound volumes, hesitated for a moment and then took two Utamaro prints down from the wall. He made up two parcels, one containing the books, the other the framed items, and then placed them in a dark wood Japanese trunk with ornamental hinges, which stood opposite his bed.

He went into the bathroom. The building that housed the Elzévir bookshop and Victor and Kenji's apartments had had running water and water closets for only two years. Kenji appreciated this luxury even more than gaslight and the hot-air heaters because he liked to plunge into a bath every day and sometimes spent so long in it that Victor would ask him jokingly if he wasn't concerned that he might melt away.

'In which case,' he added, alluding to Kenji's thin body, 'there really would not be much left of you at all!'

Whilst the copper bathtub filled up with steaming water despite the summer heat, Kenji undressed and examined himself in the mirror. With his daily ju-jitsu practice he had managed to retain a youthful and sinewy body. In spite of the grey threads in his hair and some expression lines, his face had not been very marked by age. He looked at a photo in an elaborate frame, which was on a marble shelf. A young woman with brown hair was holding close a twelve-year-old boy, who looked very much like her. They gazed out at Kenji with tender smiles. 'Daphne and Victor, London, 1872' was written at the bottom of the photograph in small spiky handwriting.

Kenji lowered himself slowly into the water, adopting a semi-reclined position and stretching his legs out with contentment. He was relaxed, free of the anguish he had felt earlier when he had seen the little redhead.

He stared at the photo. Daphne was still looking at him. Did she know that all these years since her death he had never forgotten the promise he had made to her? 'My dear, please make sure that he is happy. Don't let him marry someone who is unworthy of him.' Until now, none of Victor's mistresses had seemed worthy of him in Kenji's eyes. The most recent, Odette de Valois, a featherbrain who insisted on thinking he was Chinese and treated him like a servant, was without doubt the worst of all. But at least Victor respected a tacit agreement with Kenji that neither of them would allow their private lives to interfere with their own relationship. To the outside world they presented an odd couple, a relationship from which women were excluded. In any case, they cared little for what others thought of them. They respected each other too much to allow gossip to damage their mutual affection.

And now this impudent girl threatened to spoil everything! This thought filled Kenji with anger. He recalled a Baudelaire poem, 'To a Red-Haired Beggarwoman': '"You slyly ogle twenty-nine-sou trinkets,"' he recited to himself. Would he need to pay to get rid of her? It did not matter. He was ready to do anything.

Kenji will be pleased, I made the deal for a good price, Victor Legris was saying to himself on Quai Malaquais, greeting, as he passed, the second-hand booksellers he knew. On his shoulder he was carrying a heavy green canvas bundle full of rare books, of which Caesar's *Commentaries* annotated by Napoleon was the jewel.

Tired but happy, he greeted the assistant with a 'Good day to you, Jojo! Where is Monsieur Mori?' and hauled his canvas up onto the counter.

'A good haul, Monsieur Victor?' asked the boy.

'Not bad. Show me the newspaper.'

He grabbed *L'Éclair* and immediately began reading the front-page article. Kenji appeared, smelling of lavender. Victor shoved the paper under his nose.

'Have you seen this? When we were up on the Tower yesterday, a woman died. According to a message sent to the press, it looks like it could be murder!'

Unconcerned, Kenji opened the canvas bundle and started to sort through the books.

'Death is both larger than a mountain and slighter than a hair.'

'I tell him about a murder and he comes back with one of his Japanese proverbs!'

'Proverbs are part of the wisdom of nations,' Kenji retorted.

'Take what you can from it and don't worry yourself with journalists' rumours. They sow doubt and fear in the hearts of their readers. Good purchase. How much?'

CHAPTER THREE

Friday 24 June

As usual, Victor was woken by Jojo opening the wooden shutters of the bookshop. In his usual way, the assistant was tunelessly whistling the opening bars of '*En revenant de la revue*', clearly the only song good enough for him to start his working day. From the foot of the stairs, he called: 'Monsieur Legris! Monsieur Mori! It's eight o'clock!'

Victor groaned, threw back the sheet and put on a silk dressing-gown. He went over to the window and drew the curtains back to reveal an azure-blue sky. 'Not more sun; this is getting too much.'

'What's wrong with beautiful weather?' asked Kenji, busy in the kitchen.

Victor lazily joined him. 'What's wrong is that I'm bored by anything that goes on too long.'

'In that case you must have had more than enough of me.'

'Kenji, for the love of God, don't take everything I say so literally!'

'The wise man measures his words seven times before speaking,' retorted Kenji mischievously, as he retreated with his kettle.

'Oh, for heaven's sake!'

While Kenji was drinking his tea in his room, Victor was

alone in the kitchen, which adjoined the dining room and two bedrooms making up his apartment. He heated up a little black coffee, which had been prepared the night before by Germaine, the housekeeper, who also cooked for them. He nibbled a biscuit and then shut himself in the bathroom so that he would not have to listen to Joseph's tortured rendition of Paulus's stupid refrain.

Kenji was first to go downstairs and found Joseph leaning on the counter, reading the newspaper. 'You shouldn't be doing that now,' he murmured.

'All the newspapers are taking the same line. It's no longer an accident, now it's a case for the police!'

'What are you talking about?'

'The Patinot woman. The woman who snuffed it on the Tower.'

'Joseph! Watch your language. I need you to find space for the seventy volumes of that Voltaire.'

'Your wish is my command!'

While the assistant was busy on his ladder, Kenji looked over the newspaper, a special edition of *Le Passe-partout*. With a grimace, he shoved the daily under a large black accounts book.

Victor joined him, and after half an hour the door opened and Marius Bonnet and Antonin Clusel entered, smoking Havana cigars.

Kenji hastened towards them. 'Messieurs, I'm sorry but . . .' He indicated the cigars.

'Pardon me, what was I thinking?' said Marius, crushing his cigar out in an ashtray. 'Victor, Monsieur Mori, I need your expertise! Antonin is writing an article for us on the Congo and I thought that you might be able to show us some relevant works from your little room of wonders.'

'Let me think. Yes, we should have what you need,' Victor replied.

'Why the Congo?' grumbled Kenji. 'Is *Le Passe-partout* branching out into tourism?'

'*Le Passe-partout*?' cried Joseph, nearly toppling off his ladder. 'You work for *Le Passe-partout*?'

'I'm the director.'

'Oh! You must have the inside information on the Patinot affair?'

Marius looked triumphantly at Antonin.

'You find that story interesting?'

'Murders are my passion!'

'There's no proof that it was murder, young man.'

'But the message—'

'Joseph, there are still fifteen volumes of Voltaire to put away,' Kenji reminded him curtly.

Putting an arm around Victor's shoulder, Marius led him towards the travel books, Antonin at their heels. 'You don't happen to have the writings of Brazza, published two years ago by Napoléon Ney, do you?'

'I don't think so. I'm going to open up the holy of holies for you. There are works on Africa, but they are much less recent. Don't rearrange anything, Kenji really doesn't like people rummaging in his cupboard.'

'Did you hear that, Antonin? I'll leave you to it. I must speak to our friend.'

He went back into the main bookshop. Victor followed him, intrigued.

'I'd like you to put an advertisement in *Le Passe-partout*. It's quite expensive, but it helps the paper and produces good results for the advertiser.'

'I think that's what's known as forcing someone's hand,' grumbled Victor. 'All right, I'll get some text ready. How many lines?'

'Oh, not many, make it as short as possible. You know I'm very keen on keeping things concise.'

'I gathered that from the front-page news.'

'Yes, long articles are just so much hot air! What does the ordinary man in the street want? Gripping sensationalism coupled with popular science, which gives him the illusion of being an expert; serialised stories that take the reader out of himself and advertisements that whet the appetite. One of my colleagues was right when he said: "Let's have the courage to be stupid."'

'Most journalists don't have to try, it comes naturally,' murmured Kenji as he went to greet a customer.

Marius burst out laughing. 'You'd think Monsieur Kenji Mori didn't really like me!'

Antonin returned, all excited, with a sheet covered in scribbles. Marius snatched it from him, read it and frowned.

'What atrocious handwriting! What is that you've written? Opoé? No, Ogoé?'

'The river Ogooé, double o.'

'Are you sure it's not Ogooué, with a u?'

'I don't think so.'

'I'm going to check.'

As soon as Marius had disappeared into the back room, Joseph, who had been waiting for this moment, bounded up to Antonin.

'Tell me, Monsieur, this message that the press is publishing, have you seen it?'

'Of course. Our secretary opened it, and then she brought it to me.'

'How was it written? In the normal way?'

'What do you mean?'

'I mean with letters cut out of a newspaper?'

'Yes, actually. But how did you know?'

'Because of the books that Monsieur Legris reads. He has a large collection and he often lends them to me. *The Stolen Letter* by Edgar Allan Poe, *File 113* by Émile Gaboriau, *The Stranger of Belleville* by Pierre Zaccone . . . There are so many! My favourite is *The Leavenworth Case* by Anna Katherine Green. I adore her female detect—'

'I was right, it *is* Ogooué,' interrupted Marius, holding out the sheet of paper to Antonin.

'I'll go and close the cupboard,' groaned Joseph, put out.

'Victor, we're off. Don't forget to bring in your copy.'

'I could sort it all out with your colleague, Mademoiselle Tasha Kherson,' suggested Victor, twirling the end of his moustache.

'So, you're really taken with her, are you? You're not the only one! But alas, she's unattainable. In any case, we hardly see her these days,' he said, winking at Antonin.

'It's true. The lucky girl is spending her days at the Colonial Exhibition. For our forthcoming interview with Brazza, she's having fun drawing pictures whilst I'm wearing myself out taking notes!'

'You just need to swap your pen-holder for a stick of charcoal! See you soon, Victor. Good day, Monsieur Mori!'

Kenji gave them a stiff wave. Without pausing to put on a jacket, Victor rushed over to the door.

'Are you going out?' asked Kenji.

'Yes, I . . . I forgot to ask them something,' Victor mumbled.

'I also have to go out. I'm going to value a collection on Rue de l'Odéon.'

'I won't be long!' cried Victor. 'Joseph will look after the shop!'

Not noticing Kenji's angry expression, Victor ran after Marius and Antonin, who were already turning the corner of Rue des Saints-Pères. He had just realised that the Colonial Exhibition stretched across the whole Esplanade des Invalides and that if he wanted to find a certain red-headed girl he needed to know exactly where to look for her.

'The Colonial Palace, the Colonial Palace,' he sang to himself a few moments later when he came out onto Quai Malaquais. He paused at Père Caillé's boxes. Père Caillé, who sold spectacles and optical instruments, was the only stall-holder open at this hour of the morning. Although he didn't sell books, Victor enjoyed his conversations with him.

'How is it going this morning?'

'I'll give you the same answer as Monsieur de Fontanelle gave when he was dying. "It's not going well, I'm a day closer to death . . .'" replied the old man in the grey shirt, straight-faced.

Victor soon stopped laughing at this riposte when he caught sight of a familiar figure in a grey-checked suit, pink cravat and bowler hat, on the opposite pavement. This wasn't the most direct route to Rue de l'Odéon. No doubt Kenji wanted to enjoy the sunshine. He was walking briskly, carrying two parcels under his arm. Victor watched him, expecting him to go all the way along Quai Malaquais. He was therefore astonished to see him cross the road and continue over Pont du Carrousel. Unable to restrain his curiosity, he hurried after him.

He had never before caught Kenji lying so flagrantly and it amused him to think that, as it turned out, this man, whom he thought of almost as his father, had a hidden side to him. A mistress? Victor had often wondered about his private life. Had he given up the company of women altogether? He had hardly flaunted any liaisons in the past but Victor did not think that he was indifferent to the fairer sex. On several occasions Kenji had been overly attentive to their attractive clients, and Victor knew that he kept a large collection of erotic prints in his dresser, having admired them in his friend's absence.

A tug-boat pulling a row of barges sounded its horn. Victor stopped in his tracks, sure that Kenji was going to turn round, but he did not slacken his pace. In fact he walked faster, in a hurry to reach the Tuileries Gardens. There was hardly anyone on the paths apart from a few nursemaids pushing prams, and two or three men with neatly trimmed beards reading their newspapers on a bench. One of these cast a disparaging glance at Victor, who was looking dishevelled.

Where's the old devil off to in such a rush? he wondered, now out of breath but still hot on the heels of Kenji, who had just reached Rue de Rivoli.

Had he known that his friend would lead him from one end of Avenue de l'Opéra to the other, he might have given up his pursuit. But the further they went, the more Victor gritted his teeth, unable to stop following Kenji because of his incomprehensible behaviour, whilst the din of the coaches and omnibuses cluttering the street made his head spin. *Why didn't he take a cab? That would have been so much better. And what's he carrying?*

Finally at Rue Auber, ignoring the Opera House, Kenji reached a bookshop whose owner Victor met sometimes at the auction house. *Incredible! He's going to visit a competitor. I always thought he disliked that man.* Standing close to the shop window, half-hidden by a lamppost, Victor watched Kenji. The bookseller, a little man in a skullcap, picked up the three bound volumes, which he leafed through. Then he held out a wad of blue notes. Victor just had time to hide his face in his hands as if he were having a coughing fit. Kenji did not notice him and, turning on his heel, appeared to hurry towards the Opera House. *What's come over him? Does he really want to admire that overblown wedding cake?* Victor was hoping for a break, but was disappointed. Although he was bathed in sweat and dying of thirst, he had to drag himself as far as Boulevard des Capucines, where he saw to his envy that his friend was sipping a soda on the terrace of Café de la Paix. A stout man sporting a monocle and dressed in a light-coloured suit arrived almost immediately and sat down with Kenji. Kenji greeted him and then produced his second parcel. The man examined closely what appeared to be framed prints, offered his opinion and took his wallet out of his jacket. *What's happened to him? Is he in debt? Why is he selling off his books and prints?*

Finally, when they reached Rue de la Chaussée-d'Antin, Victor found the answer to the mystery. In a fancy-goods shop called La Reine des Abeilles, where embroidered handkerchiefs, scarves and jewellery were displayed around crystal bottles of perfume, Kenji was busy choosing various expensive gifts, which the shop assistant was carefully wrapping in tissue paper. *I was right! A woman! Kenji is in love! He's ruining himself for the sake of a mistress!*

Victor was surprised to discover that, beneath his cool exterior, Kenji hid a human heart, but he was also a little alarmed to think what other secrets he might be hiding. He also felt pleased as, in spite of his tenderness for Kenji, he sometimes felt a little intimidated by him. But from now on they would be on an equal footing.

Who can it be? Obviously someone whom he met at the shop, since he so rarely goes out! Victor's attention was distracted by the skirt of a passer-by and then by a palisade covered with posters. Cowboys in yellow, on horseback pursuing a troupe of Redskins.

That image made him think of another: Colonel Cody caricatured by Tasha. Suddenly Victor remembered why he had left the bookshop in shirtsleeves. Tasha! The Colonial Exhibition! He ran to the nearest cab rank, exhilarated by the chase that had just ended in a luxury emporium, and by the serene sky, which he no longer found so monotonous.

'Rue des Saints-Pères!' he cried to the coach driver snoozing under a black oilcloth hat.

Victor got out of the cab in front of the Ministry of Foreign Affairs. He had lunched quickly on a portion of Pont-Neuf potatoes on Quai Conti, then had gone to his flat to change and get his camera. If he was lucky enough to run into Tasha he would say that he had come to take some photographs of the esplanade.

The Colonial Exhibition was made up of numerous buildings, either standing alone or grouped into indigenous villages. Victor did not wait to look at the seven pediments of the temple of Angkor but hurried towards the red structure of the Colonial Palace, an architectural mish-mash of Norwegian, Chinese and French Renaissance styles topped by green roofing. The noise was deafening. Arab artisans were gesticulating and urging people to buy their wares, whilst customers bargained with them. Polynesian flutes and Annamese gongs mingled with Kanaka chants. Raucous children dragged their mothers towards the stalls of apricots, guavas, and sugar cane. Victor tore himself away from the displays by the lascivious Ouled Naïl belly dancers and by the rather more chaste little Javanese girls with their sacred dancing. Finally he reached the monumental entrance to the Palace, but before he could cross the threshold a black woman wearing a multicoloured madras headscarf insisted he try a piece of pineapple.

The ground floor was split into three vast halls. Victor was unsure which direction to go in. He walked around a pyramid of lacquered wooden buddhas set up under an arch of giant bamboo. But there was no sign of Tasha. Products from the territories colonised by France were stacked up all around. Carpets, furs, tobacco, coffee, furniture, silks, an eclectic sea of foodstuffs and objects reminiscent of les Halles at its busiest. Victor felt as depressed as when he accompanied Odette to the Bon Marché. He would never find Tasha! He sighed and launched himself into the crowd.

He admired the Kanaka tomahawks, the snakewood axes from New Caledonia and the muskets from Cochin China. A collection of musical instruments caught his attention, reminding him of the ones Kenji had stored in the basement of the bookshop.

'That calabash is called a *thléthé*,' murmured a soft voice in his ear.

He turned and found himself face to face with a slender dark-skinned man with grizzled hair and wearing a long blue tunic.

'What country is it from?'

'From Senegal, like me. See the jewels under this glass? I made them with my sons in our workshop in St-Louis. I am Samba Lambé Thiam and I studied with the Marist Brothers.'

'And I am Victor Legris. Delighted to meet you.'

'Victor! With a name like that you must be a gallant fellow.'

'What is so special about my name?'

'It is the name of a great man, your most prolific writer. I have read *Les Misérables*.'

'All of it?'

'Why not? We are not savages, you know. At home in St-Louis we have schools, books, a railway and houses. Here, on the other hand . . .' Samba lowered his voice, 'they have housed us in a mud hut village and we have to sleep on grass mats. Visitors to this exhibition will not have a very good opinion of us. Mind you, we feel the same way about them.'

'What do you mean?'

'I'm not saying this about you – you seem intelligent – but some of your compatriots who treat me like a monkey, imagining that I don't understand, remind us of warthogs, those stupid little pigs who charge headlong without knowing where they are going. Take, for example, the family who invited my eldest son and me to dinner, claiming that they wanted to get to know us better. Really they wanted to exhibit us to their friends. The men were in tight dark suits with gold buttons and the women wore dresses so fitted at the waist that they showed off what should have been kept covered up. Because those women were dreadfully ugly!'

He stopped to gesture with his chin towards an elegant lady who was staring at him shamelessly. Victor took advantage of this to release the shutter on his Acmé. The light was not ideal but with a little luck . . .

'You see? That woman is frightened of me. She looks like a goat watching an approaching lion. Going back to that evening, they served us pork and told us that they were sorry that we had not worn our ceremonial costumes. By which they meant our panther skins and lances!'

'And what do you think of the Exposition?'

Samba grimaced in disdain. 'A huge market where everything is very expensive and half the objects are no better than the knick-knacks brought back by explorers. As for the food galleries that they have built all along the river! I nearly died of boredom, you know, at the sight of all those endless displays of cheese!'

Victor turned sharply. There in the middle of a group of people chatting and looking around, he thought he recognised Tasha! 'Excuse me, I must go,' he said, extending his hand towards Samba.

But Samba kept hold of his hand and looked at Victor playfully. 'The next time you want to photograph me, let me know and I will pose for you.'

'I don't know what to say . . . I didn't mean to . . .'

'I must say this new fad seems very strange to me, putting people in a box to capture their image.'

Victor was in despair. The group had dispersed so he could no longer see that head of long red hair, and still Samba was not letting go.

'I like to recreate the reality that surrounds us. In the same way that . . . a painter does.'

He would have to remember that phrase and make use of it next time he saw Tasha. He withdrew his hand briskly and took a visiting card out of his pocket.

'Here is my address, if you are ever passing . . . Goodbye. See you soon perhaps!' He hurried off.

Samba stood stock-still, the visiting card in his hand. 'These white people are assuredly mad! Always chasing after their destiny! Something tells me though that maybe this one is running so fast for a reason.'

*

A tall, sturdily built man with weather-beaten features and a mane of silver hair beneath his pith helmet was wandering along the lake where pirogues, Chinese junks and sampans sailed to and fro. He turned down a path packed with noisy crowds. That day he felt, as he often did, utterly out of his element. His mind was alert, but his body was succumbing to the ravages of time. For several years now his conference tours and articles had given him a good standard of living without fulfilling him. He was only in Paris because of his medals – it was easy to attract grants if one was decorated. He was tired and took no pleasure in his success. Officials smiled at him, shook his hand and congratulated him on his achievements. Important people he had never seen before and would never see again hovered around him. What a circus! he thought. A few more weeks of speeches, openings and dinners at which he would be honoured, then he would escape this charade and taste once again the joys of exploration and adventure, which was where he really felt in his element.

He politely rejected the plate of pineapple that a woman from Martinique was offering him, and looked up at the Colonial Palace. He felt a desire to return to his hotel and pack his bags. Once again he smoothed out the wire from Louis Henrique, special commissioner of the Colonial Exhibition, who was impatient to talk to him about an important project. He straightened up and joined the crowds milling around the clumps of bougainvillaea.

Visitors knocked into and jostled him. He felt a sharp pain in the nape of his neck and threw his head back. A cold sensation began to pierce his limbs and he had difficulty breathing, even with his mouth wide open. He began to panic; he could not take in what was happening. No, surely he was not going to expire here, in this cheap bazaar! He slid slowly to the ground. Above him he could hear a loud hubbub, then his thoughts began to unravel, and the clumps of bougainvillaea were swallowed up by the shadow of night.

Victor elbowed his way through the mêlée. Blinded by the bright light, he scoured the approaches to the Colonial Palace. Suddenly Tasha emerged from the direction of the lakes, walking in a determined fashion, her little hat bobbing on her red chignon. Automatically he opened the shutter on his Acmé before she disappeared behind a cluster of bougainvillaea from where, almost immediately, shouts could be heard.

'Air! Give him some air!'

'Move away! Move away, please!'

'Fetch a doctor, quick!'

Victor hurried to the bottom of the steps and ran into a crowd of people. 'What's happening?' he cried, grabbing hold of a bystander.

'Someone has passed out.'

'Who?'

'Let go. How should I know?'

As he walked round the group of onlookers, Victor tried to spot Tasha. He suddenly saw her hurrying towards the Decauville railway, which took passengers back to the Champ-de-Mars. All his tension vanished and he sank down onto a bench. His feelings had got the better of him. Should he follow her? He did not have the strength to shadow two people in one day. What about tomorrow? He could come back, or visit the newspaper offices, or, better still, turn up at her house on Rue Notre-Dame-de-Lorette, with a bunch of flowers in his hand.

As he reached the post office his path crossed that of two stretcher-bearers and three policemen. *This is becoming a habit.* That word, habit, evoked an image that he could have done without: Odette in a state of undress. As her husband was away, he was supposed to be spending the evening and night with her. He did not derive any pleasure from the thought.

He looked at his watch: there was still time to develop his negatives before meeting Odette.

Victor had set up his photographic laboratory in the basement of the bookshop. To get to it, he had to negotiate mountains of books. In the tiny room there was a table, a chair, a sink, a paraffin lamp with a red light, and earthenware and zinc trays. Up on the shelf were scales with a series of weights, and a draining rack. His most recent works were hung on the wall: Kenji, standing ramrod straight in front of the shop; Madame Pignot on her son's arm, smiling so broadly that she almost had three chins; Kenji speaking to a second-hand bookseller; an unknown woman in a ratteen overcoat photographed as she went past on Rue de Rennes. This was his ivory tower where he created as he pleased. No one was allowed in here without an invitation. He removed his frock coat, put on a worn-out old jacket, and began to prepare the solutions, enjoying the acrid odour of the chemicals. After two hours the photographs he had taken that afternoon were almost dry. He examined the two that he thought had most contrast in them and that showed the sharpest detail. In the first, Samba the Senegalese was watching a woman with rodent features go by. In the second, Tasha seemed about to dive into a clump of flowers. The expression on her face was utterly charming, at once mysterious and provocative.

CHAPTER FOUR

Saturday 25 June

PROPPED up on a pillow in a big four-poster bed, Victor was looking at the woman with dishevelled blonde hair asleep next to him, her arm over his body, keeping him prisoner. He changed position abruptly and reached for the alarm clock on the shelf.

'Go back to sleep, my duck,' said Odette with a yawn. 'Can't you see it's still dark?'

'Yes, but only because the curtains are closed. It's twenty past ten in the morning.'

'Mmm, that's very early, my duck . . .' she muttered, pushing back the sheet and curling up around him. 'Kiss me.'

He dropped a quick kiss on the nape of her neck and got up to open the heavy velvet curtains. The sunlight fell on Odette's opulent breasts. With a little cry she covered her face. 'You're going to ruin my complexion! Pass me my négligé.'

She slipped on a ruched chiffon dressing-gown, which made her look like a lampshade, and stumbled into the bathroom. 'I must look awful. Don't move, I'll be back in a moment. We can have breakfast in bed.'

'Yes, of course,' he muttered, 'and I'll spill half my coffee on the sheets!'

Despite his irritation, he lay back down across the mattress.

He hated to start the day off in a bad mood. The previous night had been better than he had dared hope: Odette knew how to arouse his desire, and occasionally in the darkness he imagined he was holding Tasha in his arms. But now he would have to exchange lovers' caresses and fond words with a woman who, in the cold light of day, he could no longer take to be another, and all he wanted to do was escape.

He was counting up the bunches of violets scattered over the mauve fabric on the walls when Odette returned, her hair done up in a chignon. She was carrying a tray.

'I really must get rid of that Denise – she doesn't know how to make hot chocolate. She puts the cocoa in the milk instead of carefully pouring the liquid on as I taught her. Would you like a croissant, my duck?'

'Coffee will be enough.'

Dressed only in long johns, he got up and went to the window.

'Are you going to come with me, my duck?'

'I have work to do.'

'Oh, can't you get out of it for once? Don't forget I'll soon be far away from you. Your Chinaman will do your work. I so wanted you to be there for the fittings! I've ordered the same outfit as Mademoiselle Réjane, soft silk, in an utterly lovely antique blue with wisps of pink lamé. The hat is quite flat, in Eiffel cream straw. You'll love it.'

'Of course,' growled Victor as he looked for his socks.

'So, you are coming then? Afterwards I must go to Violet's to buy Tsarina face powder and also . . .'

With a weary sigh, Victor went into the bathroom. He poured water from a pitcher into a washbasin, covered his face in cream and began to shave while looking in the oval mirror. In the background, he could see Odette, slumped on an ottoman, which was overhung by a palm tree growing out of a large porcelain pot. She had opened a newspaper and was turning the pages without reading them.

'I'm pleased I've rented this big seaside villa at Houlgate for the summer. It's the right time to leave Paris – all the fashionable ladies are. Madame Azam has just invented some corsets in which you can go horseriding and play lawn tennis. I've ordered three, as well as a lace-trimmed parasol with an ivory handle. Will you come and join me soon?'

'What about your husband?'

'You know very well, my duck, Armand is in Panama, and will not be back before September. The canal, always the canal. I don't understand anything about his business. He writes that he has some little problems to sort out, but that everything is going really well for us. If you don't come, I'll die of boredom. Come now, say something, my duck.'

'Quack, quack,' he said quietly as he traced a large furrow through the lather with his razor.

Odette closed the newspaper and was about to leave it on the pedestal table when she changed her mind and took a closer look at the front page.

'My word, it's an epidemic . . . Listen to this: "Yesterday afternoon, on the Esplanade des Invalides an American naturalist died from . . ." Naturalist? Is that like Monsieur Zola, my duck?'

'Émile Zola is dead?' cried Victor as he rubbed his ears vigorously with a towel.

'You're not listening. How can you wear those awful shirts? You look like some . . . penniless artist!'

Delighted by this jibe, which seemed to bring him closer to Tasha, Victor tried to look offended. Rummaging in his frock coat, he took out a cigarette holder and a lighter, then went out onto the balcony, which went all the way round the apartment and overlooked Boulevard Haussmann. From the sea of green treetops the chalky outline of the buildings rose up, the grey roofs topped by red chimneys resembling an enormous steamship ready to sail. The hubbub from the street merged with Odette's interminable stream of chatter. Cabs rattled over wooden paving blocks, the outdoor cafés were taking over the pavements, street vendors were reciting their monotonous chants: 'Pots and pans mended' . . . 'Lovely pastries, ladies' . . . 'Who'll buy my onions?' . . . 'Glass cut here' . . . 'Ruthless, the dog shearer!' Meanwhile, in the background, Odette was droning on about green surah, draped foulards, *lait antéphélique*, lamps decorated with gauze globe covers fringed with pearls, and the Francillon bag for the theatre, which could hold a fan and a lorgnette.

Quite deafened, Victor stubbed out his cigarette butt and made a beeline for his frock coat.

'I have to go,' he said.

In consternation, Odette cast a distraught glance at the carpet strewn with clothes and catalogues. 'But . . . what about my fitting? You don't love me any more, my duck!' she whined, hanging on to Victor's arm.

He kissed her forehead. 'You know I do, my love.'

'At least promise me you'll take me to the station on the day I leave. I'll come and fetch you from the bookshop.'

'I swear,' he said, gently extricating himself and hurrying down the corridor.

He gave a friendly wave to Denise, the sad-eyed young Breton girl, newly arrived from her native Quimper and now a prisoner in a narrow kitchen with an irascible mistress.

Odette consoled herself with the thought that she would go to La Reine des Abeilles after lunch to get supplies of Fountain of Youth water and crème Farnese.

The light breeze was more reminiscent of April than June. Victor strolled as far as Rue de Rivoli. The previous day, before going to meet Odette, he had warned Kenji that he would not be returning to the bookshop until mid-afternoon. He felt as though he was on holiday and was enjoying his freedom all the more because of the frantic activity around him. The workrooms of the fashion houses on Rue de la Paix and Rue Saint-Honoré were having their lunch hour and there was a crush of apprentice seamstresses in the arcades as they stormed the soup stalls and the dairies. The less fortunate ones, clutching their lunch in their hands, scattered like a flock of sparrows all over the Tuileries, descending on the benches and chairs. A barrel organ was slowly grinding out the quadrille from *Orpheus in the Underworld*. Some children in tartan outfits were chasing a ball, which Victor stopped with his foot. Vendors were milling around with bundles of newspapers under their arms, shouting at the top of their voices.

'Get your *Événement* here! Drama at the Colonial Exhibition!'

'*Le Passe-partout*, late edition. Another death at the Expo! New eyewitness reports!'

Victor stopped a skinny adolescent, with a tangled shock of hair sticking out of his cap, to buy *Le Passe-partout*.

'AND NOW THIS!' he read on the front page, above a drawing by Tasha of a sinister bee armed with a sword charging towards the massive crowd by the entrance of the Colonial Palace. An Annamese soldier with blackened teeth, smiling beneath a plaited straw hat, pointed a menacing sabre at the monster, whilst an alarmed policeman was hurriedly climbing to the top of a coconut tree. Victor could not help laughing. With his newspaper under his arm he crossed the road, bought a pound of cherries from a fruit-seller and entered the Tuileries Gardens.

All the stone benches were taken, mostly by the apprentices, who had pieces of newspaper spread out on their laps, and were eating chips, radishes or demi-baguettes stuffed with charcuterie, when they weren't shrieking with laughter. Victor managed to find a spot on the Jeu de Paume terrace, shaded by a chestnut tree, next to two apprentices, who leant over, giggling, to get a better look at him and then spoke in hushed voices to each other.

'S'afternoon I'm going to the restocking at the wholesaler's, worse luck.'

'That's nothing. I've got to brush all the feather bagnolets. The boss says they're covered in dust. I should think so – right now we're not selling any. Everybody wants flowery hats.'

'Did you see that? He's having a good look at us!'

'He's good-looking. And well decked out. A real peach. I'd have some of that!'

Victor doffed his hat, and they giggled even more. When he started reading his newspaper, they were distracted by two non-commissioned officers on a spree, who kept walking past the bench, giving them meaningful looks. Eventually they got up and waddled off in pursuit of them. Victor took the opportunity to put the cherries down beside him. Eating them slowly, he spat out the stones at the disappointed sparrows.

The man who met his death yesterday afternoon outside the Colonial Palace had also been stung by a bee. He was an American naturalist and explorer whose identity has not yet been revealed. Recently arrived in Paris, he was staying at the Grand Hotel. On arrival at the scene, the Public Prosecutor's Office undertook a basic investigation. Eyewitnesses told our reporter that the victim was seen raising a hand to his neck and collapsed shortly after. A pineapple vendor from Martinique confirmed sightings of wasps around the displays of sweet food. It's time for the Health and Hygiene Council to take drastic measures to ensure the public's safety. But how . . .

Victor stopped suddenly to chase away a horsefly that was buzzing around his head. A resigned little donkey trotted by, ridden by a tense little girl and preceded by a cloud of flies. Further away the female workers had finished their picnics. They were still really just young girls, and they were playing hide and seek or skipping with ropes in a flurry of dresses and underskirts. Abandoning his cherries, Victor decided to finish reading the article in a restaurant in the arcades, where he recalled eating an excellent chicken with watercress followed by a coffee ice cream. Before rolling it up, he gave *Le Passe-partout* a final look. How odd: he and Tasha had both been at the scene of that incident at les Invalides the previous day . . .

Tasha folded *Le Passe-partout*, stuffed it into her shopping bag between a bunch of carrots and a kilo of turnips, and pushed open a carriage entrance. Once she was in the passage the hustle and bustle of Rue Notre-Dame-de-Lorette faded to a vague hum, which was overtaken by an irregular grating noise. Tasha stopped on the threshold of the courtyard to watch the landlady cycling around. Dressed in culottes and ankle boots, her plump calves straining to move the pedals, the sporty lady was going round in circles on the cobbles. Occasionally the bicycle wheels would get stuck between them and she would almost keel over.

'Good day to you, Mademoiselle Kherson!' shouted the woman, visibly relieved at having an excuse to allow herself a break.

She descended from her vehicle with some difficulty and leant it against a wall. 'Don't you think I'm making progress?'

'In leaps and bounds, Mademoiselle Becker. If you go on like this, you'll soon be able to cycle around Parc Monceau.'

'In public! You cannot be serious! Our misogynistic culture is not ready to accept such a revolution in behaviour and dress! And yet, believe me, trousers are the future for women! Such freedom of movement! By the way, congratulations on your drawings. I read the newspaper. I envy you having such a fine profession. What fun you must have with all those dead bodies!'

'Excuse me, I must go up. Work, you know . . . I'll give you the rent tomorrow morning, without fail.'

'Oh, I'm not worried about that. I know you are dependable, unlike certain others . . . the Serb, for example. I've got my eye on him!'

Tasha crossed the yard and opened a glass door to climb up six floors to her attic lodgings. Her door was the fourth on the right down a long, dark corridor, poorly lit by an opaque skylight. She put her shopping bag on the basin opposite her door, and searched in her pocket for the key. Just as she was about to turn the handle, the next door along opened and a bearded giant in shirtsleeves appeared, carrying a pitcher.

'Good day to you, Monsieur Ducovitch.'

'Mademoiselle Tasha! How delightful! Have you seen Madame Vulture pedalling in the yard? She worships only at the altar of the god of Rent and I'm stony broke.'

'She's just practising. Don't worry, she'll be going home soon. It's sauerkraut time.'

'Every quarter it's the same with that harridan. I daren't even go down to buy some tobacco for my pipe.'

'You have to put yourself in her shoes, Monsieur Ducovitch. Two of her tenants have already done a moonlight flit, so of course she's keeping watch!'

'Please do call me Danilo. I can tell you that I very rarely try to put myself in others' shoes, as I risk losing my own! But, God knows, I don't like her!'

'Are you still appearing in one of those Charles Garnier

historical tableaux at the Expo entrance? I've forgotten which one.'

'You promised to come and see me. I'm upset you haven't. It's an easy one to remember: I play one of those prehistoric men dressed in animal skins who live in a cave and grunt what are supposedly the beginnings of human language. And there I am dreaming of interpreting the works of Modest Mussorgsky!'

'Well, why don't you? People will be so surprised, it will make you a sensation!'

'Whilst holding a club? You must be joking! Why didn't I land a role as one of the figureheads in the medieval house or in the Renaissance home? At least there I could have given them a ritornello. Whereas in my cave I can't even read the novel you lent me. Just imagine, Cro-Magnon man reading Tolstoy! What indignity! Jack of all trades and master of none! In the ten years since I came to this city, I've only ever had odd jobs with no prospects, although I have the makings of a baritone! The body of a Goliath with the soul of a midget, that's what I am.'

He opened his large mouth, alarming Tasha, who thought he was going to demonstrate his baritone, but he only let out a pitiful cry, lamenting his miserable fate. She consoled him vaguely and picked up her shopping bag, desperate to escape his moaning. He noticed the turnips.

'You like those vegetables, do you?' he asked, suddenly cheered.

'Not really, but they are cheap and I make purées from them mixed with carrots, salt and cream.'

Danilo Ducovitch now had a greedy look in his eye.

'I'll bring you a bowl of it,' Tasha promised as she slipped through her door.

'Thank you, Mademoiselle Tasha, you *are* good! What a pickle I'm in: Jack of all trades and master of none,' he muttered as he went back into his room, pitcher in hand.

Tasha's garret was sparsely furnished with an iron bedstead, two trunks for her clothes, and an earthenware stove that gave out no heat in the winter and disappeared in the summer beneath the sketches that had been hung on its edge with clothes pegs. There was also a dresser, a round table with a wobbly leg wedged with a brick, two chairs that were losing their stuffing, a threadbare rug, and the supreme luxury of a recessed alcove in the wall where about twenty books were piled up. The chocolate-coloured wallpaper was peeling in some places, and in others was hidden by canvases, mostly of the rooftops of Paris at all hours of the day and night. Standing on a wooden stool, Tasha could see out of her dormer window a mass of red or grey roofs going up into the clouds, and had decided to devote herself for now entirely to this subject matter.

She went into the tiny room that served both as kitchen and bathroom – the water closets were at the end of the corridor and were shared by all the lodgers on the sixth floor.

She piled up carrots and turnips by a small coal stove, plunged her hands into the basin, which she had taken care to fill up before she had gone out, and wet her face and neck, trying to ignore Danilo's singing exercises in the next-door room. She returned to the main room, unlaced the ankle boots that she hoped would last her until the end of the summer, undressed quickly, throwing onto the bed her hat, gloves, jacket, skirt, underskirt, knickers, stockings, and bodice. Then she unravelled the cotton band that she wore around her chest as she could not stand the constraints of a corset. Naked, with her hair loose, she sat on the bed with a sigh of pleasure. She touched her breasts. She wanted to rediscover the feeling of Hans's caresses; she had so enjoyed making love with him. *Well, forget about that, my dear.* She grabbed a big grey paint-spattered smock, slipped it on and went over to her easel and the canvas she was currently working on: two slate roofs where pigeons were pecking about in the dying rays of the sun. She picked up a paintbrush and, after a moment's hesitation, began to retouch a gutter. A preposterous idea was going through her mind. She imagined a swarm of vengeful bees flying out of the left corner of the chimney, intent on ridding the city of those stupid individuals who understood nothing about art and were only interested in money. She could not resist the temptation and, with the tip of her paintbrush, she added some tiny yellow and black marks above the gutter. Her thoughts turned suddenly to her father. Was Pinkus still in Berlin? She had heard nothing from him for a year. *As long as he hasn't got involved in some murky political business again.* She shrugged. She was wrong to worry: he always managed to extricate himself from any trouble.

With a single glance through the shop window Victor established that the bookshop was empty. The sole occupant was Joseph, sitting on his stool, lost in a novel, as he was every day at this hour. From time to time he stopped to bite into an apple. He looked up at the sound of the door chime.

'Monsieur Victor! Monsieur Mori waited to have lunch with you, because Mademoiselle Germaine had made *escalopes à la milanaise*, but as you didn't come, he's gone.'

'I warned him yesterday that I would not be back until three. Did he say where he was going?' asked Victor, frowning.

'He said he had a meeting with a colleague.'

Victor thought the colleague in question probably wore a skirt and ankle boots, and would now be delightedly opening parcels from La Reine des Abeilles.

'Have you made any sales?'

'Everything went really well yesterday. It's a pity you weren't here. I managed to unload that incomplete Diderot *Encyclopédie* – you know, the one that was really damp from being in that cellar on Rue Le Regrattier – onto a provincial dealer, and then I—'

'Good, good. What are you reading?'

'*Monsieur Lecoq* – you recommended it and it's gripping.'

Victor smiled. 'You can't survive on popular novels. You need to eat, Joseph, and something more than just apples. What if you tucked into my *escalope à la milanaise*?'

'I'd rather feed my grey matter than have an overloaded stomach, which would give me heartburn. Mama always says that three-quarters of all illnesses are as a result of pyrotechnics and I—'

'Surely you mean pyrosis?'

'And anyway, this police investigation is just too thrilling. He's really good that Lecoq, the things he can deduce from very tiny clues . . . What would he say if he had my notebook?'

Joseph took a black cloth-bound notebook out of his pocket and threw it down on the counter.

'What do you write in here? The names of customers or your amorous conquests?'

'Something much better than that! I'm interested in unusual events, unexplained mysteries. I cut out articles from newspapers and stick them in. Have a look!'

Victor leafed through the notebook and read some pages at random:

> Frogs rain down at Montauban . . . Crime in a carriage . . . the headless woman of Bondy . . . a grouper washed up on the Ourcq canal . . . Merovingian jewels found in a bag of firelighters . . . murderous bees in Paris.

He looked closely at the article dated 13 May.

> Yesterday morning, at Batignolles station, amongst the spectators who had come to welcome Buffalo Bill and his troupe was Jean Méring, rag-and-bone man by trade, of Rue de la Parcheminerie, who died as a result of a bee-sting.

'That paragraph's from last month's *L'Éclair*. You think that is odd too, eh? Nobody's made the connection between the death of this rag-and-bone man and those that occurred at the Expo. Yet it's worthy of a Gaboriau novel. If only I could write!'

Victor smiled. Buffalo Bill's name reminded him of his encounter with Tasha.

'You think that's funny, Monsieur Victor? Oh, I realise I'm not an educated man, but I know all about books!'

'Oh, I'm not laughing at you, Joseph. It's Buffalo Bill, he made me think of someone who—'

'Monsieur Legris! You're here at last! I came by twice yesterday but you were nowhere to be seen!' roared the Comtesse de Salignac, slamming the door shut.

Victor started, then winked at Joseph as he squeezed past him and stuffed the notebook in his frock coat pocket. 'Don't forget to ask me for it back,' he whispered as he hurried to the rear of the shop.

'What's got into him?' cried the Comtesse.

'Nothing we need worry about – unless it's one of those bees!' said Joseph, gobbling up his apple core.

'Well, young man, can you tell me where Monsieur Legris has gone?'

'I think he's gone down to his studio in the basement, next to the stockroom. That's where he develops his photographs. Can you see the little red lamp on the chimney behind the bust of Molière? It's electric. When it's on it means that Monsieur Legris has shut himself away in his secret room and will certainly not be disturbed.'

'Disturbed – that's what he is,' grumbled the Comtesse. 'I wanted to know if he had finally laid his hands on a copy of *Eagle and Dove*.'

'Is that a book about birds?' Joseph teased, rolling the apple stalk between his thumb and index finger.

'Of course not! It's a novel by Zénaïde Fleuriot!'

*

Having shut himself away in his laboratory, Victor took down the prints he had developed the previous day, carefully noting down the time and place of the shot on the back of each one, then lined them up in front of him. There was no question about it, the precision of this portable Acmé camera surpassed anything he had previously come across: how extraordinary to be able to take photographs in a fraction of a second without the subject even knowing! Granted, the negatives of Samba the Senegalese, which did have true artistic value, could have benefited from a little more light, but the ones of Tasha had come out extremely well. Once they'd been retouched, they would be perfect. He prepared his tools – a small paintbrush and a bottle of China ink – then sat down at the table. When he dipped it in the bottle, the paintbrush came out completely clean: he had run out of ink. He put the set of photographs in an envelope and, with his frock coat on, passed through the stockroom, almost stopping to look at a pile of books. But he had to do something about the envelope. He went back upstairs and ventured carefully into the bookshop. There were no customers. Joseph was busy cleaning the bookcases with a feather duster. Victor gave a little whistle, and Joseph was soon at his side.

'Has the battle-axe gone?'

'Do you call her that too? I was the one who suggested the name to Monsieur Mori,' Joseph said proudly. 'But watch out because she'll be coming back. She's warned me she won't go home without her books.'

'If she asks for me, tell her I'm at the top of the Tower!'

Victor dashed towards the staircase leading to the first floor but suddenly stopped and retraced his steps to tap Molière on the head. This had been his good-luck charm since he had first owned the bookshop.

Victor crept into Kenji's apartment, with an excuse at the ready. It was empty. He looked in vain for *Los Caprichos* in the dresser. Some other volumes were missing too. He shut it again. Would Kenji have sold the Goya? But it meant so much to him! As he stood up he noticed that two framed Utamaros were missing from the wall. He recalled Kenji's visit to the bookseller on Rue Auber and his rendezvous on the terrace of Café de la Paix. He had then spent all the money from these sales at La Reine des Abeilles. The name made him feel uneasy. Of course, one had to realise it was just a coincidence, but bees had been impinging on his life a little too much recently.

On the table, protected by a large green blotter, a set of calligraphy brushes were arranged alongside a ream of rice paper and bottles of different coloured inks. He picked up the black ink and noticed *Le Figaro de la Tour* dated 22 June, which had fallen out of Kenji's pocket on his birthday. In the margin, there was a mysterious sentence written in a familiar angular hand: 'Meet J. C. 24-6 12.30 p.m. Grand Hotel Room 312.' J.C. like Jesus Christ? he joked to himself. But then he had a sudden thought. He took *Le Passe-partout* out of his pocket and reread the article with the headline 'AND NOW THIS!'. The naturalist who had died outside the Colonial Palace had been staying at the Grand Hotel.

That's quite a coincidence, he thought. Though no more than me being at the scene of a crime twice in succession. He shrugged his shoulders, more concerned than he dared admit to himself. As he moved round the oak table, on the floor by the armchair he saw a half-open leather bag from which protruded a number of parcels wrapped in mauve tissue paper. He kneeled down to inspect the contents: a box of face powder, a foulard, a miniature Eiffel Tower and a bottle of Jasmin de Provence perfume. All these presents carried the seal of La Reine des Abeilles, an elegant gilded label in the shape of a shield. He whistled through his teeth. *My goodness, he's really spoiling his lady-love! I'd give anything to know who she is!*

'As I say, Monsieur Legris assured me that he was in a position to find both of them! *Eagle and Dove* and *Bad Days*! Valentine can confirm it; she was with me!' shouted the Comtesse de Salignac into Kenji's face as he wrote out record cards.

'Shouting won't help, Madame Battle-axe,' whispered Joseph, stifling a laugh.

The Comtesse's niece, a thin young girl with a long nose and spotty cheeks, was fiddling self-consciously with her parasol. 'Never mind, Aunt, we'll come back,' she murmured.

'No! Have I nothing better to do than come here? Well, sir, what do you say?'

'That this is not a station library, but a bookshop,' Kenji declared drily.

The Comtesse turned puce and opened her mouth, but before she could protest Victor's voice was heard coming from behind her. 'My dear Kenji, you have no idea! These novels are so refreshing, they are what see us through the hot weather and give us a change from the vulgar writings of Monsieur de Maupassant and Monsieur Zola!'

Haughtily rising to her full height, whilst her niece looked at Victor with adoration, the Comtesse refused to be so easily mollified.

'Vulgar is a weak word. Rotten seems more appropriate to me. Just like this rag in which some illustrator who thinks he's witty pokes fun at the authorities. This is why we are headed towards chaos and disaster,' she concluded, throwing the latest edition of *Le Passe-partout* onto the desk.

Kenji calmly picked up the newspaper, unfolded it, looked over the front page, lingering over the drawing, and the signature 'Tasha K.' written across a coconut. 'It's very educational. I had no idea that coppers were so good at climbing trees.' He folded up the newspaper again and went back to his work.

Victor coughed politely. 'I'm so sorry, Madame la Comtesse, I haven't yet found the two Zénaïde Fleuriots. I can offer you some Raoul de Naverys, equally pleasant reads, which your niece will really enjoy.'

Valentine looked gratefully at Victor before feigning a sudden interest in the handle of her parasol.

'Joseph, go down to the stockroom, the complete works of Raoul de Navery, they're in the bilge section.'

'Bilge? What does that word mean?' asked the Comtesse.

'It's . . . er . . . it's a way of . . .'

'It's how we booksellers describe our very best purchases,' ventured Kenji, hurrying to Victor's aid.

'Really? It's a bizarre expression,' the Comtesse replied suspiciously.

'It probably comes from the English, like the word "clown",' hazarded Valentine, earning herself a grateful wink from Victor and turning quite pink.

'I don't see the connection.'

'I have them here, Madame Battle—la Comtesse!' Joseph exclaimed triumphantly, emerging with a cardboard box in his arms.

Whilst the two women examined the dusty books, Victor went up to the desk and looked closely at the newspaper. 'What do you think? This is beginning to get worrying.'

'I'm not scared of insects. When I was young my father showed me how to squash them with the palm of my hand.'

'If we buy up all your Naverys, you will of course give us a discount?' grumbled the Comtesse.

'That goes without saying,' Victor answered, impatient to rid himself of both the books and the lady.

'And you'll arrange for them to be delivered?'

'Joseph will take care of that. He'll deliver them to your home this evening,' Kenji promised, making an effort to be polite again.

She graciously smiled at him and made a majestic exit, with her niece at her heels. Valentine's pointed nose lingered a little too long on the other side of the shop window, but Victor did not even look in her direction.

'Watch out, a slip of the tongue and you'll call her "Madame Battle-axe" to her face one of these days!' he said to Joseph with a laugh.

'And on that day, you will be dismissed!' Kenji declared severely. 'Victor, I hope you are free tomorrow. You haven't forgotten we are stocktaking, have you?' he added as he got back down to work.

Did he want me to be away? Victor wondered while countering, 'Of course not. By the way, you haven't told me, was the Rue de l'Odéon library at all interesting?'

'No. Too expensive. Much too expensive.'

What a pro. He just lies through his teeth! Victor thought. 'Whilst I remember, could you lend me your copy of Goya's *Caprichos*?'

Kenji leant even more keenly over his card file and answered neutrally, 'That's a bit tricky. I recently gave it to the bookbinder on Rue Monsieur-le-Prince. He's so busy right now it'll probably be some time before it's ready.'

CHAPTER FIVE

Morning, Monday 27 June

THE previous day had been exhausting, what with stocktaking in the bookshop and laying out the new titles.

'It makes you think,' Kenji had remarked, 'knowing that all these books that everyone is talking about today will be languishing tomorrow on the second-hand stalls . . .'

With aching back, Victor was once again going up Rue Croix-des-Petits-Champs where, at this early hour, there were just a few costermongers' carts to be seen. Despite feeling tired in the evening he had had to write both the literary column and the advertisement that he had promised Marius, all in the sole hope of seeing Tasha again. He had been surprised to discover that his mind was not feeling as slow as his body and had in fact been able to produce an article of some quality. Perhaps I ought to be a writer? he had thought as he reread his work. Then he remembered Kenji's words: 'It makes you think . . .'

A storm was brewing and the heat was oppressive. He stopped for a moment at a florist's where two women were arranging carnations in vases. If Tasha was not at the news-paper offices, he would take a bouquet to her lodgings and leave it for her at the entrance with a light-hearted invitation to dinner. *No, you fool, first you'll knock on her door* . . . He shrugged. It was too early in the day to be having these kinds of thoughts.

The buzz of activity in the offices of *Le Passe-partout* reminded him of an operating theatre. Surrounding the Linotype operator like nurses round a surgeon, Eudoxie Allard and Isidore Gouvier were paying close attention to the comings and goings of the machine typographers.

Victor had to tap Gouvier on the shoulder to get his attention. The old man looked up with his round-eyed bulldog face, an unlit cigar under his drooping moustache.

'Good day, Monsieur Lenoir.'

'Legris.'

'Do excuse me, it's this job. It does for your brain. Eudoxie . . .'

The secretary, who was wearing a dark faille dress, which served to emphasise her *femme fatale* air, glanced at Victor with indifference and gave him a perfunctory nod.

'I'm going to finish the correspondence,' she told Gouvier, who was not listening.

She went off to a side door, then turned back to appraise Victor like a housekeeper considering produce in a shop window, and seemed to revise her opinion of him. Smoothing back her glossy dark hair with one hand and fiddling with the brooch on her bosom with the other, she lingered on the threshold. Sensing that she was watching him, Victor in turn considered her. She gave him a slight smile and then fled like a nervous schoolgirl.

'Would you like me to explain it all to you?' muttered Gouvier. 'There you have the marble, which is in fact just a polished metal plate. It can hold four formes the size of a newspaper page. Inside the formes are the lines of type for the headlines as well as the plates for the illustrations.'

Victor watched distractedly as the operator turned a small handle several times to lock the lines in place. The formes disappeared inside the machine. Gouvier cleared his throat. 'Good, now you place the sheets of damp card on the—'

'Is Marius here?' interrupted Victor.

'Wait, I haven't finished,' growled the old man. 'The dried board comes back out of the press, can you see? It bears the impression of the page. Now we take it across the courtyard to the printer. Clusel is down there. He's taken over from Bonnet, who has gone to a reception for the Prince of Wales. Follow me.'

Leaning against the rotary press, wearing an English suit from Etheridge's, Antonin Clusel was looking over the front page and chewing the end of his cigar.

'These two deaths are our *pièce de résistance*. We've hit the jackpot!' he exulted to Victor, who held out the two pages of his literary review without a word.

Clusel ran through it and, with an embarrassed laugh, spat his cigar out onto the floor, crushing it with the toe of his shoe.

'Excellent diatribe against school teaching. Very amusing, that suggestion of yours to banish the "ismes" to the isthmus of Panama. But I'm sorry, it's too late for today's edition. It will have to go in tomorrow.'

'You can add this too.'

Clusel cast an eye over the notice.

ELZÉVIR BOOKSHOP
V. LEGRIS – K. MORI

Founded in 1835
New and antiquarian books
First Editions
Catalogue available
18 Rue des Saints-Pères, Paris VIe

'Perfect, perfect. Eudoxie will open an account for you.'

'So, any news?'

'I should say so! The man who died at the Colonial Exhibition has been identified, an American named Cavendish. Apparently also stung by a bee. Gouvier has been laying siege to police HQ, but they don't have any more information than that. The police are saying nothing, rather like the army! They prefer to play safe and stick to the story of killer bees. They get the blame for everything, those honey-gatherers!'

'But it's all suspiciously obvious,' put in Gouvier. 'Two stiffs in the same place in three days, and then there's that anonymous letter, for heaven's sake!'

'They want to feed us information bit by bit. Well, they'll soon see. I'm going to give them news, all right, and not in dribs and drabs!' Clusel added heatedly. 'Rummaging around at the faculty, I discovered some very interesting facts.'

He took the front page and read out loud: '"It is sometimes said that frail individuals can suffer an epileptic fit after being stung by a bee. However, the only fatal cases were reported by a colonial doctor three years ago. Two African children succumbed to tetanus after being stung by a bee.'"

'Tetanus?' repeated Victor, frowning. 'I am no expert, but . . . would an infection like that show up so quickly after the sting?'

'I was coming to that! The incubation period for tetanus varies between a few hours and two weeks before the first symptoms begin to appear. Now, our two victims kicked the bucket there and then. So tetanus is not the explanation! We can therefore deduce that either these are murders – and Gouvier is right, the anonymous letter favours that hypothesis – or, we are dealing with the early signs of a mysterious epidemic. In either case the authorities do not want to make the public panic and endanger the Exposition. They are deliberately playing things down by blaming the bees. It would not be the first time that the interests of the common people came a poor second to those of the bigwigs who govern us.'

'That's a rather cynical view,' commented Victor.

'Feed the flames of controversy, Monsieur Legris, that is the job of the press! It's all in here!' cried Clusel, waving *Le Passe-partout*. '"DEATH STALKS THE EIFFEL TOWER AND THE COLONIAL PALACE." Quite a headline, don't you think? Our circulation figures are going to go wild. Listen to this: "On June the twentieth, John Cavendish arrived from London to stay at the Grand Hotel, room three twelve. Four days later, in the early afternoon, he . . ."'

Victor was no longer listening. Clusel's words faded into the background. Staring blankly, Victor tried to remember.

'J.C. . . .Grand Hotel . . . Room . . . J.C. . . .' John Cavendish? No, impossible!

He leant sharply forward. 'The Grand Hotel? Which one?' he asked in an altered voice.

'The one on Boulevard des Capucines, of course. Where else? That's where all the Yankees stay when they are in Paris. That is, those who can afford it. I could live for two weeks on what it costs to stay there for one night.'

'I must go. Tell Marius I'll call by later.'

Clusel held out his hand, but Victor kept his own in his pocket. It was trembling too much. Without so much as a goodbye to Gouvier, he raced off. Gouvier and Clusel exchanged knowing looks.

'You need to be one of us to really understand the underhand ways of journalism,' Gouvier remarked.

Room . . . room . . . what was the room number? wondered Victor as he hurried through Galerie Véro-Dodat where the sound of thunder reverberated. The storm broke as he came out onto Rue Croix-des-Petits-Champs. The only way he could find out for sure was by going back to the bookshop. He had forgotten all about Tasha.

For the first time in several days, Joseph was surrounded by customers, and, not knowing which way to turn, he had asked Kenji to come to his rescue. When the door opened and in came a drenched Victor, they both looked at him hopefully but, ignoring them, he hurried up to the first floor, vaguely murmuring something about an umbrella.

He took off his wet shoes, went into Kenji's room and marched straight up to the oak table, but *Le Figaro de la Tour* had disappeared.

Cross with himself, he paced up and down the room. He decided to open one of the drawers, then closed it and opened another, but he could not get over his reluctance to spy on Kenji in this way! Even if he was only seeking to reassure himself, it felt terribly wrong. He was all set to abandon the search when, with a final impatient gesture, he lifted up the blotter. There was the newspaper: 'Meet J.C. 24-6 12.30 p.m. Grand Hotel Room 312.'

3, 1, 2. Eyes riveted on the numbers, fists clenched, he felt almost at breaking point. There was no mistaking it, all the facts led to one dreadful conclusion. Kenji had met John Cavendish. He put the blotter back in place and, leaving his friend's apartment, returned to his own.

If Kenji's furnishings displayed a taste for the French style of the time of Louis XIII in the seventeenth century, Victor's showed him to be unashamedly nostalgic for the country where he was raised – England.

Starting with the dining room, with its massive table and six dining chairs, through the bedroom containing a bed, bedside tables, a wardrobe and a chest of drawers, to the study, which was equipped with a roll-top desk, a solicitor's filing cabinet and a breakfront bookcase, everything was made out of mahogany. Petrol lamps hung down from the ceiling, and on the floor were carpets of vaguely oriental design. On the walls hung Constable watercolours and two Gainsborough portraits inherited from his father, Edmond Legris, who, although he had known nothing about art, had followed the advice of Daphne, his wife, in making his purchases. A very beautiful red chalk drawing of the young woman hung over the bed, mounted in an oval frame. The only concession to France was a series of framed pen-and-ink drawings, arranged on either side of the desk and showing various aspects of Fourier's phalanstery. Before leaving the bookshop to his nephew, Uncle Émile, a fervent Utopian, wanted to make sure that he would never part with his sketches, nor the assortment of objects and books stored in the basement. And when Victor came to be with him in his final moments, he made him swear an oath to that effect.

The overcast sky let hardly any light into the small room where Victor sat at his desk. He decided to try out the Rochester lamp that Odette had given him. He filled it with petrol and lit the wick by turning a button. A bluish light appeared in the lampshade and for a moment Victor felt less worried. He was reminded of a winter morning shortly after his father's burial, which for him had been a deliverance. He saw again the now lifeless face of the man he called 'Monsieur'. Twenty-one years had passed but the memory of Edmond Legris's coldness had never faded. Kenji had freed Victor from his fear. Day after day, in his company, he had discovered a taste for life. By the light of the chandeliers, bright with candles, in the little first-floor drawing room above the bookshop in Sloane Square, Kenji would read him accounts of his adventures, teach him the arts of paper-folding and of calligraphy, whilst the sound of Daphne's melodious voice humming 'Greensleeves' rose up from the ground floor. One evening Victor realised that he was hearing his mother sing for the first time.

With a vaguely sick feeling in his stomach, he picked up a black notebook that had been lying on the table and wrote down the note from the margin of *Le Figaro de la Tour*. He then drew in pencil a row of increasingly large question marks. The light from the lamp flickered for a brief moment. He must protect Kenji. Whatever he might have done, Victor had to look after him, just as Kenji had looked after Victor as a child from the day his stern father engaged the young Japanese man, newly arrived in London, as an assistant. Above all, he must find out what had happened and calm his own, probably misplaced, fears. He had a sudden thought. Café de la Paix was part of the Grand Hotel. The stout man with the monocle who had bought Kenji's prints – was he Cavendish? What time had Victor seen them together? Ten thirty, eleven o'clock? Not half-past twelve, in any case. At that moment he remembered he had been eating a portion of Pont-Neuf potatoes on Quai Conti before taking a cab to the Esplanade des Invalides.

Abandoning his damp frock coat, he slipped on a tweed jacket and dry shoes, and went back downstairs. Intrigued, Kenji left the two affluent men he had been serving leafing through an eighteenth-century atlas, and came to stand in front of Victor to block his path. 'Is anything the matter?'

'No, everything's fine. I just have an urgent errand to run, so have lunch without me.'

'What about your umbrella?'

'Oh, it's not going to rain any more!'

Kenji went to the window to watch the young man as he strode towards Boulevard Saint-Germain.

The Grand Hotel wasn't just a palace, it was a town in its own right. Its eight hundred luxurious bedrooms were spread over five floors where an army of bellboys, chambermaids and waiters were engaged in the business of ensuring the comfort of its classy, cosmopolitan clientele. The Grand Hotel enjoyed an impressive reputation across the Atlantic for its excellent cuisine, fine wines, splendid ballroom, reading rooms and music. It was also known for its American bar, where guests could be entertained by violins from a Tzigane orchestra, for its bureau de change, and both men and women's hairdresser. You felt you need never leave – everything was there, including nature in the form of a jungle of palm trees and a multitude of rubber plants in pots.

As he entered this caravanserai, Victor felt as if he were embarking on a transatlantic voyage. He was almost a little giddy, though this was because of his state of mind, rather than anything to do with the hotel. He paused in front of reception and waited for one of the black-liveried clerks to turn to him. Victor asked for Monsieur Belot, Antoine Belot, just arrived that morning from Lyon. The name was duly searched for in a register, repeated several times, only to be met by perplexed expressions and the shaking of heads.

'I'm sorry, Monsieur, we have no one under that name. One moment, I'll check our reservations . . . No, no Monsieur Belot.'

'Are you sure?' asked Victor. 'That's strange. I received a telegram from him yesterday evening. Monsieur Belot arranged to meet me here in room three twelve. We were going to lunch together at Café de la Paix.'

'Three twelve? That's impossible, sir.'

'Why impossible? Room three twelve, Monsieur Belot, wine merchant. Would you like to see the wire?'

Victor said this with such assurance that he almost convinced himself of Antoine Belot's existence! Without waiting for an answer, he took out his wallet. The employee winked almost imperceptibly at a colleague, who immediately intervened.

'Don't trouble yourself, sir. There must be some mistake. We have no vacant rooms at the moment; everything has been reserved for months because of the Exposition, you understand. Room three twelve was . . . is occupied by an American, Mr Cavendish, who—'

'Was? Mr Cavendish? *The* John Cavendish, who's been mentioned in the paper?' cried Victor. 'Would you believe it? Are you trying to tell me that Antoine is sharing a room with . . . a dead man?'

The employee looked about him anxiously, then leant over the counter and said in a low voice: 'Ah . . . we don't really want to broadcast that unfortunate news. I'm sorry to insist, Monsieur, but are you sure that your friend did not go to stay at the Grand Hotel des Capucines? It's very near here and, if you would kindly wait a moment, we could telephone . . .'

'You must be right: I must have confused the hotels. How stupid of me!'

Moving away a little, Victor opened his wallet and pretended to consult a piece of paper inside it.

'Good God, that's unbelievable, I ought to wear glasses, it is indeed the Grand Hotel des Capucines.'

Relieved, the employee's face took on a sympathetic expression and he pointed vaguely towards the door. 'Just a bit further down, sir, at number thirty-seven.'

Victor went back up the street and then branched off to Rue Daunou. At Avenue de l'Opéra, he went into a restaurant, where he ordered the dish of the day, rabbit in a mustard sauce. He closed his eyes, and imagined the corpse of a monocled cowboy garnished with green beans. Cowboy, cowboy, who had mentioned that word? He pulled himself together and leant back in his chair. *Kenji, what have you got yourself involved in? Who did you see at Café de la Paix? Why did you meet John Cavendish a few hours before his death? Was it only you who met him? You must know he's been killed, so why haven't you spoken to me about it? I could have reassured you and helped you come up with an alibi . . .*

The waiter placed before him a steaming plate and a small jug of wine. The sight of the meat made him feel queasy so he made do with picking at the potatoes with his fork. *One potato, Kenji is not a murderer; two potatoes, how can I be sure? Three potatoes, Kenji has secrets, a mistress and a past I know nothing about; four, eat something, the waiter is watching you.*

He managed to swallow the potatoes, but as for the rabbit, when the waiter wasn't looking he wrapped it in a napkin and rolled it under the seat.

'An ice cream for Monsieur? It's included in the price.'

With his spoon in his tutti-frutti ice cream, Victor turned and tried to make out the front-page headlines of *L'Événement*, which the man at the next table had opened to read.

'DEAD MAN AT COLONIAL PALACE NONE OTHER THAN EXPLORER JOHN CAVENDISH,' announced one headline in thick letters. The man put down the paper, threw a few coins into the saucer, and got up.

'What's happening in the world?' asked Victor.

'General Boulanger is refusing to leave London, even though he has many supporters in France . . . We need a man like that, what with all those suicides because of Panama. The saddest thing is that it's the small investors who have lost everything. It's the same old story: they staked everything on those shares and now the canal's failed, they're sunk. No, it's not very good news at all, Monsieur,' the man said as he put the paper in front of Victor. 'Here you are, I'll leave it for you.'

'Would you like anything else?' enquired the waiter, looking disapprovingly at the ice cream Victor had barely touched.

'Just coffee and the bill.'

He scanned the article on Cavendish. The American naturalist had been invited to the Exposition by the Minister of Foreign Affairs and was to have been made a Chevalier of the Légion d'Honneur and a member of the Geographical Society the very day that he died. His accounts of his numerous expeditions, translated into French, had been published regularly in *Le Tour du Monde, Nouveau Journal des Voyages*, the earliest ones going back to the beginning of 1857.

There followed a brief biography of the man. Born in Boston in 1828, he had travelled through the Indian Peninsula,

Cambodia, Siam and Burma from 1852 to 1860, and had collected specimens of plants for pharmacopoeia. In 1863 he was in London for a series of conferences. He had then stayed in England until 1867, writing several books about his expeditions. On his return to America his government had given him the task of cataloguing the flora and fauna of Alaska, the vast territory recently bought from Russia by the United States . . .

Victor put the paper down. His father had engaged Kenji in 1863. So he had been in London at the same time as Cavendish. Before that, he too had travelled extensively in Asia. In his youth, Victor had loved listening to the tales of these wanderings, although he could not now remember exactly where he went and when. And besides, Kenji himself had made these facts difficult to recall by captivating the English boy with the suspense of a tiger hunt or a shipwreck on the China Seas. Victor opened his notebook and wrote under the sentence from *Le Figaro*: 'Kenji, Cavendish, expeditions before 1863?' He felt as if he had scented the right trail and he was at once excited and fearful. He paid and left.

CHAPTER SIX

Afternoon, Monday 27 June

O N Boulevard Haussmann, Victor calmed down. It was all a
misunderstanding. The receptionist was probably right,
and it was a different Grand Hotel. How many were there in
Paris? Well . . . the one on Boulevard des Capucines . . . the one
at the Trocadero . . . and also the Grand Hotel de l'Athénée, Rue
Scribe . . . the Grand Hotel Paris-Nice, on Faubourg Montmartre
. . . Kenji had met with a certain J.C. in a room number 312.
Unless it was a woman: Joséphine C., Jeanne C., Judith C. To be
certain he would have to question the receptionists at all the
Grand Hotels in the capital and its surrounding area. No, he had
to stop this dangerous train of thought. The mind can play
wicked tricks. Only last year, hadn't he been convinced that he
was seriously ill, when he experienced exactly the same gastric
symptoms as someone with a malignant tumour? How ashamed
he had felt when, with a smile, Dr Reynaud had diagnosed a
common or garden tapeworm and recommended he take a
vermifuge! Though he always seemed impassive, Kenji would
not have had enough self-control to feign indifference when the
Comtesse de Salignac had thrust the newspaper right under his
nose. If he had not reacted, it was because he was unconcerned.
He probably thought that Cavendish fellow had suffered a
straightforward heart attack, as had the woman on the Tower.

'At times the truth can seem very unlikely' – how many times had this line by Boileau been borne out in the past? How many innocent people had been the victims of miscarriages of justice because of an investigator's overactive imagination? Kenji had travelled, as had Cavendish, but so what? They had both been in London in 1863, but why was that significant? In any case, the date on which Monsieur Legris had engaged Kenji's services, which Victor had come across by chance in an accounts book, did not prove that Kenji had not been in England for some time already. Anything could seem true or false at a given moment; the facts could be viewed in differing ways.

Half convinced by his reasoning, Victor hurried on. A tram horn brought him back down to earth, and he nearly walked into a lamppost. Straightening his hat and smoothing his moustache, he finally looked up and saw the church of Notre-Dame-de-Lorette. Was this chance or had he been led here by his subconscious? He headed straight for the nearest florist.

They were little white suns with yellow centres, more than thirty of them, marguerites, wrapped in lacy paper and held in a man's hand. Beneath a hat with a broad brim, dark eyes looked out at her from a slightly tense, moustached face. It was him.

She stepped back. 'Excuse my appearance. I must look awful. I was painting.'

Victor stifled a laugh. Awful. That was women for you. Odette had used that very word when she woke up. Even done up in an oversized smock, barefoot and hair held up with combs, Tasha looked adorable. All the more adorable as he could make out her naked silhouette, or very nearly, beneath the stripy cotton material.

'It's hot. Would you like to have a drink with me?'

She bit her lip. He was a complex character, you could see that by the way he was holding the flowers, not quite sure whether to hand them over to her or not. *Careful. Remember your disappointments with good old Hans.*

'I'm disturbing you,' he added gloomily.

She made up her mind and took the bouquet. 'Yes, I'll come down to the café with you, but just for an hour. It's the only day of the week when I can paint. I'm going to get dressed.'

'I'll wait for you downstairs.'

Without a word she pulled him into the room by his sleeve, and slammed the door. She gathered up the clothes scattered on the bed. The sight of the underskirt and the knickers forced Victor to turn away and pretend to be interested in the earthenware stove. She threw the flowers onto one of the straw-seated chairs, as the other one was covered with canvases. Victor looked around the place, noticing the paper peeling off the walls, the piles of books in their recess. The paintings on the floor, on the furniture, on the easel, were all of rooftops: painted using impasto, the bluish grey of the zinc accentuated the pallor of the sky, that distinctive Parisian sky that even on clear days could suddenly turn rainy.

'It's not very elegant, but it's all I have,' she said, arranging the marguerites in an enamel pitcher. She observed him out of the corner of her eye. He held himself very erect and, with his hands in his pockets, looked every inch the mannequin. 'Make yourself at home. I'll be five minutes.'

She pointed towards the bed, which was the only available seating. He sat right on the edge, feeling gauche, ridiculous. She had shut herself away in the small room and he could hear the sounds of a receptacle being filled with water, then a splashing noise. She was having a wash. Although he was entirely indifferent to Odette's ablutions, he was now having erotic visions of Tasha engaged in the same task. Had he been the self-assured man that he had always dreamt of being, he would have opened the door and looked at her boldly. He might even have gone a step further. But he chose not to run that risk, as it was probably the best way of permanently alienating her.

Used as both a studio and living space, the room was twice as cluttered as it should have been. Clearly Tasha was not an orderly woman, more one of those bohemians whose lives Victor liked to read about in serialised stories but who alarmed him when he came across them in real life. On a sideboard crammed with paintbrushes and tubes of colour, he noticed the remains of some ham and dried-up purée on a chipped plate, and a stale crust of bread. She was not eating properly. A big iridescent glass bottle attracted his attention: an expensive perfume with the seal still on the stopper. A gift from an admirer? From a lover? He suddenly thought how easily she had let him in. *More dragged in, really.* Almost against his better judgement, he got up and went up to the recess to try to arrange the books into alphabetical order: Hugo, Tolstoy, Zola . . . He noticed a black-and-white reproduction pinned to the wall: it showed a man who had collapsed over a table. It was impossible to say whether he was asleep or overcome with despair. Around him, almost touching him, circled a cloud of menacing nightbirds. Underneath, written in pencil, were the words: 'The extravagance of reason creates monsters.' I know that, he said to himself. Where have I seen it before?

She shouted through the door: 'How did you get my address?'

He started and returned to his seat. 'Marius Bonnet gave it to me. Do you mind?'

'Why? Should I?' Her smiling face appeared from behind the door. 'Could you pass me those clothes on the chair? Thank you.' A naked arm grabbed the fabric bundle. There was a rustle and then she stamped crossly. 'Oh, hang it! Stockings are such a nuisance! I envy your being a man, you don't know the torture of this fashion invented by men to ruin our lives! Do you know what my landlady thinks is the future for women? Trousers!'

'Good Lord, I hope not. That would be a nightmare.'

'A blessing, you mean. I'm just doing my hair.'

The sound of a brush in her hair was even more distracting for Victor than hearing her wash or the swish of her clothes. To divert his thoughts he picked up a sketchbook from the bedside table. Leafing through it from the end, he was surprised to see a number of rough drawings of his own face. So she had been thinking about him; he was wrong to be so reserved. He found the drawing she had been looking at on Rue du Caire: the dead woman on the Tower, a corpse lying out on a bench, three children with frightened expressions. Then three lovely studies of Redskins. The last sketch reminded him vaguely of something, but not something real. The same Redskins, drawn full-length now, stood before a railway carriage and were looking at a recumbent man and another one kneeling next to him in the midst of assorted objects – bundles, baskets, a rocking horse with its stuffing falling out, a chair with three legs. Before he could give it any further thought, Tasha emerged from the bathroom-cum-kitchen and pirouetted around the room as she looked for some knick-knack or other.

'I'm nearly ready.'

He hid the sketchbook under a newspaper, which was also on the bedside table.

'Where have those gloves got to?' She turned abruptly towards him, and noticed his hand on the newspaper. She laughed. 'Oh, I know, it's absurd, but a friend of mine really wanted to sign the Golden Book. He asked me to accompany him and I gave in. Oh, well, so what? I'm only missing my gloves!'

He picked up the newspaper.

LE FIGARO

UNIVERSAL EXPOSITION 1889

SPECIAL EDITION PRINTED ON THE EIFFEL TOWER

This edition has been presented to Mademoiselle Tasha Kherson as a souvenir of her visit to the *Figaro* Pavilion on the second platform of the Eiffel To—

'Oh, leave it, it's silly!' she said, taking *Le Figaro* from him. She threw it onto the bed and started rummaging in the wicker trunks. 'By the way, have you written your literary column for *Le Passe-partout?*'

'Yes, but I don't know if my grumpy tone will amuse the readers. I'm taking a stand against the growing number of literary movements such as romanticism, naturalism, symbolism, and I deplore the bastardisation of the language.'

'You're just nostalgic for the old days. So what do you make of Victor Hugo?'

'Nothing. I admire the man he was, I deplore his somewhat overemphatic tone, in other words I'm no *hugolâtre*.'

'*Hugolâtre?* I don't know that adjective. Is it in the dictionary?'

'At the rate the language is evolving, it won't be long before—'

'Found them!' She waved several pairs of lace gloves about triumphantly. She chose one pair and then threw it back into the trunk with the others, shutting the lid. 'They're not the ones I wanted.'

'Do you collect them?' he asked, amused.

'No, I haven't the money. They're my inheritance from my mother. She loved beautiful clothes . . .'

She suddenly recalled Djina, her mother, filling a suitcase in their sparsely furnished home on Rue Voronov. She frequently relived that day from the winter of 1885 in precise detail. 'Go, my little Tasha, go and live your dream. Go to Berlin. Aunt Hannah will help you. From there you can get to Paris. There's no future for you here.' Everything that had happened – her parents' separation, the closure of the Puschkinskaia school, the move to her grandmother's home in the hostile town of Jitomar – all of it motivated her to go. She felt guilty at deserting her mother and sister, but her desire to leave was too strong. She touched in her pocket her last letter from Djina. Four long years had passed since she had last seen her.

Victor's presence brought her abruptly back to reality. He was looking at her with a puzzled expression.

'Hang it all! I can't even find my everyday gloves! When I left Russia, I couldn't carry much luggage, so I just brought the gloves. That's why my hands are in better condition than my feet!' she concluded, wiggling her right ankle boot. The tip of it had completely lost its shape, thanks to her big toe.

They both laughed, and she adjusted her hat in the cracked mirror that hung by the recess. Fascinated by the little curls on the nape of her neck, Victor had to try hard not to reach out and touch them.

'Have you known Marius long?' she asked as she opened the door.

As he did not move, looking at her almost as if he was in pain, she stepped towards him. 'So are you coming then? Oh, here are my gloves. You were sitting on them!'

The storm had passed, leaving behind an agreeable freshness. Victor still did not dare take Tasha's arm. She led him down Rue des Martyrs where she knew a brasserie that Baudelaire had frequented.

'I met Marius eight years ago in Ernest Meissonier's studio,' Victor said, in belated reply to her question.

'That most illustrious specialist of military frescoes?'

'I wasn't there to admire his paintings, but to see a projection of animated photographs. Have you been to a zoogyroscope show yet?'

'What kind of animal is it?' she exclaimed, entering the café and giving the waiter a friendly wave. 'You know, little women like me understand nothing about new technology . . .'

He ignored the sarcasm of her remark. 'It's a sort of perfected magic lantern. It gives the illusion of movement,' he explained, offering her a seat.

His gallantry amused her; she was not used to being treated with so much consideration.

'What will you have?'

'They make very good lemonade here,' she said, like a regular.

He ordered a cognac. Marcel, the waiter, recommended the home-made pastries. Victor declined the offer but noticed Tasha's momentary hesitation.

'Don't hold back, it's my treat.'

'In that case . . . do you have rum babas today?' she asked Marcel, with a greedy glint in her eye.

'So you're a gourmand then,' Victor said.

'Oh, yes. And also on some days when I'm broke or I'm too idle to cook, I just eat puddings. They keep you going.'

He grew more relaxed; she was good company. With her expansive gestures and her familiar language, he felt as though he had known her for a long time.

'So you and Marius became friends then?' she asked with a full mouth.

'Does that surprise you?'

'A little. You're so different from him. You seem to attach a lot of importance to the small things in life, though of course that's just my impression of you. But Marius doesn't care about anything except his newspaper.'

'You're right, maybe I take life a bit too seriously. You're very independent and original. I really like your pain—'

But he did not have time to finish. A hirsute, bearded giant, with an impressive black eye, descended on them.

'Mademoiselle Tasha!'

'Danilo! What happened to you?'

'May I?'

Without waiting for an answer the new arrival sat down next to Victor, who angrily shifted over.

'Have you been in a fight?'

'Yesterday, at the Exposition, during my lunch break, I had gone down to the Seine to practise the aria from *Boris Godunov*. Of course I didn't get changed, so I was still in my Cro-Magnon furs. To give more resonance to my voice I raised my club, when a woman screamed: "Help! A maniac!" Immediately three officers of the law set upon me. Ever since two idiots decided to snuff it in the vicinity, the Champ-de-Mars is stuffed with policemen. They really went to town on me! But I didn't just take it lying down. I think I may even have knocked one out. Then, realising their mistake, they excused themselves and assured me that they would refund my medical expenses. I'll be back in my cave tomorrow,' he finished gloomily.

Tasha made the introductions. On hearing that Victor was a bookseller, Danilo became animated. 'You don't happen to need an assistant, by any chance? I have an extensive knowledge of literature.'

'Thank you. I have one already.'

'A beer, with no head!' Marcel announced, setting down a

tankard in front of Danilo, who murmured pensively: 'Jack of all trades, master of none, such is my lot.'

'I must go,' said Tasha, 'I've got a lot of work to do.'

Glad to be leaving the Serb, Victor quickly followed her. 'Do you know him well?'

'He lives on the same floor as me.'

'Do you let him into your room?'

'Never. I'd be too frightened he'd sing me the aria from *Faust*!'

An idea began to form in his mind. What if he rented a small apartment? He had the means to do it. What would she say? He tested the water. 'Haven't you had enough of living in that cramped room and depriving yourself of food?'

She stopped to give him an ironic look. 'Well, of course I'd prefer the Royal Suite at the Grand Hotel!'

Why there? he wondered, suddenly guarded.

'But I have to consider my situation from a practical point of view,' she added as she walked on. 'Until I'm established as an artist, I'll have to make do with Helga Becker's attic room. At least I've got a good view of the rooftops.'

'When are you going to come by the shop? Yesterday, we were stocktaking. I put by some books illustrated by Gustave Doré for you, as well as some Jérôme Bosch reproductions. You'll have to wait for *Los Caprichos* – they're at the bookbinder's.'

She gave him a sideways look and did not reply. They walked in silence as far as number 60. Victor no longer knew whether he found her attractive or exasperating. But when she held out her gloved hand and promised to come to Rue des

Saints-Pères as soon as she was able, he felt happy. He watched her disappear into the far end of the courtyard, then walked slowly back as far as the Trinité Church. Stopping by a high-class grocer's, he suddenly felt the urge to give her a present. He thought of the bottle of perfume. He would make do with cakes, and she would appreciate them far more. Pink macaroons from Rheims? He was about to open the shop door when he saw a slight silhouette reflected in the window. He turned. Along the facing pavement, Tasha was hurrying towards the cab stand. With a few quick words to one of the drivers, she got in. Without stopping to think, Victor rushed across. 'Follow that cab!' he cried, diving into the next one.

Tasha alighted near the Parc Monceau rotunda. Once she'd got her bearings, she rang the bell of a private house that looked like a Hindu palace. Victor waited for her to go inside before he got down from his cab. His pulse was racing as if he had run all the way. He took a few steps alongside the railings without daring to venture into the shade beneath the trees, and kept his eyes fixed on the huge front door. He didn't like this new neighbourhood on the Plaine Monceau at all, with all the grand mansions built by the *nouveaux riches* springing up everywhere, even if some did belong to talented artists. As a sign of the times, land that had been worth forty-five francs a square metre in 1870 was now valued at more than three hundred francs, and nobody knew how high this speculative fever would go. Even the flunkeys here think they're above us ordinary mortals, he thought as he saw a valet in a stripy waistcoat come towards him, stiffly walking two Afghan hounds to the park. Victor stood in the middle of the pavement, forcing them to stop.

'Excuse me, I've just arrived from Limoges and I'm a little lost. Who does this great edifice belong to?' he asked, pointing to a house opposite the Hindu palace.

'That is the residence of Monsieur Poitevin and of his cousin, Monsieur Guy de Maupassant.'

'Guy de Maupassant, the writer?'

'Yes, Monsieur,' replied the valet with a touch of irritation. He wanted to be on his way, but Victor took his arm. 'My wife thinks he's a genius; she's always talking about a story concerning a ball and bat. And that house, over there?'

'*Ball of Fat*, you mean, Monsieur. Monsieur Dumas the younger lives there.'

'Oh yes, *The Lady of the Hydrangeas* . . .'

'*The Camellias*, Monsieur,' the valet corrected as he tried to calm the dogs, who were pulling on their leashes.

'One last question. What about this overelaborate construction? Does some nabob live there?'

'The house of Monsieur Constantin Ostrovski, a major art collector,' replied the valet with a disdainful sniff.

'Art! What more is there to life? Are there other painters in this area?'

'Monsieur Meissonier lives not far from here, on the other side of what was the outer boulevard, right next to the brick mansion belonging to Monsieur Gaillard, whom I have the honour of serving. Calliope! Polycarpe! We're going back home!'

Victor transferred his attention to the Hindu palace. He waited a good hour before he saw Tasha come out. She crossed

Boulevard de Courcelles. He hesitated. Should he follow her? No. He would learn far more from a meeting with the nabob.

Victor handed his calling card to a vivacious maid, who left him in the entrance hall, having offered him an imposing high-backed chair, which he refused to sit in. It was too much like his doctor's waiting room. He had time to examine at his leisure a collection of ancient weapons: sabres, muskets and pistols, which hung on the walls between paintings of rural scenes. The owner of this place seemed to favour comely milkmaids viewed from above. Amidst all this eclectic collection was *Le Figaro de la Tour*, prominently displayed for the benefit of visitors and framed like a certificate. The lead article began with the words:

PERSONALITY OF THE DAY:

CONSTANTIN OSTROVSKI

It is with great interest that we have followed . . .

Victor had to stop reading, as the hall door opened and a stout, bald man in his fifties entered, wearing a monocle and a jovial expression on his face. In a flash Victor could once again see Kenji showing his framed Utamaros on the terrace of Café de la Paix. He recognised the buyer.

'What can I do for you, my dear Monsieur . . . Legris?' asked Constantin Ostrovski, reading Victor's calling card.

Victor tried to maintain his self-control.

'So you are the personality of the day?' he asked, pointing at *Le Figaro.*

'The very same! My ego has become as inflated as La Fontaine's frog. I'm trying to deflate it before it bursts!'

Victor returned to the newspaper, skipped the lines about the collector and read the list of signatories of the Golden Book printed under the article:

Si-Ali-Mahaoui, Fez. Udo Aiker, editor of the *Berliner Zeitung.* G. Collodi, Turin. J. Kulki, editor of *Hlas Navoola* of Prague. Victorin Alibert, bandleader. Madeleine Lesourd, Chartres. Kenji Mori, Paris. Sigmund Pollock, Vienna, Austria . . .

The rest of the text was obscured by the edge of the frame.

'You haven't answered my question, Monsieur Legris.'

Reluctantly, Victor turned to him and stammered, 'I've come on behalf of . . . Kenji Mori.'

'Kenji Mori? Pardon me, I have no memory for names. Is he an Asian?'

Victor nodded. 'Japanese.'

'That doesn't ring any bells. I may have met him at Siegfried Bing's on Rue de Provence, you know, the dealer in oriental art.'

'He told me he had sold you some Utamaro prints.'

'It's possible. I *am* buying left, right and centre. Do you have something to offer me?'

'Well . . . it's a little delicate, you see, I—'

'Don't tell me I've been buying stolen property!'

'No, no, it's just that I have certain works that I would like to sell as privately as possible, you understand . . .'

'Come, we will be more comfortable in the sitting room. You have nothing against tea, I hope? In this sort of heat boiling hot tea is the ideal beverage.'

Ostrovski led him through rooms cluttered with Chinese trinkets, Greek antiquities, Sèvres plates, Renaissance furniture, and stuffed animals. They finally came to a room with enormous picture windows, overrun by luxuriant plants, which were growing right up to the ceiling. On the walls, which were decorated with brightly coloured glazed earthenware tiles, hung dozens of pictures whose tones clashed with the colour of the décor. The simplest was a still life of a bunch of grapes, the largest showed the Battle of Sebastopol. Framed by two icons, a row of hermetically sealed little pots stood on the shelf of a credence table. A corner sofa, four chairs and a cane table placed around a gushing fountain completed the arrangement. Victor stopped in front of the sofa, over which hung a large oil painting of a naked oriental dancing girl draped in transparent veils twirling around under the covetous eye of a sheik.

'The humidity . . . Isn't it bad for your canvases?'

'Daubs!' said Ostrovski with a laugh. 'I am taking my revenge on all those pretentious cretins who have had houses built around me, the Duezes, the Gervexes, the Escaliers, the Clairins . . . These lords of the palette are always selling me the poorest study for an exorbitant price so that they can buy themselves Japanese curios at the Magasins du Louvre! They boast of how their paintings are prominently displayed in my home. What they do not know is that this room was conceived not for them but for my dear plants. Let's sit down.'

Constantin Ostrovski clapped his hands. The vivacious maid appeared instantly.

'Sonia, some tea, please. Rare works, you say?' he resumed, turning towards Victor.

'Manuscripts . . . antiphons . . . a thirteenth-century illuminated Book of Hours.'

'Oh, books?' he said, pulling a face. 'I'm sorry, I'm not really interested in books, least of all religious ones.'

'The last one I mentioned is very precious. It belonged to Louis the Ninth; its binding is a little marvel.'

Ostrovski intertwined his fingers and rested his chin on them. 'And of course you'll be wanting a good price for it.'

'Nothing too excessive for such a fine piece.'

'My latest passion is for exotic objects. This bow and quiver, there on your left, taken from the enemy, was a gift from my friend Nate Salsbury, the manager, as he likes to call himself, of Buffalo Bill. But books, I must admit . . .'

Victor felt sick. This forest of twisted shapes was for him like a strange hothouse conceived by an artist in the grip of paranoia. The tree fern was unfurling its canopy in the shade of bamboos; the Indian palm tree stood alongside Mexican cacti; African zamias and cycads were mixed up with Brazilian orchids. This incongruous combination of plant species, which violated the laws of botanical geography, made him feel as if he was suffocating. He noticed a display cabinet full of glass containers where monsters that looked like foetuses preserved in alcohol were sprouting. He was reminded of his meeting with Tasha in the Palace of Liberal Arts. Tasha . . . Why had she stayed so long at this man's house? Had she reclined on the sofa underneath the naked dancer? Had the man's podgy hands been exploring her body? *She got rid of you. She lied to you.*

'Monsieur Legris? Monsieur Legris, are you listening to me?'

'Please excuse me, I was admiring . . . your dispensary over there on the credenza, a very fine series of pots . . .'

'A little weakness of mine. As a child I dreamt of being an apothecary. Not an idiot like that Homais caricatured by Flaubert, no, a highly gifted dispensing pharmacist who would discover all the secrets of plants and would know how to extract both what was good and bad from them. Now, that's something that might interest me! An old pharmaceutical codex. You don't happen to have any you could sell me? No? What a shame . . .'

He pushed a box of cigars towards Victor.

'Here's a beneficial plant. Please have one.'

'No, thank you. I only smoke cigarettes.'

Sonia brought them tea, a black steaming liquid with slices of lemon floating in it. Ostrovski crunched a lump of sugar, drank a big mouthful of the burning liquid very noisily, put his glass down, and gestured around the room to indicate the plants.

'Do you know why they fascinate me, Monsieur Legris? Because they are like us. You know, in tropical forests the smallest of them cannot survive without light. They wait for a giant tree to fall to find their place in the sun. Of course, many will not have that opportunity. It's a race to the top. The first to get there grow side branches, condemning the losers to darkness and death. One also finds species that do not need light, such as saprophytes and parasites. They feed on decomposing matter. Here, everything flourishes – I make sure of it. Do you like plants, Monsieur Legris?'

'Er . . . yes, I mean the ones that aren't dangerous,' was Victor's careful reply: he was beginning to have doubts about the mental health of his host.

'Dangerous? It all depends how they are used. Only man is dangerous, don't you agree? Well, I have your card, so the ball is in my court, and I shall contact you. Very pleased to have made your acquaintance.'

Constantin Ostrovski stood up as a sign that the interview was at an end. They shook hands. Gracing him with a silent smile, Sonia accompanied Victor to the door.

He headed into the park, taking deep breaths. He felt both disappointed and relieved. Tasha and Kenji had both met Constantin Ostrovski. What was so extraordinary about that? Ostrovski collected anything and everything. Tasha was an artist, and Kenji was converting his prints into cash so that he could spoil his mistress.

Victor sat down on a bench near the little lake and watched some small children playing with their buckets and spades as he tried to marshal his thoughts. What if Kenji's treats were intended for none other than Tasha?

'Can this really be? No! Impossible!'

A nanny on duty by the sandpit turned to look at this man who was talking to himself. Embarrassed, Victor stood up.

'No, that's absurd!'

He rejected that thought, otherwise he was going to end up losing his mind. As he walked towards the cab stand, he thought of the page of *Le Figaro de la Tour* on show at Ostrovski's home.

Was John Cavendish also amongst the signatories of the Golden Book? And what about Eugénie Patinot? *I need evidence, real evidence.*

Victor checked again that Kenji had not followed him upstairs: no, he must still be sitting at his desk with his record cards. He'd hardly reacted when the door chime had sounded. He lifted the blotter and uncovered the *Le Figaro de la Tour* headline:

PERSONALITY OF THE DAY:

CONSTANTIN OSTROVSKI

followed by the Golden Book signatories:

Madeleine Lesourd, Chartres. Kenji Mori, Paris. Sigmund Pollock, Vienna, Austria. Marcel Forbin, lieutenant of the second cuirassiers. Rosalie Bouton, laundress, Aubervilliers. Madame de Nanteuil, Paris. Maric-Amélie de Nanteuil, Paris. Hector de Nanteuil, Paris. Gontran de Nanteuil, Paris. John Cavendish, New York, USA . . .'

The letters blurred before his eyes into one grey mass. For several seconds he stood completely still, his mind empty of thoughts, his ears buzzing. He managed to recover himself, and made himself read it again from the beginning, following the text with his finger. All three of them were there: Ostrovski, Kenji, Cavendish. And Eugénie Patinot? Not there. Nowhere to be seen. For Eugénie Patinot the first platform had been high enough. He put the newspaper back in its place and smoothed the blotter. Had he stepped into a nightmare? Straightening up, he noticed that the empty spaces left by the Utamaros had now been covered by two new prints, nocturnal landscapes by Hiroshige. He felt a dull pain in his forehead. Kenji's face looked out at him from a silver frame, with a typically mixed expression, both serious and ironic. *How can one possibly suspect someone with smiling eyes, of murder?*

Seized by doubts once again, he opened a drawer and found a railway timetable for the London and Dover Railway. The apartment door creaked behind him. Closing the drawer, he jumped round. Kenji was staring at him, surprised.

'Are you looking for something?'

'I've got a migraine. I was hoping to find some medicine. I haven't any left in my apartment.'

'You know I never take medication. I'll send Joseph down to the pharmacy, you go and lie down.'

'Don't bother Joseph. I must still have a little cola nut left. Oh, so you've changed over your prints,' said Victor, desperately trying to sound casual.

'Habit is like an old mistress, it's good to shake off its yoke sometimes.'

Irritated by this proverb, which Kenji had probably invented on the spot, Victor returned to his apartment with Kenji right behind him. 'Come to think of it, I've met an amateur print collector who's mad about Hokusai. He'll buy at any price, especially animal images. He's called Ostrovkine, or something like that. Do you know him?' *Quick, lie down, close your eyes.*

'I'm not a print dealer. I'm going to make you some tea.'

Victor wanted to refuse but Kenji had already gone. He

remembered the adventures of the King of the Apes, Souen-Wou-Kong, the hero of Chinese legends, which Kenji had read to him once upon a time. *He's cleverer than a barrel of monkeys. You just can't corner him. Does he know Tasha? Are they lovers?*

Kenji returned, carrying a tray with a teapot, a cup and the bottle of medicine. 'It was next to your washbasin. I can't believe you didn't see it. Drink it while it's hot.'

Victor forced himself to sip the green tea in spite of his complaining stomach. As he put his cup down, Kenji suddenly clapped his hands loudly. It made Victor jump and he almost knocked everything over.

'What's got into you?'

'A mosquito,' Kenji said, wiping his hands. 'As a boy, I was very good at doing this.' He returned to the kitchen. Victor used the moment to empty the teapot in the bathroom.

'I won't be dining tonight! I'm going to bed!' he shouted.

He was starving, but a one-to-one meal with Kenji was more than he could face.

He closed his bedroom door, sat down on the edge of the bed, with his notebook on his knees and wrote, 'What links Tasha and Kenji? Tasha and Ostrovski? Kenji and Cavendish? Was Patinot murdered, as Gouvier and Clusel suggest? Did Cavendish suffer the same fate?'

He lay back on the pillows. *Where did I put the newspaper that had his biography? He wrote articles for* Le Tour du Monde . . .

His eyes were closing. Just before he fell asleep, he wondered at what time he could safely go to raid the larder.

CHAPTER SEVEN

Morning, Tuesday 28 June

VICTOR slept badly because of the heat, and got up early. After making sure that Kenji was still asleep, he took a piece of bread from the kitchen, slipped out of the bookshop and walked up to the Seine.

'Who'll buy my coffee? Ten centimes a cup.'

On the riverbank a coffee seller, carrying his tin stove, was offering his bitter beverage to the dog shearers and the mattress-makers, who were already at work near the Pont du Carrousel. Victor helped himself to a large cup, swallowing it in one gulp. Then, eating his bread, he walked along the river. It reflected the cloudy sky as a metallic mosaic in which millions of luminous particles coalesced, then parted again. *Just like this situation I'm in. I mustn't jump to conclusions, I must consider the two of them separately: Tasha on one side, Kenji on the other. And first and foremost, Cavendish.*

When he arrived at number 77 Boulevard Saint-Germain, the Hachette bookshop, home of *Le Tour du Monde*, had just opened. He went over to the reception desk and explained what he was researching to a secretary, who showed him into the archive room. The archivist made a note of his request. A few minutes later he put down in front of Victor several cardboard files containing all editions for the years 1857–1869, lavishly illustrated with engravings. Victor leafed through the first edition. One article caught his attention:

JOURNEY TO SIAM, LAND OF THE WHITE ELEPHANT

BY JOHN RUSKIN CAVENDISH

I was in Bangkok in December 1858 when a friend suggested I accompany him to Western Laos to attend a tattooing ceremony. This very painful process is endured by young men in order to please . . .

Victor turned the pages. South-East Asia was laid out before him – Cambodia, Malaysia, the Philippines, Borneo, Java . . . Two words caught his attention, 'blue mountains'. He read:

In Java, the granite summits of the blue mountains rise to 12,000 feet. Their slopes contain gold and emerald.

Kenji's face, as clear as a photograph, came to him. He was leaning over his childhood bed telling him a story: 'The blue mountains are home to flying dragons. When the sun beats down, they flap like bats around the fortresses built on the slopes of the volcanoes. The people of Java shoot arrows at them to chase them away. Once, a long time ago, one of these monsters braved the arrows and snatched up a human between its claws. That's how Princess Surabaja was carried off. She was more beautiful than the dawn, livelier than a squirrel and she sang better than a cicada. Taken by her grace, the dragon Djepu carried her off to his nest on Krakatoa. I must tell you that this

Djepu was in fact a valiant warrior turned into a dragon by a wicked witch. So . . .' That very evening Victor had vowed that one day he would ascend Krakatoa. Thirteen years later the terrible eruption put an end to his dream.

JOURNEY TO THE ISLAND OF JAVA

BY JOHN RUSKIN CAVENDISH, 1858–1859

Victor could not take his eyes off that heading. He made a rapid calculation. Kenji was born in Nagasaki in 1839. At the age of nineteen, after studying history and geography, he had spent several months travelling around South-East Asia. The tale of the blue mountains meant one could assume he had visited Java. That could have coincided with Cavendish's presence on the island in 1859. *They may have known each other for thirty years! In 1863, the year that Father engaged Kenji, Cavendish was in London* . . . Overwhelmed, Victor was not prepared to accept what he had discovered. He tried to tell himself that the dates did not fit, but clearly they did.

Victor continued to read. What followed in the account raised some difficult questions for him. He made some notes in his notebook but, oppressed by both the heat and feelings of apprehension, he had to take a break.

He went outside, leaving the other articles for later. He wandered as far as Boulevard Saint-Michel and then up towards the Luxembourg Gardens. The pavement was overflowing with people strolling, errand boys and workmen in a hurry. In the pavement cafés, groups of students, engaged in animated discussion, were gathered alongside melancholic old men. A street vendor selling gas-filled balloons came towards him, brandishing her multicoloured wares. Victor moved aside to let her pass.

'Who'll buy my beautiful balloons? There's one for everybody! Red, green or blue, which one's for you?'

Blue. A blue balloon attached to the wrist of the dead woman on the first platform of the tower. Victor could picture the scene clearly. Then he remembered the little boy with the blue balloon whom he had seen that very day on the same floor. The child had shouted: 'He was a cowboy, he comes from New York,' and then: 'He's part of Buffalo Bill's troupe.' New York!

Suddenly he decided to go to the home of the woman – what exactly was her name? Eugénie Pa . . . He could not remember her exact name or address, but these details had been in the newspaper reports of her death. As long as Joseph had kept them!

As its name indicated, Avenue des Peupliers in Auteuil was lined with poplars, behind which stood elegant villas. Victor first passed number 35, which bore the nameplate: 'M. et Mme de Nanteuil', thinking that Joseph must have given him the wrong address. A few metres further on he turned round and walked slowly back. He was about to pass number 35 for a second time when he noticed a broad woman on the other side of the road, trying to pick up some apricots that had dropped into the gutter. Her stoutness prevented her bending properly. He hurried over to help her. She turned away to set down her basket, gave her pale cheeks a quick pinch and then thanked him demurely.

'I have difficulty bending so far down because of my rheumatism. Luckily, only one's been crushed. They're so expensive right now, you know!'

'Do you live in this neighbourhood?'

She gave a little laugh, and simpered. 'I would be lying if I said I didn't.'

'I'm looking for Eugénie Patinot's house.'

'Eugénie? Wait a moment, you're not a policeman, by any chance?'

Her friendliness had vanished. Now she was wary.

'Yes, I . . . I work at police headquarters.'

'No one asked me any questions after her death, which is a pity as I was certainly her best friend around here.'

'Where did she live?'

'You mean you don't know?'

'I was told to go to number thirty-five. But the nameplate says "Nanteuil".'

'Oh, I see, you're new to this, aren't you?'

She was now regarding him more kindly. Victor tried to look stupid.

'They treat us novices harshly. When they send us on an investigation, they don't give us enough information . . .'

'An investigation? I knew it! The anonymous letter mentioned in the papers! The one that said that Eugénie knew too much. I really don't see what she could have known. She was always the last to hear the neighbourhood gossip. In any case, her family have taken it very badly. Oh, the shame of it! Is that what you are investigating?'

'No, no, they just want to test my abilities.'

'Right. Well, Eugénie worked for the Nanteuils. She put on airs and graces, but there was no reason to: she was working as a maid, just like me – my name's Louise Vergne. Monsieur Nanteuil works at the Ministry. He's really only a pen-pusher, but he lives in style, thanks to his wife's inheritance. Eugénie was Madame's half-sister, a penniless relation, a widow taken in out of charity. Her job was to entertain the children. I did warn her, going to the Expo with all those foreigners there!'

'The foreigners were nothing to do with it. She was stung by a bee.'

'That's what they say, but one day I saw an Indian man at the market. He was playing a flute to charm his cobra. What if the cobra decided to stay in France? It's the same with those bees – how can you prove that they're really French?'

'Thank you very much. I'd better go and ask the Nanteuils some quest—'

'You won't be able to. They aren't there. They have gone to choose the marble for the grave – so they say,' she added in a lowered voice. 'I shouldn't be surprised if they made do with granite. They're a bit careful with money.'

'In what way?'

'They're mean. They paid Eugénie a pittance. Personally I ruined myself buying a beautiful geranium to take to the cemetery, but they just took everlasting flowers. It's cheaper that way. You can ring the bell. The governess is there – she will let you in. But watch out, she's a terrible woman. She couldn't stand poor Eugénie. Mademoiselle Rose, she's called. What a joke! She's nothing like a rose, apart from her prickliness!'

Victor bowed and crossed the road.

'If you need to ask me any more questions, I live at number fifty-four, at the Le Massons'!'

He rang the bell. The gate opened and he crossed the garden, which was filled with box and ornamental pots. A maid was waiting for him on the doorstep.

'May I speak to Mademoiselle Rose? I'm from police headquarters.'

The governess received him in the parlour. She was tall, bony and ill-tempered. She resembled a cactus more than a rose, and even had hair on her chin.

'Monsieur and Madame are not here. They will be home this evening.'

'Perhaps you could give me some information on Madame Patinot?'

'I have already given information to the police. I didn't know her very well. I have only been with the Nanteuils since . . .'

Three children, two boys and a girl, came tumbling into the room, shouting and laughing. The youngest, armed with a cardboard revolver, was chasing the others. They began to run around the governess, who cried, 'Marie-Amélie! Control yourself!' and tried to catch the child as she ran past.

Victor recognised the children he had seen on the first floor of the Tower.

'Hector! Come here!'

'Can't, we're playing Buffalo Bill, they're the ferocious Indians Black Beaver and Red Wolf!' shouted the little boy, breathlessly.

The governess succeeded in pinning him to the wall, and took him firmly by the wrist.

'Gontran, I am ordering you to come here.'

Red Wolf slowed down and looked sadly at his sister. She disappeared down the corridor.

'Excuse me a moment, Monsieur. I have to have a little talk with these gentlemen in their bedroom,' scolded Mademoiselle Rose.

'Please.'

She left the parlour, holding the boys by the hand.

'What a way to behave, now your aunt is in heaven. I'm going to ask the inspector to lock you up with bread and water.'

A door closed and Victor heard no more. A rustling noise made him turn. Open-mouthed and tousle-haired, the little girl had sidled into the room and was watching him.

'Are you really a policeman?'

He nodded.

'Have you come for . . . me?'

'That depends, Mademoiselle.'

'I didn't mean to take it, you know. Only it was so pretty, I just put it in my bag. I didn't steal anything.'

'Tell me all about it.'

'The other day, at the Eiffel Tower, there were so many people and I wanted to see everything. We took the lift to the second floor and we queued up to sign the Golden Book. I saw how you make a newspaper. Afterwards we went down to the first floor to buy a present for Mama in the shops. My aunt was tired so she sat down. Hector gave her his balloon and he went off with Gontran. But Aunt didn't want me to leave her. I was fed up, as the boys could do what they liked, but not me; I could only watch them. Suddenly my aunt cried, "Ow!", something had stung her on the neck. She said it was a bee. At the same time someone fell on her: that made me laugh. Then Aunt leaped to her feet. It was funny; she looked like a jack-in-the-box. Then she sat back down. I saw that she was sleeping and very quietly I went over to the shop window. When I came back she was still asleep, but I was hungry. I wanted a toffee apple so I shook her to wake her up. Then I saw something by her feet. It looked like the handle of a nail file, but it was broken. I picked it up, that's all. I didn't do anything bad.'

'I would like to see it.'

'Not in front of Mademoiselle Rose. She should be called Mademoiselle Thorn. She's a real telltale – she tells Mama everything. Watch out, there she is!'

'Find a way of going into the garden. I'll meet you by the front gate.'

The governess bore down on Marie-Amélie and tried to catch her, but the little girl was too quick for her and bounced out of the room.

'Go to your room! Immediately!'

'In five minutes! First I'm going to take my doll for a walk.'

'No!'

Marie-Amélie had disappeared. The governess let out a sigh.

'That child is the limit.'

'I don't want to take up any more of your time. I'll come back again,' said Victor, taking his leave.

She did not see him out. At the bottom of the garden, as he reached the gate, Marie-Amélie ran to him, her doll in her arms. 'You won't say anything to Mama, will you?'

'Cross my heart and hope to die, if I tell a lie.'

'Here it is.' Onto his outstretched palm she put a metal rod inside a tapering ivory handle, which was etched with deep grooves and broken exactly in the middle.

'What is it?' she asked.

'No idea. It looks like a . . . no, I don't know. I'm going to take it to the prefecture for analysis. I will give it back to you later. In future, don't go picking up things lying on the ground.'

'Bang, bang! You're dead, Black Beaver! Buffalo Bill got you!' yelled Hector, who had escaped and was racing towards them, the governess in pursuit.

Victor made off, slipping the object into his pocket. He directed his attention to the important piece of information the child had given him: Eugénie Patinot had signed the Golden Book on 22 June. *Patinot. Kenji. Cavendish . . . Tasha? Her name doesn't figure on the list but she went up to the* Figaro *Pavilion, and yesterday in her apartment I saw a copy of the newspaper. She snatched it out of my hands before I could read the date. Was it from 22 June?*

The yellow blur of an omnibus appeared at the corner of Rue d'Auteuil. He ran towards it, waving his arm.

By the time he reached the second platform, he was exhausted. A particularly dense crowd was pressing around the feet of the metal monster, awaiting the arrival of the Russian Lieutenant Azeef, who had come all the way from Pultava on horseback in just a month, by riding eight kilometres an hour for eleven hours a day. It was also announced that six British firewomen would climb the Tower. Fortunately no one was at all interested in Victor Legris's visit to the Tower so he was able to wander as far as the kiosk that housed the *Figaro* offices. Through the glass wall, he saw the sub-editors, printers and stereotypers. A clerk pushed the door, which caught a gust of wind and Victor went in.

'I am a reporter for *Le Passe-partout* and I need some information about the Golden Book.'

'No time, I'm in a hurry. The Cossack is nearly here.'

Victor produced a five-franc piece, which had an immediate effect.

The boy murmured: 'That'll do nicely,' and pocketed it. 'Couldn't be a better time. Let's hide. If someone complains I'll say: nothing on the horizon.'

'How many signatures do you get each day?' asked Victor.

'Several hundred. People queue up for hours! They sign and fill in their surname, first name, occupation and address. At the beginning it was yours truly who copied out the information into the register. It gave me cramp in my wrists! The Golden Book weighs more than the Nautical Almanac, you know. I was like a slave. I handled the great slab of a tome and made entries in my best copperplate: Monsieur So-and-so, Rue Such-and-such, manager of Such-and-such shop, and then ran it over to the compositor. It was penal servitude! Now I have an easier time of it.'

'Why?'

'Because now we have loose sheets, which are filled in by the public and which we give directly to the printer. Then they are added to the Golden Book. Soon I am going to put in the ones from this morning.'

'Could any get lost? Names that don't get included?'

'It's rare, but it does happen.'

'Can I see the twenty-second of June?'

'Oh, I'm not sure about that . . . In principle, it is not allowed.'

Victor put another coin into the boy's hand, which he pocketed with alacrity.

'There go my principles,' he muttered. 'Come on, we need to be quick.'

They went into the inner sanctum. A huge register lay on a desk, much like a Bible on a lectern. Victor looked over it, turned the pages and eventually found those for 22 June. He began to decipher the names one by one. First page, second page, third page: nothing. Some signatories had added a comment or a sketch. He started to read the fourth page and there it was:

> . . . Marcel Forbin, lieutenant of the second cuirassiers. Rosalie Bouton, laundress, Aubervilliers. Madame de Nanteuil, Paris . . .

Alias Eugénie Patinot.

> . . . Marie-Amélie de Nanteuil, Paris. Hector de Nanteuil, Paris. Gontran de Nanteuil, Paris. John Cavendish, New York, USA . . .

His eyes went to the next page.

> Constantin Ostrovski, art coll—

Ostrovski! So he signed it too.

For several seconds Victor did not move, except for his hands, which were trembling. He made no attempt to pull himself together. He looked at the signature again:

Constantin Ostrovski, art collector, Paris. B. Godunov, Slovenia . . .

But where is Kenji? Then his heart gave a lurch.

'What is it?'

In the shock of the moment he had almost cried out. There was a ball in the pit of his stomach.

'You shouldn't be surprised,' said the boy. 'Some people do drawings; they think they're artists. Naturally, we don't reproduce them.'

Victor looked back over the page. He could not believe it. There, just after Cavendish's signature, was a caricature of the Eiffel Tower wearing a tutu and, with spindly legs, doing the splits over the River Seine. There was no name, but he recognised Tasha's signature at once. Feverishly he looked at the sixth page. Kenji must be there somewhere; he hadn't dreamt it!

Si-Ali-Mahaoui, Fez. Udo Aiker, editor of the *Berliner Zeitung*. G. Collodi, Turin. J. Kulki, editor of *Hlas Navoola* of Prague. Victorin Alibert, bandleader. Madeleine Lesourd, Chartres. Kenji Mori, Paris. Sigmund . . .

Something was not right: in *Le Figaro de la Tour* Kenji featured before Cavendish, he was sure of that.

'Are the names of the signatories printed chronologically?'

The boy sighed in exasperation.

'That would be asking too much. Sometimes the printer might get the sheets mixed up because he's overworked. The main thing is that everyone appears in the newspaper, isn't it? Now, have you finished?'

'Just a minute, I need to take some notes.'

Victor almost missed the lift. There was a real scramble and a woman cursed him roundly. 'You crush my feet and you don't even apologise! You cad!'

Tasha, Tasha . . . Tasha, Kenji, together on the Tower the day Eugénie Patinot died! . . . I'll go to Tasha's house.

By the time he finally managed to extricate himself from the crowd of spectators who were cheering Lieutenant Azeef, he had regained his composure.

She was not there. A note was fixed to her door with a drawing pin:

Dear Danilo,

I am at La Chapelle de Thélème. Come and join me at eight o'clock at the Café des Arts at the Expo, opposite the Press Pavilion (which is beside the Palace of Fine Arts). My boss has organised an audition for you tomorrow for a place in the Opera chorus.

Tasha

He would not be able to wait until the evening; he was plagued by too many unanswered questions. He went back down, wondering which church that chapel could be in. On the first-floor landing, a women in breeches, pushing a bicycle, appeared from one of the apartments.

'Excuse me, Madame, do you know Mademoiselle Kherson?'

She stared at him over her spectacles. 'She's my tenant.'

'I'm a friend of hers. She asked me to meet her at La Chapelle de Thélème but she forgot to give me the address.'

'Hm, a friend, eh? She has many of those. What are you? A painter? Journalist? Singer?'

'A columnist.'

'Oh, so you must know what they aren't telling us about the Expo murders! I dream about them at night; I do love a good mystery.'

'No, I'm afraid I have no information, I only write about literature. Whilst you on the other hand—'

'Mademoiselle Kherson does not keep me informed of her comings and goings. You should ask the owner of the art shop on Rue Clauzel. He is the confidant of all the so-called painters in this neighbourhood!'

Not knowing exactly what the cyclist was referring to, Victor went on his way. He soon found the tiny shop selling paint, brushes, pencils and other artists' supplies.

He was greeted by a stocky man of about sixty, with close-cut hair, who gave him a friendly welcome.

'La Chapelle de Thélème? Yes, of course I know it. Rue Lepic, right at the top. I couldn't tell you what number it is, but when you leave Boulevard de Clichy, it's on the right as you go up the hill.'

'Is it a religious institution?'

'Not at all!' laughed the man. 'You know the famous Thélème monastery created by Rabelais in *Gargantua*? Well, La Chapelle is an eclectic coterie of artists who share the same approach to art. That's why they use a name that evokes a clan, a brotherhood. You see, nothing monastic about that, especially as the chapel in question is the back room of the bistro Le Bacchus. It was founded by Maurice Laumier, a rising young artist. The members meet each week to paint a life model. The first time Laumier came here, I sent him packing. He had the nerve to ask for a tube of black paint. Black! Whereas I believe wholeheartedly in the dazzling colours used by the Impressionists! Then he came back and we sorted it out. I even traded the paint for one of his pictures.'

He pointed to one of the shop walls that was covered in portraits, landscapes, and still lifes. Disconcerted, Victor went up to a small, delicate picture. It depicted the head and shoulders of a naked woman fixing her hair in front of a mirror, her arms raised, her firm round breasts in full view. It was Tasha!

'Is it for sale?' Victor asked in a neutral tone.

'They're all for sale! Laumier and his associates have talent, but the best are these masterpieces that have not unfortunately found a buyer – this one for example.' The man pointed to a small square canvas of irises in a vase. The red, yellow and white flowers seemed to want to leap out of their blue background.

'Vincent Van Gogh, a genius, misunderstood like all geniuses. I'll wager you've never heard of him. No one paints flowers better than him. They're so beautiful! Each time I look at them, I'm filled with wonder. And to think that he hasn't sold a thing! Not a single canvas! People think he's mad. But that's the kind of madness I would be happy to have round to supper. And what about Cézanne! There's another one who doesn't sell, and to think that all the ones I admire, and who leave me their pictures in exchange for paint, will never earn me a bean. Never mind, any man who lives on more than fifty centimes a day is a scoundrel! But tell me, have you ever seen such wonderful art?'

Victor glanced distractedly at the paintings of pears or apples in dishes, of crooked houses and of mountains in geometric shapes. The richness of the tones did not distract him from the portrait of Tasha. The shopkeeper sighed.

'Oh, you're just like all the others! It doesn't matter, just mark my words, one day everyone will be talking about those two and fighting over their works, even if it is after they die. So, you like the Laumier, do you? It's not expensive. Twenty francs . . . fifteen. Oh, have it for ten, if you like.'

'It's not a question of money. I am not arguing about the price, it's just that . . . I'm not sure.'

'That's the problem. No one is ever sure. You'll see, soon museums will be fighting each other for the privilege of exhibiting these canvases. Believe me, Monsieur.'

Out on Boulevard de Clichy, home to dance halls, cabarets and music halls, Victor stopped outside a tavern named Les Frites Révolutionnaires. A tramp, hanging about near the entrance, told him that the establishment was owned by an ex-colonel from the Commune, and in return cadged a few sous from Victor.

'Tell me, my friend, Le Bacchus, is it really at the top of Rue Lepic?'

'Never heard of Le Bacchus, and I've been working this area for thirty years and been in every alehouse. Don't you mean Bibulus?'

'What?'

'Bibulus. Yes, the owner is a native of Flanders, like King Leopold. Bibulus is the name of a dog in a book, and that dog is as keen on beer as an old drunk. The geezer who wrote the book, he's Belgian as well.'

'*Tyl Ulenspiegel.*'

'What on earth's that?'

'The name of the book. This bistro, is it far?'

'Go back up Rue Lepic as far as Rue Tholoze. Turn right there and you'll see the sign, you can't miss it.'

Constructed under Napoleon, Rue Lepic was named after a Napoleonic general. Wider than the twisty alleyways of the neighbourhood, the street rang with the clatter of the coaches and cabs that horses struggled to drag towards the summit of Montmartre. After the Carrefour des Abbesses, Victor passed tall brand-new buildings, which in their immaculate whiteness towered over the two-storey hovels, the windmills and the dives with their wooden shutters. This strange assortment of buildings was dominated by the construction site of Sacré-Coeur, where work had started fourteen years earlier.

Le Bibulus, which advertised itself to customers with a sign representing a suckling dog, was a smoky bar with a low ceiling, and barrels for tables. The owner, a fat man with a ruddy complexion, was rinsing glasses and pontificating behind the bar.

'I'm a friend of Laumier's,' said Victor, 'I—'

'At the back, on the right,' mumbled the man without even looking up.

Victor went down a narrow corridor that reeked of cabbage. At the end there was a door with a glass panel. He pressed his nose against the misty square of glass and discovered a long room littered with easels. A group of young people, about ten of them, were painting enthusiastically. On a trestle table stood a man posing in the bare minimum of clothing. Shocked, Victor noticed Tasha, very much at ease, engaged in studying the model from every angle. A large long-haired, bearded man went up to her, slipped an arm round her waist and murmured something that made her roar with laughter.

Victor's shoulders drooped. She was nothing but a whore! One of those easy girls who would sleep with anyone. He desired her so intensely that he could not bear to see anyone else with her. He could picture himself punching the large bearded character, who was now looking at Tasha with a proprietorial air.

Victor hurried out of the bar and found himself standing outside on the pavement. *To hell with her!* He strode off, his face flushed, breathing hoarsely. He told himself that she cared nothing for him. But he still wanted her. *Eight o'clock, Café des Arts . . .*

Without realising, he had returned to Rue Clauzel, to the artists' supplies shop. The owner was chatting to two young artists.

'I'll buy the Laumier,' said Victor. 'Here's twenty francs.'

'It's not worth that much. I don't want to fleece you.'

'It is worth that. Take it.'

'You're sure you wouldn't prefer a Van Gogh?'

'Could you wrap it for me?'

The shopkeeper shrugged and picked up an old newspaper.

'See you soon, Monsieur Tanguy, we'll be back,' called the young people, as they left the shop.

Victor put the little picture away in the pocket of his frock coat.

CHAPTER EIGHT

Evening, Tuesday 28 June

IT was late afternoon when Victor reached the Expo. The cannon fire from the Tower's second platform made everybody look up and he almost collided with a street vendor selling bread rolls, saveloys and fresh herring. He looked at his watch: 5.45 p.m., two hours to kill. Moving away, he wondered where on earth fish could be fried here. No doubt in the troglodyte habitat.

He wandered through a forest of pylons and overblown constructions. The flow of visitors on their way home crossed with those out for the evening festivities. Armed with baskets brimming with provisions, they had taken over the History of Habitation and settled on the ancient ruins, transforming the dolmens into dining rooms. The passengers on the little Decauville train en route for the Esplanade des Invalides shouted a few insults in their direction as they went by.

Victor walked back towards the Tower, but there too the picnickers had taken over, laying siege to the lower steps of the staircases. The Press Pavilion offered him a refuge and he dived straight in. On the first floor there was a library, flanked by two big rooms, the first for foreign correspondents, the second for French journalists. He was heading straight for a comfortable armchair when he recognised Antonin Clusel, immersed in a dictionary. He quickly did an about-turn, returned to the ground floor and, having crossed the telephone hall, entered a restaurant that was full to bursting. Above the sound of conversation and laughter, an orchestra was playing an Offenbach Allegro. A head waiter came up to him.

'Are you a journalist, Monsieur?'

Victor shook his head.

'I'm very sorry, Monsieur, but this restaurant is only for members of the press and their guests.'

'Victor, what are you doing here?' Marius Bonnet and Eudoxie Allard were leaving their belongings at the cloakroom. She dragged her fingers through her black curls, and looked at him, pouting.

'Georges,' said Marius to the head waiter, 'I would like to dine well away from the orchestra.'

'That is not a problem, Monsieur Bonnet. Please follow me.' He led them to a quiet table and sought Marius's approval.

'Perfect, Georges, perfect.'

'It's an honour, Monsieur Bonnet. I buy your newspaper, I share your opinions. One wonders what the police are up to. These deaths are very bad publicity for the Exposition.' He pulled out the chairs, dusted the tablecloth and laid out the menus. 'I'll send the wine waiter over,' he said as he left.

'Good Lord!' Victor exclaimed. 'Have you got shares in the place?'

'I am in possession of the secret formula: everything can be bought, everything is for sale, even people. Will you join us?'

'No, I must go.'

Marius took him to one side. 'Stay, you'll be doing me a favour. Eudoxie has set her cap at you. I'm just a stop-gap. And in any case, she's not my type. I prefer them more . . .' His hands moved eloquently.

'Sorry, old man, I'm not for sale and I've got a rendezvous.'

'Blonde or brunette?' asked Marius.

Victor withdrew, his mind busy with plans. What would he say to Tasha? 'Well, what a surprise, who would have thought it, you're here for the fireworks display too?' No – too banal!

It was oppressively hot. He pushed back his hat and dabbed his face with his handkerchief. At the entrance to the restaurant he got caught up in a large group of chattering women outside the ladies' lavatories.

'Certainly, Monsieur Ostrovski, it's a pleasure, please do come this way . . .'

Stunned, Victor turned. He saw the head waiter in his white jacket lead a man with a tonsured pate towards the back of the restaurant.

Ostrovski? He recalled his feelings of unease during the visit to his house. He managed to break free of the crowd in order to scan the tables, but a group of revellers pushed him against the cloakroom counter and obscured his view. Feeling suddenly very weak and lethargic, he made for the revolving doors.

Outside in the fresh air he felt better. He lit a cigarette, stayed a moment to look at the great crowds, much denser now than in the early evening. Ostrovski! Who was he meeting?

*

Against a red and white stripy background the sign declared:

THE IMPRESSIONIST AND SYNTHETIST GROUP
CAFÉ DES ARTS

MANAGER: VOLPINI

UNIVERSAL EXPOSITION, CHAMP-DE-MARS

OPPOSITE THE PRESS PAVILION

EXHIBITION OF PAINTINGS

Paul Gauguin	Émile Schuffenecker	Émile Bernard
Charles Laval	Louis Anquetin	Louis Roy
Léon Fauché	Daniel	Nemo

Irritated by these '-ists' and deterred by the names of unknown artists, Victor resignedly crossed the threshold of Café Volpini. In the centre of a brightly lit dance-floor, a Russian princess with golden hair was conducting a group of young female violinists in Muscovite costume. On the lookout for a red chignon, he went past sideboards and beer pumps, and collided with the counter, from which the well-endowed torso of the cashier rose up. A waiter charged out of the pantry, bumped into another coming in the opposite direction, and the two trays crashed to the floor. The cashier heaved herself up over her till, grabbed a saltcellar and sprinkled the unfortunate waiters with it. Victor slipped in discreetly amongst a group of hotheads who were gesticulating and talking loudly.

'You don't understand! Individual initiative is trying to do here what incalculable administrative idiocy would never have allowed to happen!'

'But the Palace of Fine Arts—'

'Don't give me the Palace of Fine Arts!'

'That chamber of horrors!' yapped a small thick-lipped man, wearing a bowler hat and pince-nez. 'They managed to rid themselves of Cézanne, by hauling his *Hanged Man's House* right up a wall to just beneath the ceiling, so that nobody would notice it there. Meanwhile, there's a crush to see the official exhibitors. Ooh! *Joan of Arc Entering Orléans* by Scherrer. Aah! *The Death of Ivan the Terrible* by Makowsky! Messieurs, it is worthy of Cormon's mammoth hunts.'

'My dear Henri, you speak wisely. It's thanks to a café owner that we've managed to create a rival to that exhibition!'

What have I done to deserve this? wondered Victor. He felt as though he had woken up suddenly on the stage of a vaudeville show and was trying to work out which role each person was playing.

In simple wooden frames, a hundred canvases covered partitions hung with dark red fabric. Some resembled stained-glass windows, their warm palette creating an unusual effect, their pronounced line depicting an impression of subjects without attempting to render the objective reality of a landscape or a model.

What is he trying to express? Victor wondered, looking at a canvas signed 'Gauguin: *The Sea*'. A naked woman with loose red hair was surrendering herself to the caress of the waves. The unusual tones, the economy of method evoked a sensual pleasure in the viewer. The old man of the Rue Clauzel had been right: it was physical. He stared down at the floor but the feeling did not go away. He looked back up at the painting; the sensation persisted.

'It seems that Gauguin has gone off to Brittany to nurse his resentment.'

'It's his new passion. Armorique does rhyme with Martinique, after all. He painted *The Mangoes* there. Have you seen them on the left?'

Shut up, please make them shut up! Victor moved aside to escape these remarks.

'What's this then? *Painting with Petrol?* Why not in charcoal? And who is Nemo?'

Victor withdrew to the back of the room, in desperate need of a tonic.

'You! What are you doing here?' Hanging on the arm of the bearded painter he had seen in Montmartre, Tasha did not hide her surprise. 'Maurice, this is Monsieur Legris, bookseller and amateur photographer. Monsieur Legris, this is Maurice Laumier, painter and engraver.'

Victor reluctantly shook the outstretched hand. He instantly took against Laumier: Tasha spoke to him in a familiar way and called him 'Maurice'!

She noticed Danilo Ducovitch, lost in the sea of tables. 'I'll be back. Why don't you get to know each other?' she said to them as she walked away.

Laumier laughed disdainfully. 'Bookseller-cum-photographer, eh? There certainly aren't many of you around!'

Victor sensed that Laumier had decided to provoke him. He restrained himself and tried to be friendly instead. 'I spend more time in libraries and dark rooms than in galleries, and I'm very ignorant about artistic terminology. What do you understand by synthetism?'

Laumier pushed back the hair from his forehead. 'Do you know Berthelot? No? He successfully performed the first synthetism experiments in organic chemistry. We now know that there is no living organism that cannot be reconstituted by science. Some painters, of whom I'm one, apply this discovery to their work. So we manage to recreate external reality by using modern techniques.'

'Forgive my naïvety, but what's new about that? Isn't the only thing an artist can truly express: here is how I see and feel about the world at a particular moment in my life?'

Laumier did not favour him with a reply.

'Despite modern methods, my latest negatives merely reproduce what I saw through my viewfinder,' Victor continued. 'They were clean, sharp and artificial. I had not been able to imbue them with the slightest puff of life and—'

'You are surely not claiming to raise photography to the level of painting!'

'I would never dare risk making such analogies. They each take different routes.'

'You're playing with words! It takes months of labour to produce a pictorial work: one's hand, heart and spirit are all involved in its creation. What you do takes no skill: you just press a button.'

'What rubbish! One has to know above everything what one wishes to express. One has to get inside the subject, be aware of shadow and light and find the right angle at the right moment. And wait. Sometimes when I'm developing my photographs, I feel a tremendous joy. I think: the photograph of this man or that woman is expressing some profound truth. I'm not touched just by the expression on a face, or a pose, it's what they suggest to me and what my personal vision, my own sensibility, has screened out. This fleeting moment may have a different meaning for one, ten, a hundred other photographers and the public—'

'The public! They are always thirty years behind! When they finally understand the artistic revolution of the 1880s, research will have advanced so far that the Academy painters, who are now so fêted and have so many commissions, will seem like prehistoric men!'

'When contemporary painters accept photography is an art, they will nearly be fossils too!'

They had defied each other and both now turned away. Laumier stomped off.

'So you got on well, then?'

Victor looked down and his eyes met with a low-cut neckline. Nothing more charming in the world than a bosom, half-hidden, half on view. 'How long have you been standing here?' he murmured.

'A moment or two. You reminded me of a swashbuckling pirate tickling his adversary with the tip of his foil.'

'Do you think I injured him?'

'Oh, he's tough, he'll get over it. Are you interested in synthetism?'

'No, I had a business meeting at the bar with an amateur collector of ancient books, a Russian – maybe you've heard of him.'

'Lots of Russians live in Paris. I can't be expected to know all of them!'

'No, of course not, but this one is an eccentric. He lives in a rather unique house in the Monceau neighbourhood, stuffed with trinkets, antiques, paintings, plants. The atmosphere there is suffocating.'

'And what's this strange bird called?'

'Constantin Ostrovski.'

'Ostrovski? Who doesn't know him! He's been by the studio several times. Laumier sold him some canvases.'

'And you?' Victor asked in a strained voice.

'Oh, I'm just feeling my way at the moment. I'm far from being ready to show my own work.'

'Even your *Macbeth* illustrations?'

'Oh, I do that just to earn a living.'

'I'd still like to see them. Did you get much work done yesterday after our outing to the café?'

'I painted until dusk.'

He was staggered at her sang-froid. She was such an accomplished liar! She looked up at him with a totally innocent expression.

'We have one thing in common, don't we, Monsieur Legris: light.'

There was an ambiguous gleam in her eyes. He put a hand on her arm and felt his grip tighten. He became tense; his casual nonchalance had evaporated. The smell of her body at such close proximity awakened his desire. 'Tasha . . . this may seem . . . my God, yes, silly, I imagine . . .' He stopped, surprised at what he was about to say, and hurriedly continued: 'What's your perfume called?'

She looked as though she could hardly believe her ears,

asked him to repeat his question and gave a little laugh. 'Benjoin,' she said. 'It's also called Encens de Java.'

His fingers pressed even harder. Java, Kenji! Benjoin . . . What was the name on the label he had found in Kenji's apartment? It sounded the same . . .

'Can you let me go please? I need to say hello to some friends.'

He let go of her arm, touched the pocket of his frock coat, which was misshapen with the little canvas bought in Rue Clauzel. Her voice seemed to come from far away.

'Don't forget my *Caprichos*, Monsieur Legris,' she ventured.

He did not hold her back. He was relieved she had left with a light-hearted remark. However, his jealousy had grown even stronger.

His head was spinning. He needed to get out of this damned café. He was looking for an exit when somebody rocked him with a slap on the shoulder.

'Monsieur Bookseller! How delightful! Are you leaving? I'll come with you. Too many people here. Mademoiselle Tasha is my salvation: thanks to her I'm going to sing at the Opera House. Just think, the Opéra-Garnier! I have to audition tomorrow. If my voice is right, and it will be, goodbye to jack of all trades and master of none! Do you sell opera scores?'

'No, only books,' Victor said quickly. 'The second-hand booksellers along the river sell them.'

'Are you sure you don't need a second assistant? I've read a lot, you know. Mademoiselle Tasha has lent me works. Oh, Balzac, Tolstoy, Dostoevsky! Stories of blood and madness! Where is your bookshop?'

'Rue des Saints-Pères.'

'I'll come and see you . . . I'll come and see you.'

'Of course,' muttered Victor.

The freshness of the night took him by surprise. He shivered.

'How beautiful!' cried Danilo, looking up.

Like the blade of a shining dagger, the Tower tore through the dark sky.

They walked along the French garden. Projectors were casting coloured lights on a monumental fountain with an allegorical theme. Around Humanity, sitting naked on a sphere, five female figures were arranged, each symbolising a continent: dreamy Europe, resolute America, voluptuous Asia, submissive and fearful Africa and savage Australia. Leaning on America's thigh, an old man dressed in an African tunic watched the people go by.

'Good evening, Monsieur photographer, do you remember me?'

'Yes . . . yes . . . Lamba . . .'

'Samba Lambé Thiam. Have you my portraits?'

'They're at home; I'll give them to you. May I introduce Monsieur Danilo . . .'

'Ducovitch, lyric artist,' finished the Serb as he crushed Samba's hand in his own. 'Which country are you from?'

'From Senegal. I live in St-Louis.'

'Is there an opera house in St-Louis?'

'We have the governor's mansion, barracks, a hospital, a church and more than five hundred shops. Two schools, a— Oh, it looks like it's on fire!'

Immense fireworks were erupting from the Eiffel Tower. There were cheers and applause.

'Have you been up there?' asked Samba. 'I haven't dared.'

'Several times. I've had free tickets. I've even signed the Golden Book, though going up the star attraction to enjoy the view is hardly something to boast about! I find there's rather too much emphasis on consum—'

Victor had pricked up his ears. The whole world seemed to have signed the damned book! He put his hands in the fountain, and the coolness of the water went through his whole body. He was in the wrong mood to spend time in the company of the two men, but he remained there, thinking about Tasha, recalling her attitude, working out the meaning behind her replies and every flutter of her eyelashes. *She'll have to leave in the end. She'll pass close by here and I'll go up to her and . . . If only this idiot would stop spouting nonsense!*

'. . . and there are medals on sale for those who want to impress people,' Danilo went on. 'Bronze for visitors to the first-floor platform, silver for those on the second, gold for those on the third, except that they are meaningless. You can buy them for half the price on the Boulevards!'

'So it's the same as the Légion d'Honneur,' Samba countered. 'Apparently one can also buy those. I've heard that the former President of the Republic's son-in-law had been dealing—'

'Shhh. No need to shout it from the rooftops. Walls have ears,' Danilo whispered. 'The Expo is stuffed with informers and policemen, and in the evening there are reinforcements.'

'Wise precaution,' Samba approved. 'Where there's money you'll find thieves like flies around a honeypot. Flies are a big problem in my country.'

'Imagine if a madman took the life of the Prince of Wales or the Shah of Persia, the police could easily blame it on foreigners, and, you know, I want to make a career for myself here in France. Who knows, maybe it's the nihilists or anarchists who've trained killer bees to do away with people.'

Victor could feel himself becoming tense. This fool was really getting on his nerves. To think that Tasha showed him kindness!

'You have an overactive imagination and a very strange way of reasoning, Monsieur Ducovitch,' he ventured, slapping the water with the flat of his hand.

'Oh, I know what I'm saying, and I say what I know. I've already been taken for a maniac by a woman. Me, a man who has nothing but respect for the weaker sex!'

'The weaker sex? What's that?' Samba asked.

'Women,' grumbled Victor.

'Women – weak? Maybe in your country, but in mine, in Senegal, they lift loads that not even a mule would carry!'

'Gentlemen, I bid you good evening,' said Victor. Having begun to walk away, he changed his mind and turned back. 'Monsieur Ducovitch, how long have you known Mademoiselle Kherson?'

'Since I've been lodging at the German woman's place. Let's see . . . nine months and five days. Ah, Mademoiselle Tasha . . . that adorable nymph, my guardian angel! She washes my shirts, she feeds me, she appreciates my singing exercises, I think she's in love with me! In fact, have I told you that, thanks to her, I'm to be taken on at the Op—'

But Victor had gone.

'The Op? What's the Op?'

Danilo turned to Samba. 'The Opera House. So, you say that St-Louis has no lyric temple? Something ought to be done about that.'

The cannon fire from the Tower at eleven o'clock took Victor by surprise on the Quai d'Orsay. The Expo was about to close. He walked on, arms swinging, remembering Danilo's words in time to his steps: *they trained killer bees to do away with people.* Killer bees. Patinot, Cavendish, both stung by bees? Antonin Clusel was right, you don't die from a bee-sting. Other than that wretched Golden Book, what might link a penniless widow, an American globetrotter, a Japanese bookseller, a Russian collector . . . and Tasha? Thinking of her in her little grey dress made him feel as sad as when he had seen her go into Ostrovski's house.

He arrived at the Pont d'Iéna. At that very same moment the Decauville train whistled past. A plume of smoke stretched up to the tricolour beam projected from the Tower's beacon. Victor froze. A train, a station, of course . . . He remembered the article Joseph had shown him in his precious black notebook. Batignolles station. An article from *L'Éclair,* 13 May '89, 'Killer Bee in Paris'. The dead man had a name like something sweet: Macaroon? Calisson? Marzipan? Meringue . . . Méring, that was it, Jean Méring.

CHAPTER NINE

Morning, Wednesday 29 June

VICTOR woke with a start. As soon as he opened his eyes, the dream receded, leaving only a bitter aftertaste. He got up and drew back the curtains. Day was dawning and it was already very hot. After washing quickly, he put on a clean shirt and trousers and chose a comfortable pair of shoes. His frock coat was much too heavy for the season. He rummaged in the pockets, throwing his notebooks, wallet and change on the bed, and struggled to pull out the picture wrapped in newspaper. He put on a summer coat and leafed through the notebooks, keeping the one belonging to Joseph. Then he pocketed the various items strewn on the bed and went into his study, where he put his own notebook, along with the picture, at the bottom of one of the drawers of the roll-top desk. He heard Kenji at his ablutions on the other side of the partition and slipped out quietly.

The river had a greenish hue, which was darker under the bridges. Victor paused a moment, long enough to see a barge glide by, a dog running to and fro on its deck.

The booksellers and vendors of sheet music had not yet set up, but all along the riverbank, the carpet cleaners were getting to work, armed with their beaters. Victor crossed Carrefour Saint-Michel, which was crammed with handcarts, trolleys and omnibuses. Not knowing the area well, he decided to branch off towards La Maube.

Below Quai Montebello was the domain of the stevedores. They negotiated like tight-rope walkers the gangways linking the boats to the quay. With bent backs, they carried wicker baskets full of coal or cement on their leather, caped caps. Black dust floated in the air. Victor rubbed his eyelids, swollen from lack of sleep. At Rue de la Bûcherie, with its run-down houses, he passed a succession of shady hotels and cheap eating places offering rotting meat for four sous, and turned right towards Place Maubert. A roadsweeper was gathering up cigar butts from the gutter.

'Excuse me, where is Rue de la Parcheminerie?'

'You have to go back the way you came and get back onto Rue Saint-Séverin. You wouldn't happen to have a couple of coins on you? I've got a terrible thirst. Thank you kindly, guvnor!' cried the man, pocketing the money. 'I'll drink your health at Old Lunette's!'

Victor strode up Rue Lagrange, only recently built through the middle of the slums. As he entered the network of alleys behind the church of Saint-Julien-le-Pauvre, he reflected that in large cities there were invisible boundaries around affluent neighbourhoods through which one passed suddenly into areas of degradation and misery. Rue Galande looked very much as it would have done in the Middle Ages. Fried-fish vendors and left-over food sellers were setting up their stalls in the wind. Dishes of beetroot sat alongside rounds of cold black pudding.

Victor felt as if he were back in Whitechapel. The drinking dens, the low doorways in decrepit façades, the stands selling second-hand clothes and scrap iron, all set the scene perfectly for a Parisian Jack the Ripper. In the evening the pavements must have been crawling with whores and other shady characters. But at that hour of the morning, only a few tramps the worse for wear after a hard night's drinking were on the damp pavements.

The contrasting light promised to create some interesting effects, and Victor resolved to return with his Acmé.

Like the neighbouring streets, Rue de la Parcheminerie was doomed to poverty and filth. A rat disappeared into a crevice. At the back of a courtyard, a bareheaded woman was washing laundry in a tub, ignoring the cries of a new-born baby. Victor asked her if she knew Jean Méring. She indicated the tall silhouette of a leprous building a little further down. He returned to the street, stepping over a pile of rubbish and passing a wretched-looking carpenter's workshop, before going down into a passage leading to a second courtyard.

'Where are you going?' demanded a rasping voice.

The concierge was eyeing him from the doorway of her lodge. Her long apron covered her from the chest down like a sort of armour. The get-up was completed by a broom, intended to chase away intruders as well as stray sheep.

'I'm going to visit Jean Méring.'

'In that case you'll be needing to go to the cemetery.'

'Is he dead?'

'And buried. What did you want with him?'

'I'm a journalist. I had some questions to ask him.'

'It's a bit too late for that. But you could ask old Capus. They were sharing lodgings. When Méring died, Capus stayed, just my luck. Shame it wasn't the other way round.'

'Why?'

'Because in spite of his line of work, Monsieur Méring was tidy and polite, while that Capus stinks the place out with his chemicals, not to mention his unsavoury trade. I'm always afraid that he will get Mac-Mahon; he lures him in with meatballs. One day he'll skin him. In fact, I haven't seen Mac-Mahon this morning. Mac-Mahon! Mac-Mahon!' she bellowed.

'And where does he live, this Monsieur Capus?'

'At the back, the ground floor, on the right. Mac-Mahon!'

Surely ex-president Mac-Mahon would not have premises in this hovel? Of course not! thought Victor, knocking.

'Come in, it's open!'

The smell, a mixture of alcohol and carbolic acid, took him by the throat. The bedroom was badly lit by a narrow window. It was crammed with two beds, a bench covered in strange objects, a long tinplate cylinder on the floor near some rubber boots, buckets, butterfly nets, a small charcoal stove, glass jars standing on wooden planks, and some clothes hung on nails. Sitting on a chair in front of a little wooden table, a man was absorbed in reconstructing a tiny skeleton. Without looking at Victor, he pointed to a stool.

'Are you from the Faculty? What are you after?'

Busy making a mental note of the little room's contents, Victor did not reply. He noticed that on a bench next to some fossils there were sheets of cork with insects nailed to them.

There was also a large herborisation box and books with dog-eared pages, both novels and scientific works.

'So you're a collector?' the man went on. 'I don't have much at the moment – a few beautiful specimens of butterfly, a praying mantis. You could place an order.'

Victor bent down to inspect the glass jars: he could make out some green and yellow shapes floating in a cloudy liquid. He deciphered the labels: 'Frogs from Seine-et-Marne', 'Lizard from Chantilly', 'Adder from Marly'.

'Actually I've come about something entirely different.'

The man put down the tweezers he was using to move the bones around, and stared at him. He could have been anything between fifty and sixty years old. He was thin, with a lined face, and the way his moustache drooped onto his salt-and-pepper beard gave him a melancholy air.

'Oh, yes? And what's that?'

'I have to write a series of articles on unusual Parisian occupations for my newspaper and if you would agree to talk to me about your work, I would be happy to pay you.'

'It's a deal! What would you like to know?'

'How did you come to be a laboratory supplier?'

'I was trained in phar—'

He was interrupted by a hollow meowing. A vast tabby cat had just extricated itself from under one of the beds and was rubbing up against the door.

'Mac-Mahon! You were hiding again, you miscreant! He must have got in when I took out the rubbish,' Capus grumbled.

He pushed the animal outside and sat down again.

'Where was I? Oh, yes. The pharmacy. I couldn't face spending my whole life behind the counter of a pharmacy. So I became a purveyor of small animal species for the Museum of Natural History and for lecturers in physiology. That was much better as I had my freedom. I also supplied private individuals. I'm always going here, there and everywhere, at least I used to. Now I can't come and go so easily because of the damned rheumatism in my pins.'

'What do you hunt for?'

'Larvae, insects, vipers, toads . . .'

'And this?' asked Victor, pointing to the skeleton.

'A bat. There are bats in the walls of the fortifications around Paris. University lecturers write to me from the provinces. I have a reputation; I'm known.'

'I'm sure that you know as much, if not more, than some lecturers. I'm interested in something on which I'd like your opinion. You must have heard about the brutal murders at the Exposition. It's been claimed that the victims were stung by bees. Do you think that's possible?'

'It's ridiculous! Just as it was with Méring, but no one believed me.'

'Who is Méring?'

'A friend of mine. We lived here together. Sometimes I accompanied him on his forays. He was a rag-picker. When he made a find we would share it fifty-fifty.'

'What sort of find?'

'Fossils. There are many amateur collectors. Once he discovered two shaped flints. They were worth quite a bit.'

'Has he moved out?'

'No, he's dead. I was right next to him when it happened. The police called me in and when I told the commissioner that it was not a natural death, he laughed at me in disbelief and told me that I must have bats in the belfry. But he said that was hardly surprising considering that I work so closely with small animals. And then he added: "The other witnesses swear that your friend the rag-and-bone man was stung by a bee."'

Capus leant forward and grabbed a bottle of red wine, and two glasses, which he filled. 'Your health. Méring, poor chap, also thought it was a bee. But I know what I'm talking about, and by God, that was no bee.'

Victor drank barely a mouthful.

'Are you sure?'

'For heaven's sake, it's what I work in! I tell you, Monsieur, I prefer the company of animals to that of imbeciles. Yes, even that tomcat belonging to that loud-mouth of a concierge, and too bad if she does think I'm going to flog it to a laboratory for vivisection! I have respect for animals and I only sacrifice a small number so that I can afford to live. He was an idiot, that commissioner. He didn't want to hear my opinion, case closed. No point writing about it in your newspaper.'

'What did happen then?'

'Maybe I know, maybe I don't. It's too late for an autopsy. Poor Méring has been pushing up daisies for a while now. If he'd been from the right side of the tracks, a pen-pusher, a merchant, a soldier, I'll bet you anything that old fool of a policeman would have bent over backwards to open an investigation,' Capus finished with a disdainful pursing of his lips.

Victor put a banknote on the table.

'Tell me about Méring.'

'He was a good sort, not very talkative, a loner. He put up with me, I suppose. But ten years of hard labour in New Caledonia, that changes a man. Before the Commune he was a cabinet-maker. He set himself up in the room next door about three years ago. I think that he had been married but he preferred not to talk about it. We kept each other company and now . . . What a rotten old life!'

'What happened to him?'

'That day, I had gone with him. I needed some crickets and they are often found on the railway tracks, especially in the sidings where it is warm. Méring had filled his basket and he had gone on ahead because he wanted to see Buffalo Bill arrive. When I joined him, he was lying on his back and there were people almost trampling on him, making it hard for him to breathe.'

Capus poured himself another glass. 'Aren't you drinking?' he asked, looking at the liquid. 'It's funny, the strangest thoughts occur to you at moments like that. My friend was suffocating in the middle of a wild crowd and I was noticing insignificant details: the gravel on the track, the moth-eaten mane of a rocking horse, the ankle boots of the person who thought they were being helpful by offering advice. I could hear someone's voice but all I could see was what they had on their feet, those yellow kid-leather boots. And then the world seemed to restart and Jean murmured: "A bee." Naturally my first reaction was to try to remove the sting: but there wasn't one. So I looked for the bee itself or for some similar insect: nothing.

The poor fellow could no longer move. He was breathing very slowly with his mouth open, he was dribbling and his trousers were wet. I spoke to him and from his eyes I could tell that he understood, but he couldn't answer. I examined his neck. He had certainly been stung, but I can assure you that it was not by a bee, definitely not. He had a red mark about the size of a hundred-sou piece. Very quickly the edges of the sting swelled up and soon the whole thing was bluish and puffy and about two centimetres in diameter. I touched it with my fingertips. Jean didn't react, he couldn't feel anything. A bee-sting is quite different. All you see is a little white lump about two or three millimetres across with a grey point, which is the sting. The swelling increases, the skin stretches and you feel a sharp pain, which itches and hurts.'

'You're certain there was no trace of a sting?'

'Yes. Instead there was a hole, as if someone had pushed a large hollow needle into the flesh. His eyes had become glassy and he was suffocating. His heart stopped. By the time the police arrived, he was dead. I told them that it was very strange to die just from a bee-sting, but they replied that it was not the first time that a drunkard had kicked the bucket all of a sudden.'

He guzzled the rest of his drink, then put the glass down abruptly. 'So there you are! Ever since I've had nightmares. Because . . . what can I say? It was no accident.' He banged his fist on the table. 'Good God! What kind of swine would do that? And why?'

'Did he have any enemies?'

'I have no idea. Take your money – I don't want it. Which newspaper do you work for?'

'*Le Passe-partout.*'

'I hope to read your article soon, Monsieur . . . ?'

'Victor Legris,' he replied, not having the presence of mind to give a false name.

'I'll make a note of that,' said Capus, snatching up a pencil and a school notebook. 'That way, I can always complain to the paper if you twist my words.'

With her cat on her lap, the concierge was keeping watch. Victor saw that the passage led to another courtyard, which opened onto Rue de la Harpe, opposite the restaurant Le Père Chocolat.

Surprised by the brightness of the light, he joined Boulevard Saint-Michel, shaken by what he had just learnt. Jean Méring had died in exactly the same way as Patinot and Cavendish. Capus seemed convinced that someone had poisoned his friend with a needle. What sort of poison would produce such a rapid effect?

The boulevard gradually coming to life made Victor feel slightly better. He felt as if he was emerging from a bad dream and he could still taste the sourness of Capus's wine. At the corner of Boulevard Saint-Germain, he jumped into a cab to get back to the bookshop as soon as possible.

Alone with his apple and his book, Joseph rose to greet him.

'Monsieur Legris, your article has appeared in the paper. I read it, it's spot on! You've really outdone all those other puffed-up scribes! Do you know what? You should write about mystery novels in your next column.'

'Is Monsieur Mori here?'

'He's gone to have lunch at Rue Drouot with his colleagues. Germaine has left you some cassoulet.'

'In this heat? I'll see, maybe later. If there are any customers, you look after them. I'm going down to the stockroom.'

'Oh, Monsieur Legris, you forgot to give me back my notebook, please . . .'

'Your notebook? Yes, yes, here it is,' said Victor, putting it on the counter. He hurried off without even tapping Molière's head.

'Everything's changing . . . and those two are abandoning me. If this goes on, I'll be in charge of everything,' grumbled Joseph, reimmersing himself in *The Chamber of Crime* by Eugène Chavette.

Victor had not found what he was looking for. Yet somewhere on those shelves there had to be a book on the subject. Sometimes he would buy lots at auction that no one wanted, in the hope of finding a hidden gem. Most of the time he drew a blank and the unsaleable stock would gather dust in the dark recesses of the stockroom. Joseph had suggested opening an annexe called Books by the Kilometre.

Crouching down, he manoeuvred his way under the staircase where hundreds of paperback and hardback books were haphazardly piled. The odour – of leather, dust, and wax – made him feel dizzy. He had almost reached the bottom layers when he felt the spine of a large book: *Dictionary of Drugs and Poisons*. He'd found the damned book at last!

He turned off the gas-lamp, climbed the few steps leading to the shop and pushed the door open just enough to see what was going on. No customers. He swept past Joseph, perched on his ladder, and rushed up to the first floor.

Anselme Donadieu was snoozing in the seat of his cab, having arrived much too late at the station on Place Maubert. His black oilcloth hat had slipped over one ear. Hiding behind a lamppost, a little boy aimed a stone at Anselme's headgear, tipping it into the coachman's lap. He awoke with a start.

'Little devil,' he muttered, covering his head again.

He looked at the cigarette-butt sellers filling their haversacks with the butts of partly smoked cigars and cigarettes, and cast a hopeful look at a hesitant couple who chose to get into the cab in front. He cursed into his beard. He was old and tired, and afflicted with persistent sciatica. His horse, an emaciated ten-year-old mare, was scarcely any better. Everyone chose the younger coach drivers and their horses with glossier coats. Anselme Donadieu could see the anxious day coming when no one would want to hire him any more. Then he would be good for nothing but the workhouse and Polka would be destined for the knacker's yard.

He had been idle for two hours when a man wearing a wide-brimmed hat and an Inverness cape approached his vehicle, holding a piece of paper. Blinded by the sun, Anselme could not make out his features but he thought he was dealing with a foreigner who spoke no French, probably British, so he looked at the note. Having read it, he nodded his assent. Before getting onto the running board, the man slipped him the fare for the journey with a generous tip on top. As their hands touched, Anselme noticed that the foreigner was wearing gloves of a slightly coarse texture. He cracked his whip and shouted, 'Gee up, Polka!' loud enough to make the poor beast's ears tremble.

As soon as he began reading the *Dictionary of Drugs and Poisons*, Victor realised he was heading into dangerous territory. He couldn't explain his determination to get involved in this business. Did he just want to prove he was wrong to suspect his nearest and dearest? Was he trying to establish Kenji's innocence? Or wasn't it more a simple desire to impress everyone? As a child he had so often dreamt of shattering his father's total indifference with some great achievement.

The air was stifling. He opened the window slightly.

Bent over his desk with his collar open and his hair in disarray, he read through a number of articles that were brief but enough to give him an idea of the subject. Capus had stated that Jean Méring died rapidly with no spectacular symptoms. What kind of poison could have such a devastating effect? He read on. After half an hour he had already eliminated several toxic substances, including Spanish fly, digitalis and arsenic, all of which acted too slowly. As he skimmed through an article on strychnos, he made a discovery.

Strychnos is a climbing plant that winds itself around the trees of South America. The Indians living in the lands between the Orinoco and the Amazon use it to coat the tips of their arrows. It is also found in the intertropical countries of Asia, in Cochin China and on the island of Java. The natives poison their arrows with upas antiar extracted from the bark of *Strychnos tieute*.

Upas antiar. The letters danced in front of his eyes. He had already seen something about that – he had even copied it down. Taking his notebook from its pigeonhole, he leafed through it until he came to the notes taken from *Le Tour du Monde*.

JOURNEY TO THE ISLAND OF JAVA

BY JOHN RUSKIN CAVENDISH, 1858–1859

I was present at the death of one of the unfortunate victims of upas antiar. At first he showed the characteristic symptoms of that poison: anxiety, agitation, shivering and vomiting. Then he arched his spine sharply, clenched his jaws and the muscles of his limbs and chest stiffened. The poor man's face became flushed and his eyes looked as if they would burst out of their sockets. He had three choking fits and then . . .

That was where he had stopped in the middle of the sentence, in a hurry to leave the Hachette bookshop.

He wiped his face with his handkerchief and put his notebook away. *That doesn't tally with Capus's description. So it can't be upas antiar.* He went on reading the dictionary.

Also extracted from strychnos is ticuna or curare, which is found in Para and in Venezuela. This preparation arrived in Europe either in little clay pots or in calabashes. It looks solid and sticky, is of a blackish brown colour like liquorice, and is soluble in distilled water and in alcohol. Like aconitine, the Calabar bean and cicutine, curare paralyses nerve function. But while the first three substances provoke physiologically violent reactions – spasms, vomiting and muscular contractions – curare acts without pain, and death occurs within half an hour following the injection.

In 'The Master of Curare' Alexandre de Humboldt reports the comments of Indians who say: 'The curare that we prepare is superior to anything that you know how to prepare. It is the essence of a plant that kills quietly.' (*Journey through Central America*)

'Curare,' Victor murmured

He was convinced that he had found the cause of the death of Méring, Patinot and Cavendish. There was no proof, of course. It was just a hunch. He reread the page out loud and suddenly, as he was saying: 'either in little clay pots', he pictured himself in the Hindu palace. The Battle of Sebastopol. The plants. The sideboard covered in . . . in pots, firmly closed little earthenware pots.

Ostrovski, Constantin Ostrovski . . . I told him that I liked plants that were not dangerous and he replied: 'It all depends . . . it all depends how they are used. Only man is dangerous . . .' Could he be mixed up in all this? He was also up there on the Tower . . .

He felt totally confused. He needed to lie down a moment to think, to decide on a course of action. He closed the dictionary.

*

Though usually so meticulous, he had thrown his clothes carelessly down on the furniture and now lay on his bed, dressed only in his long johns, with a damp towel to his forehead to stop a migraine developing. The situation had become too much for him, and a feeling of listlessness was growing in him. He would doubtless have fallen asleep, had he not been looking at the Constable watercolour on the wall facing him. If only he could escape into that peaceful countryside, far from this city of stone and iron, which had cast an evil spell on him! He felt a longing for that emerald-green countryside where the cottages held the promise of pleasant dreams. He was floating towards the watercolour, entering it . . . He pressed the towel to his head. He must calm down. He needed to go back over everything that had happened from the beginning up to his interview with Capus. Capus . . . He had said something important and Victor had tried to make a mental note of it, but he could not now recall what it was. He remembered Kenji's teaching about memory: 'Our mind is a succession of rooms where we put our memories. Some of them are stored in full view on the shelves but others are thrown in a jumble at the back of dusty attics. When you can't find one of them, you use your inner eye like a lamp and visit the rooms one by one, carefully following the beam of light that you're casting on your memory. In this way you will eventually find the memory you are searching for.'

He closed his eyes in concentration. Ostrovski, the little terracotta pots on the sideboard – was it curare? The Russian had signed the Golden Book just like Patinot, Cavendish, Kenji and Tasha. Of these five people, two were dead. Perhaps Kenji and Tasha knew each other. After all, Kenji had bought perfume whose name seemed similar to Tasha's – Benjoin. Kenji had apparently had a meeting with Cavendish and sold some prints to Ostrovski. Ostrovski had received Tasha at his house. Tasha . . . What was it that linked these facts and people to some deaths that only intuition suggested might not be from natural causes? The threads were becoming tangled and his migraine was taking hold. He groaned.

'Tasha . . .'

He found the strength to get up and fetch the little canvas he had bought by Laumier, which he unwrapped and looked at for some time. Why was he attracted to this woman? What did she have that others did not? Was it her pretty face? Or breasts as round as peaches? Perhaps it was her personality? He remembered her turning Bill Cody's portrait into a caricature with two lines of her pencil, and his thoroughbred into a ridiculous old nag. The word struck him so forcefully that he had to sit down. That was it! *My friend was suffocating in the middle of a wild crowd and I was noticing insignificant details: the gravel on the track, the moth-eaten mane of a rocking horse . . .* Capus's words resounded in his head, illuminating a half-forgotten image: a drawing he had glimpsed two days before in Tasha's notebook. A train, some Redskins, a man lying on the ground, baskets, a chair with three legs, *a rocking horse.* She had also been there when the rag-picker died! It couldn't be a coincidence. The Indians . . . Buffalo Bill! *Méring wanted to see the arrival of Buffalo Bill,* Capus had said. So had Tasha. Did she go of her own accord or was she sent by *Le Passe-partout?* In the latter case her drawing would certainly have been published. He would have to go back to the newspaper and look at the issues of 13 and 14 May.

He dressed in a hurry. As he was leaving, he caught sight of Laumier's picture on the bed. He leant it against a clock on the chest of drawers and considered it again with a wry smile. Tasha had been present at all three murders. Was that why he found her so disquieting?

CHAPTER TEN

Afternoon, Wednesday 29 June

As he did every day, a nondescript man, dressed in nondescript clothes, was limping up and down the corridors of police headquarters. Some years earlier, when he had been a secret police agent, a violent thief had broken his tibia and his days of tailing and interrogating were brought to an end. Isidore Gouvier was then transferred to the office researching family interest cases, where he remained dejectedly for almost five years. Following his resignation he became a private investigator before offering his services to *Le Temps*. Marius Bonnet had persuaded him to join him in the *Le Passe-partout* adventure.

Isidore Gouvier did not spend much time with the other journalists, whom he found too blasé, too cynical, too full of themselves. There was nothing exceptional about him, and it might seem surprising to some that he was always better informed than anyone else. The explanation was a simple one: always unhurried, unflappable and clear-sighted, he was invariably in the right place at the right time.

On that 29 June, he went from one office to the next, sneezing into a check handkerchief. He had been struck down once again with his annual hay fever. Hobbling and sniffling, Isidore Gouvier waited patiently for a hansom cab driver called

Anselme Donadieu to come through the next-to-last door at the end of the corridor on the second floor of police headquarters.

Le Passe-partout was closed. On the door was scrawled in pencil: 'Isidore, meet us at Le Jean Nicot.'

Disappointed to be denied access to the newspapers, Victor easily found the café, which was right next to Galerie Véro-Dodat. Marius, Eudoxie, Antonin Clusel and Tasha sat at the pavement tables with their aperitifs, along with two typesetters, who were slightly separate from the group.

'Victor!' shouted Marius when he saw him. 'Come and raise a glass with us!'

'What are you drinking to now?' he asked, with a quick wave to the team and a long look in Tasha's direction.

'To the success of our articles on "A Day at the Expo with Brazza", and our next guest, Charles Garnier, the architect of the History of Human Habitation, who's just confirmed that he will do it. For an epigraph, we'll use one of his many plays on words which apply so perfectly to our newspaper: "The dirty rag had mopped up more than the clean one." *Le Figaro* will scoff. Antonin is beginning the interviews tomorrow. Tasha will go with him. By the way, your column was a great success. When can I have another?'

Victor finished ordering a vermouth and cassis, and frowned. 'I haven't had time to think about it. I have a vague idea about novels that have crimes and murders as their subjects. What do you think?'

179

Marius gave him a surprised look. 'I didn't know you were interested in that sort of literature.'

'That genre has existed since the dawn of time. Just remember the Atridae,' Victor replied. He stared at Tasha, who looked down.

'Don't you think there's already enough violence in life? Think of wars, or simply the terrible crimes in the news, like the stiff 'uns at the Expo,' Antonin Clusel remarked.

'These deaths are shocking, but they also spice up everyday life by forcing you to ask yourself certain questions,' Eudoxie said with a half-smile in Marius's direction.

'Children, don't forget that for the moment there isn't the least proof that they are murders, apart from that anonymous letter, which could be the work of a lunatic. In the last few years there have been several complaints to police headquarters. There are a great number of wild beehives in Paris, particularly in the sugar refining area. Workshops, lodgings and gardens are all infested by bees, so much so that the chief of police has just banned beekeeping in the capital. A lot of people have been stung, and not just once. There are reports of epilepsy in young children, adults having convulsions, and bites sometimes causing eyesight problems and—'

'But you're contradicting yourself,' Antonin Clusel objected. 'You said—'

'Oh, I know what I said. You have to say something to increase circ—' Marius stopped, his eyes fixed on the facing pavement. A breathless Gouvier was crossing the road and hurrying towards Le Jean Nicot. 'Have I got a story for you! Pens at the ready: there's another dead body!'

This news was received with cries of astonishment. Satisfied, Gouvier continued: 'It was discovered in the early afternoon, in a hansom cab, stiff as a board. I gave the driver the third degree when he came out of police headquarters. I was the only journalist there at the time. So we've got an exclusive, until proved to the contrary, and we need to get a move on!'

'Eudoxie, get your pen and pad and write everything down. Who was it?' Marius asked.

Gouvier blew his nose and looked down at his scattered notes. Antonin watched him impatiently, drumming his fingers on the table.

'Constantin Ostrovski, Russian, with a large fortune, a very large fortune . . .'

Victor choked on his vermouth and cassis. Murdered. He was stunned at this incredible revelation. Dead, Ostrovski made a pretty poor suspect. His hypothesis was falling apart. Back to square one. He glanced at Tasha, who was holding her portfolio. Her knuckles had turned white. Gouvier went on unhurriedly deciphering his scraps of paper.

'Known to art dealers. On first inspection, it looks like a heart attack. That has a certain similarity to the preceding deaths, except that this time there's a suspect. The driver, who was waiting around at Place Maubert, took a fare to Parc Monceau. Once there, a second fellow – Ostrovski – joined him, heading towards the Magasins du Louvre. The first passenger got off and the driver went on to the Champ-de-Mars, to the Expo entrance at Quai de Passy. The fare had been settled in advance. The driver is called Anselme Donadieu, a fateful name as it turned out. Sixty-five years old. Lives in Ivry.'

Victor could not stop looking at Tasha. She kept tying and untying the strings of her portfolio nervously.

'Ostrovski, how's that spelled?' asked Eudoxie, leaning over her pad.

'As it's pronounced, with an i.'

'What are the police saying?'

'They're keeping to their "bee" story. My contact knows what's going on: he tipped me off. For the moment nothing is being leaked, no statements to the press, there's just a lot going on behind the scenes. Everyone is under great pressure. But according to my contact, they've got no real leads, they're playing for time.' Gouvier finished his account with a resounding sneeze.

'I stand by what I said: these are murders,' Antonin asserted. 'Lecacheur knows it. Don't forget he's a follower of the Goron method.'

Victor paused as he raised his glass to his mouth. 'Goron?'

'The head of the secret service. When Paris wakes up to the announcement of a death in suspicious circumstances, he immediately needs to find a culprit. In five days, on the Fourth of July, on the Grenelle Pier, a scaled-down Statue of Liberty is going to be unveiled, a gift to Paris in friendship from our American community. It would be a shame to spoil this historic moment with some sordid business, because, don't forget, John Cavendish was a United States citizen. So not a word to anybody. The police are investigating on the quiet and feeding false information to the press. Once again honest Lecacheur is pointing the finger at the bees – bees, I ask you! But, I repeat, these are murders.'

'Without any obvious injuries?' asked Victor in surprise.

'Oh, you can easily poison somebody with a syringe or needle if you set about it the right way!' muttered Gouvier. 'Antonin, remember the story you told us last year?'

'Which story?'

'You know, the one about the Spanish woman.'

'What's Spain got to do with anything? Your hay fever's affecting your brain.'

Gouvier blew his nose again and gulped down some beer.

'It happened in Seville about fifty years ago. The woman was called Catalina, and she'd fallen for a handsome hidalgo who rejected her advances. She was hot-blooded, and stabbed him in the arm with her hatpin, which was tipped with a poisonous substance – extract of white hellebore, I think.'

'Did he die?'

'The pin had gone through a sleeve, so the material soaked up some of the poison and he narrowly escaped death after several days in a coma.'

Marius cackled. 'A *Sleeping Beauty* for our times.'

'If you like. But our victims at the Expo were not so lucky. They won't be seeing in the new year.'

'We'll do a special edition!' Marius exclaimed. 'It will cause a sensation amongst the post-theatre crowds! Come on then, everyone back to work!'

The two typesetters got up and went off. Marius took the pad from Eudoxie and began to compose his article. Slowly Gouvier unfolded another piece of paper.

'As to the driver's testimony, it's all written down here. He didn't see his first customer's face because the sun was in his eyes. He looked like some kind of English type: big hat, Inverness cape, gloves. Clothes that surprised him, as it was so hot.'

'Is that everything?'

'The English fellow said nothing, the itinerary was written on a piece of paper. Full stop.'

'It's odd, but I've just remembered something,' Victor said thoughtfully. 'Last month, one of our customers reported a man being stung by a bee, a rag-and-bone man, I think, and that he'd died. But another rag-picker who was present at the time of the incident swore blind that his friend had been poisoned, and not by insect venom.'

'Who was it? Where did it happen?' asked Antonin.

'I can't remember. At the time I paid no attention. One hears so much idle chatter in a bookshop.'

Once again Victor was watching Tasha's reactions. But she remained huddled up with her elbows on the table and her chin in her hands.

'I know,' said Gouvier. 'It was the day Buffalo Bill arrived.'

Immersed in his writing, Marius slowly looked up. 'Listen, children, I'm trying to concentrate on my article, what are you talking about?'

'Nothing, nothing, it's not relevant,' Gouvier went on. 'As is my duty, I carried out a little investigation of my own. The fellow was sick, very sick, a heart problem. And there's no cure for that. He had spent ten years in New Caledonia, as a former Communard. I spoke to the doctor who examined him.'

'There we are, I've finished!' Marius exclaimed. '"Crime in a Carriage" – not bad, eh?'

'Inspired, Boss,' Antonin approved as he looked through the article, 'but you said it yourself, there's no proof, so I suggest a more neutral tone. We don't want any backlash.'

'Oh, but I've only put down the facts. To work!'

They got up and smoothed down their clothes. Only Tasha remained seated.

'What's wrong, my dear?' Marius asked.

'It must be the sun, I . . . feel a little dizzy. I'll be with you in five minutes.'

'Absolutely not. You go home and rest. We really need you at the Expo. I can manage without a picture this evening, I'll just need one for the next edition. Oh, these flowery ladies' bonnets,' Marius added, indicating Tasha's hat. 'It's decorative but gives no protection at all from the sunlight!'

As Tasha tottered off, Victor took his leave of the team.

'Yes, to the penny-dreadfuls, but hurry up and write me something!' shouted Marius as he left.

Where was she? Over there, outside the baker's. For one moment he was tempted to follow her, but he needed to be alone to consider the new information. A walk would do him good.

He made his leisurely way as far as Rue de Rivoli, passing by the Magasins du Louvre with signs up for summer sales and special offers. The pavement was full of people. In a window devoted exclusively to travel items, a male mannequin wearing a pith helmet stared back at the curious onlookers with expressionless eyes.

Victor watched a group of sandwich men pass, strapped into advertising boards that covered their chests and backs. Without thinking, he read:

LA GRANDE REVUE PARIS & SAINT-PETERSBURG

Bi-monthly publication out on 10th and 25th of every month
EDITORS: ARSENE HOUSSAY & ARMAND SILVESTRE

Poli . . .

Saint Petersburg. A fat self-satisfied face superimposed itself on the mannequin's. Constantin Ostrovski was staring at him with a mocking expression. It was curious, all the same . . . Had Ostrovski arranged to meet his killer? Was it a friend? An accomplice? An accomplice who had eliminated him because he knew too much and was becoming a liability? One could only wonder. Those little pots on the credenza, what did they contain? Curare? *I feel I've got something here . . . some proof. But have you? The police could go wild over something like this. The police! What's that inspector called? . . . Lecacheur? Lecacheur is following a lead. It won't be long before he establishes a link between the signatories of the Golden Book. That will take him back to Kenji, Tasha . . . and me! I left my calling card at Ostrovski's home.*

His temples were throbbing and his forehead was on fire. He crossed the pavement and entered the Tuileries Gardens, collapsing onto a chair. He needed some respite to recover both physically and mentally. What was this all about? Who would suspect a bookseller who was a go-between for a collector?

He rubbed his neck. His imagination was racing. Kenji was implicated. And Tasha. A woman could easily be the perpetrator of such a murder, as that scorned Spanish woman of Gouvier's proved. A simple hatpin! It would be easy to get one's victim in a crowd, just by starting a commotion. *Suddenly my aunt cried, 'Ow!' . . .* Those were the words of Eugénie Patinot's niece. The little hypocrite had added: *Someone fell on her: that made me laugh.*

Somebody? A man or woman?

Back to Avenue des Peupliers.

Kenji was taking a break outside the bookshop. Through the glazed door he could see Joseph doing battle with three customers. He entered discreetly and gave him a little sign.

'Where's Monsieur Legris?'

'No idea. I'm not clairvoyant, you know. He comes and goes, he can't keep still in one place,' Joseph answered sullenly.

'Did he come back for lunch?'

'He can't bear cassoulet in the summer, and I can sympathise. He shut himself away in the stockroom, then he went up. Who knows if he came back down? I was out for five minutes to get some apples from Mama. You know, Monsieur Mori, you should try and reason with him, because I can't be everywhere at once.'

'And did you see him this morning when you opened up?'

'No. When he wants to make himself scarce he'll take French leave, escaping down the apartment stairs. I know that trick. Hey, don't you leave me too!'

'I'll be back. Take care of your customers,' Kenji said as he went up the steps.

He went along the corridor that separated the two apartments, up to the front door, which opened onto the first landing of the building. Of course, yet again Victor had slammed the door without locking it. He slid the two bolts and entered Victor's home. The bedroom was unusually untidy. The curtains were half drawn, the bed unmade, clothes scattered all over the room. He noticed a coloured rectangle leaning against the clock in the glass case, an oil-painting of a nude, a young red-headed woman whom he immediately recognised with displeasure. He was about to leave when his eye fell on the desk. The top was open. Next to a basket overflowing with jumbled post, marked 'Incoming and Outgoing', he caught sight of a blue envelope resting on a dictionary with: 'Photos taken on 24 June at the Colonial Exhibition' written on it. He reached out, lifted the flap, and his sleeve caught a dark object, which crashed to the floor. He bent down and picked up an order book. On the first page he read: 'Meet J.C. 24-6 Grand Hotel Room 312' followed by some question marks. He pulled the armchair out and sat down.

It had gone four in the afternoon when Victor knocked on the Nanteuils' gate. A fat woman with a pallid face came to open it. He recognised Louise Vergne.

'You again! It's a disgrace! Digging up a good Christian soul and chopping her up into pieces. When I think that you're paid for that dirty work, you ought to be ashamed. You're worse than cannibals!'

'I have no idea what you're talking about.'

'Are you sure you belong?'

'To what?'

'To the police! Because if you really did, you'd know all about the *autopsy*!' She had stepped back to get a better look at him.

'Oh – *that*! Of course, the autopsy,' he said. 'I thought you were talking about another murder!'

'Why? Have there been more?'

'Well . . . I can't say anything as an officer in the police service . . .'

'During a service? Oh, there's just no respect for anything any more! Killed in a church!'

'Er . . . please don't repeat any of this. I would like to have a quick word with Mademoiselle Rose.'

'Some hope. That beanpole handed in her notice, declaring that she wouldn't stay a moment longer in a house whose dead were dug up to examine their entrails! So then the Nanteuils begged the Le Masson family to lend me to them for a few days, long enough to find another governess, and I said yes. Madame Nanteuil is shut away in her bedroom. She won't receive anybody.'

'In that case . . . might I see her daughter?'

'Who? You don't mean Marie-Amélie?'

'She's a key witness.'

'I don't know. You stop at nothing, do you? Interrogate a young girl, indeed . . .'

'I won't be more than five minutes and you can listen in.'

Louise Vergne hurried off to call Marie-Amélie, who arrived quickly, eating bread and jam, which was also smeared all over her cheeks.

'I already told you everything the other day.'

'Yes, except for one detail. You told me that just as your aunt was stung by a bee, somebody fell on her and that it made you laugh.'

'That doesn't surprise me from this one,' Louise Vergne muttered.

'It's very important. Take a moment to think. Was it a gentleman or a lady?'

Marie-Amélie frowned. A fly landed on her bread and jam and she shooed it away. 'Oh, I don't know . . . I think it was a gentleman . . . Yes, it was, it was a gentleman! Can I go now?'

She ran back to the house. Louise Vergne shook her head. 'I always knew that under that prim exterior, Eugénie led men on!'

Avenue des Peupliers suddenly took on a festive air. If the little girl was telling the truth, if it was a man who had bumped into Patinot, then Tasha was innocent. Victor felt relieved for a brief moment, before he realised that, in that case, Kenji was once again the prime suspect.

No sooner had he entered the bookshop than he felt he had walked straight into a trap. Seated as if in a waiting room, three people looked up at him. From his stool, tying up a parcel of books, Joseph grimaced with an embarrassed smile. At his desk, holding his pen quite still, Kenji straightened his shoulders as a blonde woman, who had been slumped on a huge trunk, leaped to her feet.

'Odette,' Victor murmured in consternation.

'My duck, you did promise to—'

Kenji didn't give her enough time to finish.

'So, how was the sales room? Did you manage to close the deal?'

'Yes, not without difficulty, that's why I'm late,' Victor replied, taking the ball and running with it.

'My duck, sales room or no sales room, you must take me to the station. I've been here for an hour, and I'm going to miss the Houlgate train. You forgot!'

Odette was furiously pacing up and down in front of the trunk, which she kept hitting with the end of her parasol, as she couldn't take it out on Victor.

'I haven't forgotten. The situation is totally under control. We have more than enough time,' he said in his calmest voice, looking at his watch. 'Joseph is going to fetch us a cab.'

Only too happy to escape the storm, Jojo left his badly tied parcel and hurried outside.

'Is there at least somewhere to powder my nose?' asked Odette with a snort. 'Your Chinaman didn't even offer me any refreshment,' she added, lowering her voice.

'Yes, on the first floor, to the left, the room at the back.'

Kenji waited for her to grumble her way up the narrow stairs before saying, 'I have rarely come across a more disagreeable person. She scared off two customers. Make sure she gets on the right train. It would be a pity to deprive the Normandy coast of such a charming visitor . . .'

'You don't like her very much,' said Victor, holding back a smile.

'I think it's mutual. I'm also leaving unexpectedly.'

'Where are you going?'

'To London for a couple of days. I'm leaving this evening.'

Victor was struck dumb with emotion for several moments.

'But what do you need to go to London for?'

'A private affair. You have yours,' he added, pointing upstairs with his chin, 'and I have mine.'

'Nothing serious, I hope.'

'No, all is well. Why do you ask?'

'Just a thought . . . You've seemed preoccupied for some time now.'

'Since you mention it, I'll tell you what's worrying me: you are.'

'Me?'

'You are always out, and Joseph and I can't do everything. I feel as though this bookshop has ceased to interest you.'

'Not at all. On the contrary, I've had to value a large number of private book collections, as have you. What's more . . .'

They moved away from each other. Victor thought they were arguing like an old married couple.

Joseph came in shouting: 'Madame's cab is here!'

Odette's dress rustled on the stairs. The driver loaded the trunk onto his shoulder. Victor wanted to shake Kenji's hand but he had already returned to his desk and was instructing Joseph: 'Make that delivery straight away. I'll close up.'

Hanging on to Victor's arm, Odette kissed him repeatedly

until they had sat down in the cab, where she nestled up to him.

'Truly, truly, my duck? You really hadn't forgotten?'

'Of course not. I've been preparing myself for your departure for some days.'

'You're not just saying that?'

He dropped a distracted kiss on her forehead, wondering why Kenji was leaving for London so suddenly.

Flattening herself against a porch, Tasha watched the hansom cab move off towards the Seine. She remained deep in thought for some time after it had gone, then went back up the road towards the Elzévir bookshop. Kenji was quickly closing the wooden shutters. Catching sight of each other through the window, they were both momentarily transfixed.

Assuming a sad expression as he hummed '*Le Chant du départ*', Victor could see a tearful face hanging out of the door, and read on her lips a last 'When will you come, my duck?' her voice drowned out by the noise of the locomotive. Then everything disappeared in a cloud of steam. Normandy was not to be deprived: Odette was on her way to Houlgate.

On the platform, piles of luggage everywhere, he stopped a newspaper vendor to buy a special edition of *Le Passe-partout*. On the first page was a big headline: 'CRIME IN A CARRIAGE'.

He read the article as he walked along. When he left Gare Saint-Lazare, the lamps were being lit. He decided to walk to Tasha's.

*

A noisy mass of hurrying people filled the station foyer. Porters dressed in the uniform of the Compagnie du Nord were shuttling between the long-distance departures and the line of cabs parked in Place de Douai. Leaning against the wall near the information window, Kenji unfolded the special edition of *Le Passe-partout*.

CRIME IN A CARRIAGE

ANOTHER VICTIM FOR THE KILLER BEES

A collector who was well-known to art dealers, Monsieur Constantin Ostrovski, dies in a hansom cab a few hundred metres from the Eiffel Tower.

The article recalled that two other people had died in the previous week in similar circumstances. The police refused to make any statements. The testimony of the driver who had discovered the body followed.

Kenji read no further. He picked up his bag and put his paper in it. A steward wearing a striped cap with the word 'Interpreter' on it in gold letters offered his services. Kenji refused, then reconsidered and murmured a few words to him as he handed him a tip. The man went off, and reappeared shortly after with a piece of paper. Kenji put it in his pocket and looked at the clock: a quarter past ten. He made his way to the telegraph office and composed a message.

UNFORESEEN DELAY. WILL COME NEXT WEEK. LOVE, KENJI.
MISS IRIS ABBOTT CARE OF MRS DAWSON, 18 CHARING CROSS
ROAD, LONDON.

He handed his form to the employee, saying it was 'urgent', then paid, left the station and walked back up Boulevard Denain to the Hôtel du Chemin de Fer du Nord.

At reception he presented the piece of paper given to him by the interpreter. 'I have a reservation,' he said.

The concierge, a small woman with a weaselly face, accosted Victor from the doorway of her lodge. 'Hey, where are you going at this time of night? I'm responsible for everyone that comes and goes here!'

He leaped up the stairs, taking them two at a time. On the landing of the sixth floor he looked down into the stairwell. All the floors were smothered in darkness, right up to the empty corridor.

She was there, on the other side of the wall, fourth door along on the right. He listened: silence. But he thought he had heard the sound of bare feet running across the wooden floor. He waited, his heart full of hope. She was going to unbolt the door, he would force her to face him, to say yes or no to him . . . but maybe she was busy enjoying herself with someone else? He was overcome by a wave of jealousy that left him breathless outside the door. *I'd do better to leave rather than lose my temper. She's not back yet, that's what it is.* This thought calmed him. He banged the edge of the basin and groaned. A door opened. A ray of light.

'Monsieur Legris? Is it you? I thought . . .'

The woman was real, all right, and just here, so close . . . The basin, feebly illuminated by the skylight, seemed to fade away along with the walls. She was wearing a nightshirt with a high collar, which showed off her figure. He hesitated, then stammered: 'Tasha . . . I was worried . . . You left the café so suddenly earlier on. You're . . . you're not sick, are you?'

'Just tired. I'm working fourteen hours a day.'

'You'll catch cold.'

'It's extremely hot!'

'The tiled floor . . .'

With eyes lowered to the floor, he stared at her ankles. He suddenly moved forward, trying to take her by the shoulder. She jumped back.

'No!' she whispered.

He froze. Could she doubt how hard he was trying to resist the urge to touch her? She moved in front of the oil lamp on the table. For just a moment he clearly saw all the curves of her body through the light fabric.

'You're the one that's sick!' she cried, withdrawing further into the room.

He moved nearer to her, close enough to smell her scent. 'You knew him! You told me you did,' he murmured.

'Who?'

'The man who was found dead in a cab, Ostrovski.'

She looked worried.

'I came across him a number of times, so what? You know him as well. You were going to meet him at Volpini's yesterday evening!'

'Just came across him? Are you sure?'

'How dare you?'

He put a finger under her chin, forcing her to look up.

'When did you come across him for the last time?'

She jerked her head free. 'A couple of days ago I went to deliver a work that he had commissioned from me. Sketches of Redskins. Why these questions? Are you a police informer?'

'His death was suspicious. Sooner or later the police will want to know the nature of your relationship with him. Were you at Les Batignolles station the day that Buffalo Bill arrived?'

Disconcerted, she crossed her arms.

'What's that got to do with anything? Do you think there's a connection between that business and what's happened at the Expo? Is this why you were talking about it at the café?'

'Were you at Les Batignolles?'

'Yes, Marius sent me there for the newspaper.'

'Unless Ostrovski did.'

'You go too far!'

Pretending not to hear, he closed the door. Was she play-acting? Too forceful in her responses, but without enough conviction.

'The rag-and-bone man — were you present at his death?'

'No. I saw him fall; I thought he was having a turn. I had time to sketch something before the police arrived. There was a crush, so I left. I don't enjoy morbid spectacles!'

Pale with fury, she was defying him. Suddenly, she understood.

'My God, you think I did it! Are you about to accuse me of killing all those people? But Gouvier told you, the rag-and-bone man was sick, with a heart condition. Who put these ideas in your head? Clusel?'

'I didn't need him,' Victor muttered, turning away to stop

himself from being won over. 'I thought it over. You were on the Tower the day that Eugénie Patinot died.'

'Does that make me guilty? Lots of people were there: the newspaper team, your Japanese friend, you yourself . . . Do you think I'd really be able to cause someone harm? Have you no regard for me at all?'

'On the contrary! I have a lot of . . . respect for you. I am simply trying to protect you.'

'From whom? From what?'

'You knew Ostrovski. And then . . . I saw you on the Esplanade des Invalides a few moments before Cavendish died.'

'You were spying on me!'

'It was by chance, I assure you.'

How could he confess to her that on that day he had been hoping to meet her at the Colonial Exhibition?

'Go away. I'm tired.'

'That expensive perfume that I saw here the day before yesterday – did Ostrovski give it to you?'

'And if he had, how would that concern you? I am free, I associate with whom I wish!' she shouted as she tried to get to the door.

Leaning on the handle, he barred her way. She sighed.

'That bottle is just a sample. Last year I drew some labels for a perfumier. Now go. I never want to see you again.'

She quickly wiped her eyes, which were brimming with tears. He imprisoned her fist and raised it to his lips.

'Tasha, please . . . forgive me,' he said between kisses. 'I wanted to be sure . . . all this is so complicated . . .'

She made a feeble effort to extricate herself.

'Complicated, that's what you are,' she said in a choked voice.

He drew her to him, buried his face in her hair and breathed her scent in deeply. When his lips touched her, she resisted but did not turn away. He kissed her on her forehead, her nose, her neck and felt her let herself go. Blood was throbbing in his ears, he tightened his grip, his fingers went all down her arching back. Her cheeks suddenly aflame, she moved away from him, stood on tiptoes and, looking at him intently, slipped his frock coat off his shoulders.

She guided his hands to her hips. He embraced her passionately before carrying her to the bed. Lying next to her, he undid her nightshirt, tore off the collar, crumpling the lace. She raised herself up to look at him in the flickering light of the lamp and tried to undo the buttons on his shirt front. She was breathing faster now.

'Come,' she whispered.

He kissed her throat, caressed her breasts, descended towards the warmth of her thighs. Their naked bodies joined together in sensual harmony. Her movements were in rhythm with his. He fought against the desire to go too quickly.

CHAPTER ELEVEN

Morning, Thursday 30 June

K ENJI limbered up with some stretches. He missed not being able to take a bath. The room, with its flowery wallpaper and mass-produced furniture, was clean, but lacking in comfort. He stared into the mirror, almost hoping to find the answer to his worries, but he could see nothing except a man's face with drawn features. He had been kept awake most of the night by an oversoft bed, the noise from Rue Denain, along with the comings and goings in the hotel, and used the time to try to make sense of everything he had learnt. Now he was trying to reach an objective decision on what course he should follow. He pushed the table up to the window, picked up a file and took out three negatives that he had appropriated from Victor's apartment the day before. He adjusted his glasses and examined the photos, minutely examining every detail. Putting the photographs down, he began pacing the room, whilst weighing the pros and cons. He didn't have much to go on, just an impression. He poured himself a cup of tea and reread the article in *Le Passe-partout* that related the circumstances of Ostrovski's death. Yes, he had a hunch. It was starting to take shape in his imagination. Once he had made his decision, he put on his jacket. Better to act without absolute certainty than to carry on plagued by doubt.

*

Entangled in a sheet, one leg hanging out of the bed, Victor was floating above the scene from the opera in which a horned Mephistopheles dressed in scarlet was lustily singing *And Satan leads the dance*. . . He groaned and shifted position. The rich baritone was still singing, the sound of his voice getting louder and alarmingly close. Disorientated, Victor half opened one eye and was immediately dazzled by the bright light coming from a skylight. Why did Mephistopheles insist on invoking the golden calf? Still half asleep and confused, he hugged the bolster. The dream dissolved but the voice continued, filling and taking possession of the bedroom. *It's Hell calling you, it's Hell following you.* Now it was coming from an earthenware stove covered in charcoal sketches. Tasha! Had he dreamt her also? The space next to him was still warm and imbued with her perfume. No, last night's adventure was no illusion. He was filled with joy, similar to the joy he had felt as a child when his boarding school in Richmond ended for the summer. He rolled onto his stomach and buried his head in the hollow of a pillow.

'Benjoin,' he murmured.

What was the name of Odette's eau de toilette? Heliotrope? Odette, who had left only the day before, was already as insubstantial as a ghost. He decided to banish her to oblivion. Propped up on his elbow, he could barely make out the face of his watch: 8.15. At that moment he saw a piece of paper on the table. A note from Tasha.

Dear Victor,

They say the early bird catches the worm so I should catch quite a few today! I'd be delighted to see you later if you are free. Here, this evening at eight o'clock. There's coffee. Put the key under the mat when you leave.

Tasha

From the other side of the wall with its dreadful brown wallpaper, Rossini's *Barber of Seville* had replaced Charles Gounod's *Faust*. Vexed by that 'Dear Victor' – after everything that had happened last night! – he sat up on the edge of the bed. His underwear was hanging on an easel with an unfinished monochrome oil painting of a roof, a gutter and sky. He reached out for his socks. His eyes were riveted to the canvas: something was amiss. Those minuscule dark specks, at the bottom, on the right, were they stains? He peered closely at the painting. The specks broke up into little winged cones with black and yellow stripes. Bees. Unusual to see bees pollinating a gutter. Should he interpret them as a message? With an uneasy feeling, he decided not to answer that question, and then had to have several goes at pulling his long johns up his legs before finally getting them on.

He went into the nook that served as a kitchen, but, having failed to light the small charcoal stove and searched in vain for sugar in the midst of the forest of jars on the shelf, he decided to make do with a cup of cold, bitter coffee.

He took his shirt out from under the table, where it lay close to the brick wedged under the wobbly leg. Dust and breadcrumbs littered the floor. As he got up he reflected that Tasha was not one for the joys of domesticity. Opposite him, a picture of a man weighed down by terrible grief was pinned up by the book-filled alcove. Probably a drawing by Grandville; he recognised his style. He must have seen that picture in an old copy of *Magasin Pittoresque.* That flock of nightbirds flying around the man bore a strong resemblance to the winged creatures so beloved by Goya. He felt ashamed that he had not lent Tasha *Los Caprichos.*

Through the wall, the voice of Danilo Ducovitch suddenly burst into song.

> *'Už kak na Rusi carju Borisu slava!*
> *Slava! Slava!'*

Silence, then:

> 'Glory and long life to Tsar Boris!
> Glory, glory to Boris!'

Had the Serb been taken by the Opera House chorus? Was he celebrating his triumph?

> *'Už kak na Rusi carju Borisu!*
> *Slava, Slava, mnogaja leta!'*

In any case he was no longer singing about Figaro, Victor concluded. He felt suddenly light-hearted. Now where had she put his trousers? Ah, there, on a wicker trunk, along with his cravat, his shoes and frock coat. He tied his laces. The Russian words sung by Danilo were stirring up a vague memory. An idea was taking hold, but just out of his reach. He put on his frock coat as his mind worked on. A door slammed: Tsar Boris leaving his apartment. His memory was still teasing him: it was something to do with a name he had glimpsed recently, a name . . . But what name? He was about to go out when he realised that he had forgotten to put on his trousers. *I give up. My mind's like a sieve.*

He locked the door and put the key under the mat. Tasha! He would see her this evening! He felt like singing too, but didn't, because he was always out of tune. He thought of buying flowers, chocolates, violet drops or perhaps some tea. *Yes, maybe she'd like some camomile? What an idiot I am!* He bounded down the stairs.

In the courtyard he almost collided with Danilo Ducovitch and Helga Becker. Red-faced and glaring, the small woman in her cycling clothes and the bearded giant were hurling abuse at each other.

'You evil, cruel woman!' shouted the Serb.

'You sponger!' returned the German.

Victor greeted them as he went by. They paused a moment to look at him, then continued with their quarrel.

'Vulture!'

Victor reached Rue de Clichy, passing a shop whose sign had always intrigued him: 'For mothers of children devoted to blue and white'. He turned back and, buoyed up by his good humour, opened the door and cried, 'And what about Little Red Riding Hood?'

Laughing wildly, he went on his way. A little further along, the wide windows of Prévost, the confectioner, caught his attention. He could never resist those Légion d'Honneur medallions.

The Batignolles-Clichy-Odéon omnibus came down the hill, jolting on its iron wheels. As there was no one at the bus stop, the conductor was preparing to spur on his horses when Victor appeared, arm outstretched and carrying a chocolate Eiffel Tower.

Kenji looked up at the statue, unveiled just a month ago. His back turned on faraway Notre-Dame, and proudly ensconced on a monumental plinth in breeches and stockings, the great writer and printer Étienne Dolet dominated Place Maubert. Kenji felt sympathetically towards Dolet, whose philosophical opinions had been judged heretical. He had been hanged and burned in 1546 a few steps from the current Boulevard Saint-Germain where ten or so carriages were now parked. Waiting for custom in the shade of the trees, the cabmen wagered that General Boulanger would return from exile and were generally putting the world to rights. Kenji walked up to them, holding the special edition of Le Passe-partout.

'Good day, gentlemen. I'm looking for Monsieur Anselme Donadieu.'

'He's at La Guillotine, telling his story to anyone who'll listen and offer him a drink. Some people have all the luck. Nothing like that would ever happen to me!' replied a ruddy-faced coachman.

'La Guillotine?'

'It's actually Le Château Rouge, on Rue Galande.'

Kenji raised his hat, smiling, and walked away.

'Hey, my friend, better watch out for crooks. They can be tricky with foreigners . . .'

The coachmen guffawed.

Taking no notice of Joseph's sullen expression, Victor hurried into the stockroom to deposit his half-melted tower somewhere cool. He came back up smiling.

'I must go and change, Joseph. But why the fish-eyed look? It's only a bit of chocolate,' he said, holding out his sticky hands.

'Things would work much better if I knew where to get hold of you, Monsieur Legris, now that you are famous.'

'Famous? What do you mean?'

'I mean famous – people are beginning to write to you at the newspaper . . . Here's a letter that an errand boy delivered this morning. Congratulations!'

Victor read the envelope, which Jojo was holding out to him.

M. Victor Legris
Journalist at Le Passe-partout
Rue Croix-des-Petits-Champs

'Put it in my pocket and I'll read it when I've washed my hands.'

He started up the spiral staircase.

'Tell me, Monsieur Legris, now that you work at the newspaper, you must have details about the Expo murders. What do you think? Did that Russian in the coach simply die of natural causes or not?'

'As Monsieur Mori says, death is only simple in poetry!'

'Thanks for nothing,' muttered Joseph grumpily.

In the kitchen, Germaine, with tousled hair and apron askew, was stirring the contents of a saucepan with a wooden spoon. Victor sniffed, recognising the aroma of partridge and cabbage in a cognac sauce. He would have liked to point out the inadvisability of preparing dishes with a sauce during a heatwave, but he held his tongue. Germaine, who was an outstanding cook and had worked for Victor and Kenji for seven years, was conscientious and undemanding, but she could be very touchy if criticised. In fact, the good woman turned into a real harridan who could sulk for hours, and that was very bad for her cooking.

When he had wiped his hands, Victor tore open the envelope. A line written in awkward script wandered over a page torn from a notebook.

29 June
I must see you, it's very urgent, come to my house before midday.

Capus

Had the letter been sent to the newspaper the day before? It was possible. In that case Capus was expecting him today. What time was it? Ten past eleven. Victor gave up the idea of getting changed, stopped off briefly in the kitchen to cut himself a slice of bread and a piece of Emmenthal, and went downstairs without hearing Germaine's admonition: 'Nibbling something between meals will ruin your appetite!'

Perched on his rolling ladder, Joseph was looking for an illustrated edition of La Fontaine's fables for a spotty young man. He was relieved to see Victor return, but he was already flying out of the door.

'Monsieur Legris!' shouted Joseph, seeing himself abandoned yet again. He sent up a prayer to the god of shop assistants to bring Kenji Mori back immediately to the Rue des Saints-Pères.

Outside the bookshop, a fat pigeon pecked at invisible grains. When it flew heavily off, Victor watched its flight as far as the opposite pavement, where his attention was caught by a large figure half hidden in the entrance of an apartment block. The build, the cast of countenance and the very long hair were familiar. Danilo Ducovitch. What was he doing there? He was the last person Victor would have expected to see, but he seemed to get everywhere. And with such an intense character, he was probably in love with Tasha. Perhaps he was jealous? He remembered giving him his address the other evening as they left Café Volpini. *Oh, he's probably come to ask me to take him on. I hope Joseph will be able to deal with him.*

There were just a few people on the embankment where the sun beat down. As Victor went past the Institute, he fancied he heard footsteps behind him. He stopped, and shortly afterwards the noise stopped. *So, Ducovitch is following me. He is jealous, but probably not enough for him to want to fight me.* He turned round. No one. A couple of old soldiers, maids with shawls and straw baskets passed by, indifferent to what was going on around them. Victor began walking again, not completely reassured. The impression of being followed stayed with him.

Finally he reached the district of la Maube where he saw a heavy-set man go into a café. He quickened his pace. Cupping his hands around his eyes he pressed his face up against the dirty window and saw what looked like a market porter leaning against the counter. It was not Danilo Ducovitch. *My goodness, I must be going mad, or getting paranoid! I can't have eaten enough these last few days.* In fact, his head was spinning a little.

The armoured concierge must have been sweeping the corridors, as the courtyard was empty. Victor knocked on Capus's door. He could hear the noise of the city, punctuated by the cries of a baby nearby. He knocked with the flat of his hand on the cracked wood of the door, putting his ear against it.

'Monsieur Capus . . . Monsieur Capus, are you there? It's Monsieur Legris.'

He hesitated, then quietly turned the door handle, expecting to feel resistance. The door opened. Inside, the shutters were half closed. The only movement came from the dust particles dancing in the slender rays of light.

'Monsieur Capus, it's Victor Legris from *Le Passe-partout* . . . Is anybody there?'

A grating noise and a barely discernible movement came from his left. Victor stayed still, listening for another sound. He had cramp in his calf.

'I'm getting out of here,' he murmured.

The blow struck him full on the shoulder. He staggered backwards, his arm numb. He fell heavily. There was a wild meowing, which mutated into a long wail. A shape sprang up and quickly disappeared. Victor felt the room expand. Above him a menacing shadow threw itself against the ceiling with the speed of a spider climbing its web. Instinctively Victor rolled aside, banging his head on the corner of a piece of furniture, and closed his eyes, ready for the worst. His heart was pounding so hard that he did not hear the door being locked. The pain flooded back and a black veil descended over him.

When he opened his eyes, he saw a pair of seven-league boots and shards of glass a few centimetres from his face. With a huge effort of will, straining every painful muscle, he managed to stand up by gripping the edge of a table. Once his eyes were accustomed to the gloom he noticed a bulky shape covered with light-coloured canvas on one of the iron beds. He leant over the mattress and carefully pulled back the cover, but dropped it again immediately, stifling a cry. He had touched something cold. For a brief moment he tried to tell himself that what he thought he had seen was merely a trick of the light. He breathed in deeply several times and pulled the canvas back sharply. Henri Capus lay on his back, his head thrown back. A bloody gash ran from ear to ear across his throat. A large dark stain was spreading over the bolster.

Shocked and terrified, Victor started to tremble violently. His senses refused to accept the reality of what he saw.

'Mac-Mahon!'

The shout made his flesh creep. He stayed rooted to the spot, his head gripped in a vice, holding his breath.

'Mac-Mahon! Where are you, my sweet?' wailed the concierge behind the door. 'I know you're in there, you old scarecrow. It's no use pretending. Give me back Mac-Mahon, otherwise . . . Wait a bit, I'm going to fetch Old Chocolat. That'll show you!'

A snapping sound. The woman did not seem to be moving. Too long – she was taking too long to leave. Finally her slow footsteps receded along the corridor.

The acrid odour of phenol began to irritate Victor's nose. He had to get away, quickly. Back to fresh air and life. He groped his way, arms outstretched. Feeling sick, he managed to grab the door handle. The door would not open. He tried again – nothing. He shook it frantically but to no avail. He was shut up with a dead body! If he were to explain what had happened, who would believe him?

Panic-stricken, he stepped back. He suddenly thought of Kenji recounting the Great Fire of London for him as a schoolboy: 'Think, don't throw yourself into the flames. There is often a way out.' A way out . . . the window! Of course, he risked being caught in a dead end or seen by witnesses; his attacker would have thought of everything. Even so, he had to reach the window. He stumbled against something soft: the seven-league boots. He lost his balance and almost fell on the remnants of a glass jar but caught himself at the last minute by grabbing a bedpost. Despite himself, he found he was looking at the shroud concealing Capus's body. He imagined it suspended in an enormous jar, with the label: 'Inhabitant of Rue de la

Parcheminerie'. He raised himself onto the narrow windowsill, grazing his fingers as he tried to open the window latch, which had probably been jammed for years. With clenched teeth, he set to furiously, striking the glass violently with his clenched fist. *Open, damn you!* His fist went through the pane and the glass shattered into fragments. Blood ran down his palm. In a blind rage, he tore down the dirty curtain and wrapped it around his good hand. With repeated blows he managed to force the worm-eaten wood to give way, and the window opened. To the left of the building was a courtyard, to the right, a passage. Just as he was about to jump out, two children suddenly appeared from the left chanting: 'You old drunk, old drunk, we can see you, you're covered in blood, we're going to tell old mother Frochon that you've eaten her moggy!'

Screaming horribly and terrifying the children, Victor tumbled out onto a pile of wooden crates, then rushed blindly on. He came across a narrow passage in the wall that was so low he had to duck down. Then there was another courtyard and beyond it, the street. He ran, pursued by a dog and dodging a beggar, who was rummaging in a dustbin. An alley zigzagged between humpbacked houses. He hid in a doorway, his heart racing. He really needed to pull himself together. He wrapped his injured hand in the scrap of curtain he still had. The cut was superficial and gradually the bleeding was stopping. He moved his arm cautiously: nothing was broken and the pain was lessening. He adjusted his frock coat, smoothed down his sleeves and flattened his hair. Right by him was all the bustle of the boulevard: the sounds of voices, footsteps and wheels clattering on cobblestones. He threw himself back into the flow of passersby. Once he had stepped onto the embankment at Quai Montebello, he felt much more his old self. As he recovered his spirits and hurried in the direction of Quai Conti, he was overwhelmed by the emotion that he had held back throughout his mad escape, his throat tightened and he started to cry.

The growl of thunder came, followed by the first warm drops of rain, which splashed onto the macadam as he turned into Rue des Saints-Pères. He leant against the wall and, with his head back, let the rain fall on his face. A fruit-seller hitched to her cart passed him, hurrying to take shelter under the bookshop awning. Victor saw Joseph looking through the glass door and waited until he was back behind the counter before crossing the road and going in. At the top of the stairs, he felt his pockets: no keys. Had he lost them as he made his escape or left them in Capus's home? The key ring had his name on it.

He went down again, knowing he would have to go through the bookshop. Joseph was polishing a set of bound books. At the sound of the door chime, he turned with a salesman's smile on his face, which vanished immediately.

'What on earth's happened to you, Boss? Have you been run over by a bus? Your hand's bleeding.'

'It's nothing, just a scratch.'

'You're very pale, you should go and rest. Come on, I'll help you upstairs. In any case, this weather's put paid to any customers.'

Too shaken to protest, Victor let himself be led upstairs. Joseph forced him to lie down and removed his shoes for him.

'Have a good sleep, Boss, and you'll feel better. Do you want me to call Dr Reynaud?'

'No, good heavens, no! Go back and look after the shop.'

'All right, all right, but don't complain if that gets infected. Speaking of injuries, have you heard the latest? There's been a third death at the Expo, a murder like the two others, and the paper—'

'I know, Joseph, you've already told me.'

'I'll leave you . . . He'd be better off finding himself a pretty young girl to kiss instead of finding himself face down on the pavement. And why am I always the one who does all the work around here!' muttered Joseph, loud enough to be heard.

The door slammed. Victor fell back onto the pillow. The high window let in a dull, leaden light and rain lashed the glass. He shut his eyes, then opened them quickly to escape the vision of the old man lying rigidly with his throat slit. And all the blood, the blood! He felt a dull pain in the pit of his stomach, and fear. Overcome by nausea, he just had time to get to the bathroom. A flash of lightning streaked the sky. Automatically he counted, one, two, three . . . The thunder shook the walls while a second spasm doubled him over. The heat was unbearable and he staggered to Kenji's apartment to run himself a cold bath. Sitting on the side of the bath, he watched the water rise.

He had escaped unharmed. No one had seen him other than the children. No one, that was, except the murderer. Who could bear a grudge against old Capus?

He lit the gaslight and undressed. On the shelf above the basin were two framed photographs in pride of place. One was of a small boy nestled against a young woman: 'Daphne and Victor, London, 1872', the other was of an Asian man of about thirty, straight and serious in his sombre frock coat.

Without that cat, I would probably be dead. . . Oh, my keys!

He couldn't stop looking at Daphne and little Victor. He

straightened the frame and stared at Kenji posing for the picture.

For the first time he wondered why Kenji had been so attached to his mother and him, to the point of renouncing his own private life. When Monsieur Legris senior had died, Kenji had assumed the role of head of the family in a very natural sort of way. Had he acted out of self-interest? The question filled Victor with shame and self-disgust. Could he really suspect the man who had raised him, protected him and watched over him day and night during the terrible diphtheria epidemic of 1869 . . . ? No, it was just not possible.

He unwound the piece of soiled curtain from his injured hand. No, it couldn't be Kenji, he couldn't stand the sight of blood. His blood phobia went back to his childhood when a number of his relatives who had converted to Christianity had been massacred by order of the army of the Tokugawa. It was a miracle that he had escaped.

Victor turned off the tap, got into the bath and quickly immersed himself. The icy water took his breath away and the vision of Capus's hand, cold as marble, suddenly appeared before him. He had touched it as he had pulled back the sheet covering the corpse. His mind began to race. How long after death did a body become cold, taking account of the room temperature? Eight, ten hours?

He realised that he was shivering. He got out of the bath. Standing in the middle of the bathroom, he tried to work it out. *I arrived at Rue de la Parcheminerie around midday. If my calculation is correct, Capus was butchered as he slept at about three o'clock in the morning.*

While he dried himself, he noticed the shelf where the photos stood, very white under the crude gaslight and, by a strange association of thought, that shiny shelf made him think of a bistro table. He envisaged the sunny pavement tables of Le Jean Nicot. *I mentioned Méring's death.* What had he told them? That the friend of the rag-picker, who'd been with him when he died, had sworn that his death was deliberate poisoning, not from a bee-sting. *I was not supposed to know that detail . . . Tasha! No! Surely not her, we spent the night together!*

He looked up. Gazing out impassively from his frame, Kenji seemed to be studying him. *An accomplice! She pretended to be ill and alerted an accomplice!*

He pressed his lips together to rid himself of the bitter taste in his mouth. Something was still eluding him. The killer could not have foreseen that he was going to come so why was he still at the scene of the crime more than eight hours after committing the murder?

The letter! Capus's letter. Someone had found out about it at the newspaper after the mail was distributed. Tasha. *The early bird catches the worm. Damn her! The murderer returned there to wait for me.* He dashed off to his bedroom.

The storm had calmed down, and golden streaks pierced the clouds. Victor pulled the envelope out of his wallet.

M. Victor Legris
Journalist at Le Passe-partout
Rue Croix-des-Petits-Champs

No stamp. No seal. The letter had been dropped off at the newspaper. Crumpling the envelope with his tense fingers, he fell onto the bed, where his tiredness and emotional state got the better of him and he sank into sleep. He had a dream.

He was flying pleasantly over a long steel snake. Gradually he came down to earth in the middle of a hothouse where children were dancing round in a circle chanting:

'Figaro me voici
Figaro me voilà
Figaro-ci, Figaro-là.'

He went up to them. As soon as they saw him, they broke up their circle and ran towards him, surrounding him. Confronted by their curiously misshapen faces, he gave a cry of horror: their bleeding throats were slit from ear to ear. Suddenly he sank into a tunnel peopled by anatomical models. He was clutching a shopping list given to him by Germaine. A bodice, he must buy a bodice for Odette, but he had forgotten her size. He bumped into a woman wearing a turban who greeted him with a 'Hello, my duck!' and offered him a slice of pineapple, which he raised to his mouth. But his hand began to bleed so he plunged it into a glass jar in which hundreds of droning particles were buzzing – bees. They escaped and then crashed into a poster of the Redskins running after a train. Leaning out of the carriage door of one of the coaches, a large tortoiseshell cat was waving the shopping list, shouting incoherent syllables which seemed to say: 'Glory to Boris!' Suddenly the ground seemed to rise up. Turning on his heel, he ran until he was out of breath, convinced that he would never escape. He started violently and fell out of bed.

CHAPTER TWELVE

Afternoon, Thursday 30 June

V ICTOR no longer knew his name or where he was. Why was he naked? His vision slowly cleared, but it took him a few minutes to decide that the Gainsborough on the wall in front of him was leaning down very slightly to the right. 'This is my room. What the hell am I doing on the floor?'

He went into the bathroom, splashed his face and, leaning on the basin, tried his hardest to recall what had happened. Searching for a clue, he tried to unpick his fragmented dream: children, slit throats, wax figures, a turbaned woman, bees, Redskins, a train, a cat. Some words came to him: *Figaro me voici . . . Hello, my duck . . . Glory to Boris!* In Russian . . . the cat had spoken in Russian! And . . . the list, *Figaro*, that was the important thing in all this. The list from *Le Figaro de la Tour!* Was Danilo Ducovitch amongst the signatories on 22 June?

He rushed to Kenji's apartment but, finding nothing in the drawers, went into the bedroom, to the recess. He banged his little toe against the raised floor, making his eyes mist up. Hopping around on one foot, he tripped and fell onto the mat, which slid off the bed base. One of the slats was dislodged, revealing a cavity beneath. He kneeled down and, reaching in, removed several items: a package wrapped in patterned material, a metal box, two big envelopes and the copy of *Le*

Figaro de la Tour. As he unfolded it he saw that the note about J.C. had been ripped off. In agitation, he looked through the list.

Bottom of the first column:

> . . . Madeleine Lesourd, Chartres. Kenji Mori, Paris. Sigmund Pollock, Vienna, Austria. Marcel Forbin, lieutenant of the second cuirassiers. Rosalie Bouton, laundress, Aubervilliers. Madame de Nanteuil, Paris. Marie-Amélie de Nanteuil, Paris. Hector de Nanteuil, Paris. Gontran de Nanteuil, Paris. John Cavendish, New York, USA.

Second column:

> Constantin Ostrovski, art collector, Paris. B. Godunov, Slovenia. Guillermo de Castro, student from Alicante. Tancrède Pendarus, priest from Bordeaux. Charline Crosse of Les Folies-Bergère.

He looked back. B. Godunov . . . B. Godunov . . . *Glory and long life to Tsar Boris* . . . It was Danilo Ducovitch. The pieces of the puzzle were starting to fall into place. *He was the one following me this morning* . . .

Dropping everything, Victor quickly dressed and left via the external staircase.

Admiring yet again the wide perspective of Rue de Tournon, Kenji slowed down outside Restaurant Foyot, and took a moment to spot the parliamentarians sitting around a leg of lamb. A short way further on he came to his friend Maxence de

Kermarec's shop. He was an antiques dealer who specialised in ancient string instruments.

In the shop, which was decorated in Louis XV white and gold wood panelling, there was a very good selection of virginals, spinets and harpsichords, most of them with painted cases. On tables inlaid with marquetry were displays of classical guitars, student violins, bows, balalaikas and mandolins. A harp with a sculpted frame stood guard next to a dresser full of Sèvres porcelain depicting lutes and violas being played.

The owner, a tall, thin man with a neatly trimmed beard and dressed in a strange dark red velvet outfit that made him look like a devil, was eating a sandwich as he paced up and down. Seeing Kenji enter, he raced forward with outstretched hand.

'At last a friendly face – how few I've seen during this hot summer!' He pushed Kenji into an armchair. 'Do sit down, Monsieur Mori. Would you like tea. Or coffee?'

'Tea, please.'

Whilst the dealer disappeared into the back room, Kenji smoothed out his *Passe-partout* and laid it conspicuously on a pedestal table. The devil was soon back with a silver tray on which stood a steaming cup of clear liquid.

'Pure jasmine. Now tell me your news.'

'Have you seen this? It's very worrying,' Kenji remarked, pointing to the newspaper.

The antiques dealer glanced at the main headline and smoothed his beard thoughtfully.

'Yes, I did read that. How insignificant we are in the scheme of things: one little bee and that's it. Did you have a chance to sell him the Utamaros?'

Kenji nodded.

'I knew he would like them. He won't have enjoyed them for long, though, poor fellow. I've just bought up the Duc de Frioul's collection: a marvellous pianoforte, a François-Xavier Tourte bow, a Thomas Hancock spinet. I took the opportunity of snapping up his book collection, mostly seventeenth and eighteenth century. I think you'll find it a real treat.' He gobbled up the last piece of his sandwich.

'Shame,' he said with his mouth full, 'I've lost a good customer. Did I tell you I'd persuaded him to invest in violins?'

'Yes, you did, when I last saw you.'

'These collectors, they are funny people, all the same. Here was a man who knew nothing at all about music! Let me show you what he was planning to buy if he had not been called to more urgent matters beyond the grave.'

He opened a small padded case and, with the utmost care, took out a violin.

'A Guarnerius. Isn't it magnificent? Do you know what according to some gives it its unique sound? It's a kind of mould that absorbs moisture, making the wood drier and lighter. Funny to think that its beauty and value depends on a fungus. Our friend had advanced me a large sum, which I shall have to return to his heirs, if he has any. He was expecting a large sum back at the end of the week. Your tea's getting cold.'

Kenji forced himself to drain the cup: he liked only darjeeling.

'He was short of money?' he asked.

'Not at all! He was a money-lender. He financed some businesses on the quiet – his name never appearing anywhere.

The sort of business I told you about last week. It was a game of hide-and-seek, and he loved that, even if he sometimes got his fingers burned, which was rarely, mind you, as he was such a formidable adversary. "My dear Maxence," he would say, "he who has not risked anything, has not lived. I'm like a puppetmaster. I pull the strings behind the scenes. But woe betide whoever tangles the threads, because I'll always go for a clean break rather than undo the knots." Between you and me, Monsieur Mori, do you really believe these stories about killer bees?'

'One can never be sure of what's true.'

'I can see your oriental wisdom in that comment. Oh well, never mind about the Guarnerius,' said the dealer as he put away the violin. 'I'll always find takers for that sort of item. Would you like to see the books?'

'I have to meet someone, but I shall come back. Tell me, what did he tell you exactly about this latest enterprise?'

It was barely four o'clock and yet Victor could not hear any sounds of activity. Abandoned at the end of the typesetting workshop, the Linotype machine looked like a watchful animal, with all its teeth bared.

He went back down the alley. Two men, sitting on the kerb, were playing dice.

'Isn't there anyone in the offices of *Le Passe-partout*?'

'I think Madamoiselle Eudoxie is on the first floor.'

He climbed the stairs, stopping on the landing by the sofa, which was covered in a mass of paper. Eudoxie had not heard him come up. Sitting very upright at her desk, she was typing with the speed of a virtuoso pianist whilst also crunching peanuts. Her fingers flew from one key to the next, as the shuttle rotated. Eudoxie pulled out the typed page and put it down to her right, ate another peanut, inserted a blank page and carried on as quickly as if she were working at a sewing machine.

Victor knocked on the half-open door. Eudoxie quickly hid the packet of peanuts.

'Oh, it's you! Have you been here long?'

'I was just admiring you. What dexterity!'

She chuckled and patted her hair.

'Would you like to try? It's the Hammond model, it's on display at the Expo.'

'Er, no, I think I'd be too clumsy.'

'You don't need to have a qualification. You just need to put your fingers in the right place. I'd love to show you my method.'

'That's very kind of you but . . .'

'Your hands look perfect to me. They're long, sensitive and skilful,' she remarked, adjusting her bodice.

He cleared his throat, and nervously patted the cigarette case in his pocket.

'Where are the others?'

'You couldn't have come at a better time. Everyone is out and about. Gouvier is camping on the doorstep of police headquarters. Marius has gone to the doctor.'

'Is he unwell?'

'Just a little peaky, recently. Antonin won't be back until six.

Tasha's gone to the Expo, but we'll make do without her, won't we?'

She had got up and crossed the floor. He took the envelope out of his wallet.

'I need some information – perhaps you can help me.'

'Whatever you want.'

'It's about a letter. A messenger gave it to the assistant in my shop this morning at about eight. I assume *Le Passe-partout* was forwarding it to me.'

She took him by the arm.

'Come through a minute, won't you, Monsieur Legris. The light's much better here.' With an enigmatic Mona Lisa smile playing on her lips she led him towards the desk. 'Let's see. I hope it wasn't anything unwelcome,' she said, squeezing his arm tighter.

Victor felt as if he was being trapped by a serpent. He gently extricated himself.

'No. Just a few cross words from a reader who didn't like my column. Did you send it to me?'

'Oh, Monsieur Legris, it would never occur to me to insult a man of your worth!'

'No, I didn't mean that. I wanted to know if it had passed through your hands.'

'If it had, I would have delivered it to you personally.'

'Maybe one of the team here—'

'You're joking! The post is my responsibility. I'm always here first in the morning and begin by going through it. Are you sure you don't want me to show you how to use the typewriter? It would be useful for you in the bookshop. In

New York there's not a single business left that sends hand-written letters . . .'

Whilst she went on extolling the virtues of the Hammond machine, Victor was trying to marshal his thoughts. If the letter had been taken straight to the bookshop, then it could not have been written by Capus. *I made sure not to tell him my real profession or my address.*

So there could be no further doubt: he had been caught in a trap. *How did he know? How could that bastard Ducovitch have known that I'd been in contact with Capus?* The answer was obvious. He recalled the old man writing down his name and the words *'Le Passe-partout'* in a school exercise book. *Just in case you twist my words.* Having slit Capus's throat, Ducovitch had doubtless gone back into his room and found the notebook.

Suddenly Victor felt dizzy. He leaned against the wall. How long was it since he had eaten a proper meal?

'You look pale . . . Are you all right?' Eudoxie asked, taking advantage of his weakened state to come up close and begin to undo the buttons of his coat.

He needed a good pretext to get rid of her. But before he did, he wanted to clarify one last point. Had *Le Passe-partout* covered Buffalo Bill's arrival or not?

'Would you be kind enough to let me see the first few editions of the newspaper?' he muttered hoarsely.

She stepped back in surprise.

'Right now?'

'Yes, please.'

'Well, I can't deny you anything,' she said with evident

disappointment. 'Sit down at my table – the seat is still warm. I'll move the machine over, there you are.'

She put down a dozen copies in front of him and leant over his shoulder.

'If you tell me what you're looking for, Monsieur Legris, I'm sure I can help you out.'

'Oh, nothing in particular. I just want to get a general idea of the tone of the newspaper, so I know what kind of readers I'm writing for.'

He could feel her weight against his back, her breath on the nape of his neck, and then a sinking feeling in his stomach.

'Would it be a terrible bore . . .' He stopped just in time. '. . . if I asked you to open the window? It's very hot in here.'

'I'll fetch you a glass of water. Why don't you take your jacket off? There's no need to stand on ceremony.'

Without replying he began to turn the pages noisily. She went out and he heard her opening a cupboard. Quickly, quickly . . . Nothing about Buffalo Bill. In that case what was Tasha doing at Les Batignolles station that day? The 14 May edition was dull, the one from 13 May almost entirely devoted to a birth that had taken place on one of '"the Tower lifts. The newborn baby, Augusta-Effeline, so named in honour of the man who built this marvel, will receive from Gustave Eiffel himself the . . ."' He read aloud in order to look composed because Eudoxie was on her way back, holding out a glass of water for him. He downed it in one, choked and then coughed. She slapped him on the back.

'What a way to drink!'

She sat down on the armrest of the chair so that their hips were touching.

'Very vulgar, don't you think? Going up that lighthouse when you're about to give birth. Some women will do anything to get talked about.'

'Yes, it's even more unusual than Buffalo Bill's arrival,' he said with forced casualness.

'Marius decided not to publish anything about the Redskins as all the other papers were making such a big fuss about it. You know what he's like, he always prefers to swim against the tide. That goes for me too, you know. I like to stand out from the crowd. Take for example what makes a man attractive. Unlike most women, I find that blond men leave me cold.'

He was starting to feel drowsy again and withdrew far back enough into the armchair for the other armrest to dig into his sides. With what strength he had left he said, 'I'd be glad of another glass of water.'

Eudoxie left his side with a little sigh and went out of the room. Faster even than he had left Capus's lodgings a few hours earlier, Victor made good his escape.

Poor Joseph was surrounded by a flock of ladies squawking like parakeets. He just missed having his eye poked out by the point of a parasol, and decided to take refuge behind the counter, from where he concluded that the enemy numbered too many for him to venture another sortie. There was only one thing to do, and that was to shout even louder.

'One at a time, please, or I shall have to call the police!' he roared.

The opposing ranks fell silent. After briefly consulting her friends Raphaëlle de Gouveline, Mathilde de Flavignol, Blanche de Cambrésis and Adalberte de Brix, the Comtesse de Salignac waved the white flag and withdrew her demands.

'The title of the novel is *Which One?*'

'Author?' asked Joseph stiffly.

'Georges de Peyrebrune.'

'Publisher?'

There was a sheepish exchange of looks between the five battle-axes lined up at the counter.

'Right, let's carry on. Summary of the plot?'

'It's the story of three poor, chaste young girls. Following a crime – you can guess which, young man – one of the girls becomes a mother. Which one?' cried the Comtesse de Salignac, eyeing Joseph as if he were personally responsible for what happened in the story.

'I give up,' he said, utterly worn out. 'Ladies, we will soon be closing.'

'So early? It's only five o'clock!'

'We're stocktaking.'

Making the most of this noisy invasion, which managed to muffle the sound of the door chime, Victor had sneaked into the shop. Just as he reached Molière's bust, Joseph saw him. Victor threw him a feather duster for cleaning books, put his finger to his lips and gestured to Joseph to come upstairs with him.

The chattering band was duly ushered to the door with the feather duster. Joseph locked the door, wiped his forehead and went up the stairs. Victor was waiting for him in the kitchen.

'Well, Monsieur Legris, you're just always coming and going, aren't you? It's a pity you didn't come a bit sooner. They almost killed me.'

'Joseph, please think carefully, at what time did the messenger give you the letter?'

'The letter? What letter? Oh, the letter! I had just taken down the shutters. It was eight o'clock on the dot. He wanted to give it to you personally, because it was very urgent. Urgent or not, I told him, I couldn't get you up.'

'Eight o'clock? Are you sure?'

Joseph looked offended.

'Monsieur Legris, need I remind you that I open the bookshop every morning at seven forty-five. You can set your clock by me, you should know that by now. I called you several times, but there was no reply so I was worried and I came up but there was nobody here. And I thought, Joseph, if Monsieur Legris has suddenly decided to accompany Madame de Valois to Houlgate, then you're really stuck!'

'What did the messenger look like?'

'Aggressive, like all cab drivers.'

'A cabman?'

'Yes, of course, he was a cabman. His cab stood outside the Sulpice Debauve shop.'

'Were there any passengers?'

'Look, Monsieur Legris, I haven't got second sight, you know. And anyway, I was going to tell you . . .'

Victor abruptly walked off and went into his office. Joseph went back down to the shop, grumbling, 'He needs to know what's on my mind. He can't just cut me off like that.'

He opened the bookshop door, and ventured a quick look outside: not a battle-axe in sight. In that case, boss or no boss, the shop would not close until seven in the evening.

Victor was pacing up and down, talking to himself, unable to stand still.

'At eight o'clock, Ducovitch was singing away on Rue Notre-Dame-de-Lorette. Only Tasha could have delivered that letter. Yes, it had to be her. He told her about the unexpected hitch last night or very early this morning. I didn't hear anything, I was asleep, I was exhausted . . .'

Distraught, he stopped in front of the chest of drawers and straightened the Laumier. He felt a stab of emotion: that smooth body, those round breasts . . . could it be that she was just play-acting?

You know absolutely nothing about her.

A hansom clattered past on the street. Victor closed his eyes as if a very bright light were blinding him. He looked at the little painting one more time, then went back into Kenji's apartment. He emptied the bathtub and tidied up what had been left on the floor. Fascinated by the box, he took the top off after a moment's hesitation. He found a pendant containing a miniature of his mother, as well as a photograph of a young girl. On the back was written 'Iris, March 1888, London'. Resisting the desire to open them, he put the two big envelopes that were sealed with wax back under the bed slat and quickly also replaced the parcel wrapped in material. But his hands seemed to have a mind of their own and before he knew it he had unwrapped it. He was amazed to discover Goya's *Caprichos. He told me he'd taken it to the bookbinder's*. Stunned, his mind a blank, he began turning the pages until an etching caught his attention: a man, overwhelmed by emotion, surrounded by nocturnal predators, the original of the reproduction pinned on Tasha's wall!

The extravagance of reason creates monsters. He needed to come up quickly with some reassuring thoughts to hold back the tide of suspicion that threatened to destroy his life and its certainties. He was shattered, but he went on leafing through the book to keep his hands occupied. He refused to admit that Kenji might be involved in this business, but he could not ignore the evidence: Kenji and Tasha had been colluding in all this.

She's expecting me at eight this evening! he remembered bitterly, suddenly furious. When she wrote me that note, she knew perfectly well that her accomplice was going to finish me off! But who was her accomplice?

The day's events all merged together in his mind. He put *Los Caprichos* away, arranged the mat and the blanket, and returned to his room.

At the foot of the Eiffel Tower, between the embankments and sunken paths that bordered the Champ-de-Mars, a strange village retraced the history of human habitation from prehistoric times up to the Renaissance. Built according to plans created by Charles Garnier, there were six areas, each comprising several buildings intended to attract interested visitors. But the metal monster cast its long shadow over these typical dwellings and only a few people actually wandered this far. At this late point in the afternoon, there were only two slightly odd-looking men walking in this part of the Expo to the indifferent attention of bar owners and souvenir sellers. A big bearded man, draped in a rather moth-eaten bearskin, offered his arm to an old African man wearing a boubou, and was animatedly telling him about this kingdom of wood and cement.

'Clearly, beginning at the end is not really the best way, but here, my dear Samba, everything is so fanciful that what does it matter!' remarked Danilo Ducovitch. 'Look, those squaws plaiting baskets, do you think they hail from the Adirondacks? Not a bit of it, old chap. The little one over there, next to the fellow crowned with turkey feathers, is a Spanish dancer who's usually wiggling her hips in the cabarets on Boulevard de Clichy.'

They passed the Japanese, Arab and Russian houses. Danilo stopped outside a sixteenth-century hostelry where young girls in Henry II costumes were selling Murano glass.

'Their Italian straw hats are a bit of an anachronism! And look at those Tunisians! Here are some more, in the Greek section. And again in the Persian house. There are lots of unemployed Tunisians in Paris, and now jobs have been found for them here. Let's not slow down outside the Hindu house; it's empty and is being used as a public convenience. Ah, here's the Hebrew home! It's been rented to a carpet seller from Rue Taitbout. Hello there, Marcel, how's business?'

'I don't understand,' said Samba. 'It says here this is an Egyptian tent, but there's Asian porcelain on sale inside.'

'Note how Tunisian the salesman looks. The organisers must have thought the public wouldn't notice.'

Beneath the trees alongside the Gallo-Roman huts, people were unwrapping their provisions and spreading them on cardboard beer barrels. Danilo was given a glass of cider by a Roman matron with a rounded posterior.

'Thank you, Frieda. She's Austrian, a singer like me,' he whispered to Samba. 'But not a word about my good fortune, or she'll be green with envy. Would you like to try this?'

He held out the glass. Samba took a sip, frowned, and then looked at the picnickers.

'They're eating potatoes.'

'In oil. It's a very popular dish.'

'Potatoes, always potatoes. And this is meant to be the food capital of the world! Their dogs and horses soil the pavements, their buildings shut out the sun, their streets are grey, and they dare judge me with a superior air, asking, "So what does a Senegalese make of Paris?" That's not a proper name. What if I said, "Hey, you French! Hey, Tunisian! Hey, vendor! Hey, singer!"?'

'I'll be known as the baritone,' Danilo murmured. 'My problems are at an end. Nobody is going to get in my way. I passed my audition – do you realise what that means? Passed my audition, me, jack of all trades and master of none! Thank you, Charles Garnier, for building such a beautiful Opera House.'

They reached Avenue La Bourdonnais near to the prehistoric habitats. Danilo looked enviously at the solidly built Pelasgian house and even the Palaeolithic hut. Then he stopped outside his cave

'My modest Cro-Magnon lodgings,' he announced. A visitor

went in. Hot on his heels, Danilo picked up something the man had dropped on the path.

'A lucky find!' he said, showing off his trophy to Samba. 'I'll save it for the evening following the premiere of *Boris Godunov*! I can see the poster already: stage direction Danilo Ducovitch, the Serb with the golden voice . . .'

'Oh, definitely golden,' said Samba approvingly as he looked at the band of the barely unwrapped cigar. 'It's pretty, may I have it? I can use it for my designs. I also do filigree work, which I put on walking sticks and boxes. It's one of the things I specialise in.'

'I'm going to get changed. Wait for me here. We can go and eat at the soup kitchen next to the Machinery Hall. We can splash out – my treat!'

'No more potatoes, please, for pity's sake,' muttered Samba as Danilo went back into his cave.

Danilo walked gaily into the darkest recess of his shelter. As he passed it, he greeted Attila, the stuffed boar, which he had borrowed from the Gallo-Romans to give him a bit of company. '*Salut! Demeure chaste et pure,*' he sang as he raised the curtain of the tiny extemporised dressing room in the recess of the inner wall. His singing suddenly turned into a yelp. He grimaced and quickly slapped the nape of his neck. He had been stung by something. Astounded more than shocked, he moved his head with difficulty. A dark silhouette was dancing before his eyes. He squinted at the flickering gaslight, which was becoming fainter. He wanted to make it brighter and tried to raise his hand without success. He was suddenly tremendously sleepy. *You're very tired and you need to be on top form tomorrow . . . Your first rehearsal, no good having stage fright . . .*

He gripped the curtain as he began to fall. As he gradually slid down towards the floor, he tried to hang on to one thought, and brought to mind Tasha's superb breasts: he had sometimes spied on her through a hole in the dividing wall. Around him now, colours seemed to be changing, shapes were fading like mist in the sunshine. He slowly collapsed, pulling down the curtain with him.

Sitting cross-legged on the grass, Samba was eagerly looking out for his friend's return. Lunch had been just some greasy chips, and he was hungry. He thought of a gourd overflowing with steaming white rice sprinkled with spicy vegetables. His mouth started to water.

A man appeared at the entrance to the cave. Samba got up, but was disappointed to see that it was just a visitor in a hurry.

After a quarter of an hour he could wait no longer. Overcoming his fear of closed spaces, he gingerly stepped into the cave. In the half-light he could make out a four-legged animal rooted to the spot. He shivered, but managed to control his fear. 'You old warthog, you gave me a fright!' Then raising his voice: 'Are you there, Monsieur Ducovitch?' Step by step he went further in, his eyes wide open, arms outstretched, fearing he would desecrate the sacred atmosphere of the cave.

He tripped against a big bundle of rags and lost his balance. 'Monsieur Ducovitch?'

He was lying on the floor. Summoning his courage, Samba bent down. A quick examination of the man's face convinced him that Danilo Ducovitch would never sing again. Shocked, he picked up his boubou. The place was cursed and he needed to get out of there fast!

'Boss! Boss! Can you hear me? It's important!' Joseph shouted as he banged on Victor's door.

'What now?' groaned Victor, not opening it.

'A customer – at least I think she is – a pretty little redhead. She wants to speak to you. She says you know her.'

'Send her up.'

He drew the bolt and opened the door slightly, nervously smoothing his moustache. He could hear Tasha's light steps on the stairs. She sidled into the apartment. Quite naturally, she went to kiss him but Victor stiffened, holding back. Amazed, she said nothing for a moment as she caught her breath.

'Did you see my note?' she said at last.

He nodded.

'I won't be in this evening. I have to go and dine at the Exposition with Charles Garnier, Antonin, Marius, Eudoxie and a handful of officials, for the article, you know. It's a nuisance, but I can't cry off. As soon as I knew about it, I did everything I could to warn you. I've got a couple of free hours now,' she said finally, putting her gloves and hat on a chair.

Her tousled hair, her pink cheeks . . . He must not give in to desire.

Feigning a sudden interest in the condition of his nails, Victor said in a neutral tone: 'It's good that you came by. Something's puzzling me: I'd like to know where you've seen those celebrated Goya *Caprichos*.'

'What's the matter with you? Why are you being so formal?' She burst out laughing. 'I see! Because of the mujik! Well, don't worry, he stayed downstairs.'

Seeing Victor was not reacting, she carried on more uncertainly, 'Is this a joke?'

'No, Tasha, I just want to know where . . . I saw a copy of one of the illustrations at your lodgings and—'

She cut across him loudly, 'At Ostrovski's. In exchange for my watercolours of the Redskins, he let me copy some plates from his copy of the book. And now are you going to—'

'That's not possible. Only twenty-seven volumes of those etchings were sold. They were banned by the Inquisition after February 1799.'

'And . . . ? You're not the only person to own one! Is it really yours anyway? What's got into you? This icy coldness, these statistics, all this interrogation . . . You're doubting me again, despite what we've shared!'

She sounded both indignant and sorrowful. Victor's self-control vanished.

'Tasha, I'm going to go mad. Tell me the truth: who are you?'

'Who am I? The same as ever, the very same person who slept next to you last night. And what about you? Who are you? You come knocking at my door when all the time you have a mistress decked out in plumes and jewels!'

He frowned. She had scored a point against him.

'Yesterday, after hearing of Ostrovski's death, I wandered around in a dream. There was no way I could go back home. I was too distraught, thinking about all those dead bodies . . . I thought of you, and wanted to see you and speak to you. I walked all the way here. I saw you with that woman: you got in a cab with her. Your business associate saw me too, ask him. He doesn't like me – I don't know why, maybe he's worried I'm going to trap you. Tell him he can rest easy, that's not my intention at all.' And with that she put her hat back on.

'You didn't rebuff me last night.'

'Why would I have done? You are free, I am free. Why not enjoy ourselves?'

'Exactly. Why not?'

Very taken by the lock of hair that was poking out from under her hat, he moved closer to her and pressed his lips brutally against hers. She in turn pushed him away.

'Not like that!' she protested.

She straightened her hat. With jerky movements she managed to tidy her hair up, put her gloves on and then stood there indecisively, arms dangling at her side.

'Let's not ruin everything,' she murmured.

Maybe she did feel some affection for him after all? This thought made him feel somewhat more relaxed, and he found the energy calmly to offer her a glass of something before she left.

The bitter smell of cabbage filled the kitchen. He noticed something white: a note from Germaine, saying his black frock coat was being cleaned but that she had first emptied the pockets. On the table he was relieved to find the keys to the apartment, which he thought he had left at Capus's lodgings, a handkerchief, an entry ticket for the Expo, a button and a metal rod set in a tapering ivory handle with deeply etched grooves and broken right down the middle: it was the object that Marie-Amélie de Nanteuil had given him!

His hand trembling, he filled a glass with Málaga wine, returned to give it to Tasha, and mumbled an excuse about having forgotten to warn his assistant about something to do with an order.

Joseph was putting some books away.

'I'll be closing up soon, Boss. It's quieter than the Gobi Desert here today. Would you mind if I left fifteen minutes early?'

Without replying, Victor went into the back room and opened the display cabinet where Kenji kept his precious collections. He picked up one of the tattooing needles he had brought back from Siam, and compared it to Marie-Amélie's find. They were identical. The same sharply pointed metal rods, the same handle. With racing heart he was about to close the cabinet quickly when he noticed a piece of paper sticking out from *Voyage into the African Interior*. A bookmark? He pulled it out and instantly recognised the flier announcing Buffalo Bill's parade, which Tasha had turned into a caricature in the cab, the day they first met. He kept hearing in his head a phrase he had learnt as a child: *The heart is a hollow muscle, the heart is a* . . . He was no longer in control of his mind or his actions. He slowly crumpled the leaflet and then tried to smooth it out. He abruptly accosted Joseph.

'The woman who's just gone upstairs, has she been to the bookshop recently?'

'Well, yes, she was looking for you. You'd promised her a book by Goya, but Monsieur Mori told her we didn't have it. I rummaged about in the stockroom, but he was right, we didn't. What's wrong? Shouldn't I have let her in?'

'What day was this?' Victor barked.

'Wait a minute . . . the same day that Monsieur France came in!'

'Yesterday?'

'No, last Thursday. I remember because the battle-axe had demanded *The Ironmaster* and Monsieur Mori asked me to deliver it to her Boulevard Saint-Germain apartment. It's in the order book. Why do you ask?'

'Did you open the display cabinet for the young woman?'

'Yes, she wanted to look at a book on Africa.'

'Did you stay with her?'

'I think I left her on her own for a couple of minutes because Monsieur Mori called me.'

'Had she come by before?'

'No, it was the first time I'd seen her.'

Victor raced back up to the first floor.

'A moment ago I didn't want to believe him . . . you bitch!' he thundered, grabbing her by the arm so violently that the glass fell on the carpet.

He was staring straight at her, unable to control himself. She tried to struggle, but he pulled her towards the stairs and made her go down and into the back room.

'Admit it! Admit it! It was you! You stole a tattooing needle from here, and curare from Ostrovski, you killed them, all of them, and this morning you almost got me too at Capus's. Why? Why on earth?'

He released her abruptly and she rubbed her arm.

'You're mad . . . I don't understand a word of what you're saying,' she pleaded.

Then, recovering, she slapped him hard.

'Goodbye!' she sobbed.

She ran out, bumping into Joseph, who was holding a shutter.

Devoid of all emotion, Victor stood stock-still in front of the display cabinet. He wanted just one thing: not to have to think any more. He uttered one barely audible word, which Joseph managed to make out: 'Kenji.'

'My word, you look fit to drop. Lean on me.'

He put down the shutter and took Victor into the main shop to sit him down.

'You know, Boss, it's none of my business, but it's not good for you to get into this sort of state. You could end up with cerebral congestion. And what on earth made you strike out like that at that nice little redhead? She's no thief! If anyone's to blame, it's me. I shouldn't have opened Monsieur Mori's display cabinet, but I'm sure she didn't take any books.'

'It wasn't a book, Joseph, but one of the objects in there,' Victor replied hoarsely. He was beginning to feel a little better.

'Well, in that case, any number of people could have taken it. Your friends from the newspaper – Monsieur Bonnet and the other one who dresses like an English lord – they also spent time in there on their own not long ago. And why not the battle-axe, or her niece, or even me, if you're thinking along those lines?'

Joseph touched Victor's forehead. 'You're burning hot, you've got a temperature, and Monsieur Mori's away, to boot! Can you stand up? I'll help you upstairs. You're best off going to bed.'

Victor let himself be led like a child: his willpower had deserted him. Joseph made him take two pills, undress, lie down and then tucked him into the cool bed.

Through all this, he kept on muttering, 'No more work for you, I'm telling you, and also who was that chap who pestered me for hours this morning, a lunatic who rolls his rs, and kept talking about opera and claimed you had work for him? You're not looking for a second assistant, are you? Because if you are, I'm handing in my notice! Well, you have a good sleep. I'll tell Mama I'm staying here to watch over you. I'll come back, put the shutters up and . . . where shall I sleep then? At Monsieur Mori's, I suppose, though his bed is rock hard!'

In the middle of the night, Victor awoke with a thick head. His scene with Tasha seemed just like a bad dream now. If it really was all over with her, there was still the question of the murders to resolve. Joseph had left him a carafe of water and a glass by his bed. He drank deeply, sat down at his desk, took his notebook and made himself write down some thoughts. Danilo could not have attacked him on Rue de la Parcheminerie, because, according to Joseph, he had spent the morning in the bookshop. However, nothing would have prevented him from killing Capus the night before. So . . . everything seemed to point to Kenji. But there was no tangible evidence. The same could not be said about Tasha: the Buffalo Bill flier condemned her. And yet something did not quite add up. Tasha had come to the bookshop the day after Eugénie Patinot had died, and a good month after Méring's death. The tattooing needle must already have been stolen by then. What if this had been a totally flawed train of thought? If it was, Tasha would not forgive him, and would never want to see him again.

Marie-Amélie had told him that Eugénie had been jostled by a man just before she died. The cab driver had picked up a man prior to Ostrovski's death in the hansom. A man had tried to kill him at Capus's lodgings. He wrote down: 'Kenji?'

Then he realised that anyone who read *Le Passe-partout* could have got his address from the advertisement. Including Capus . . .

Feeling dizzy again, he tottered back to bed.

CHAPTER THIRTEEN

Friday 1 July

THE Champ-de-Mars awoke to a colourless day, its party clothes in disarray following the excesses of the night before. An army of sweepers had invaded the square, dustcarts were collecting piles of rubbish, and there were gardeners raking the flowerbeds, watering the flowers and tidying up the lawns. It was barely seven o'clock. The suppliers' carts and wagons, weighed down with provisions, dispersed to the four corners of the Expo to satisfy the insatiable appetite of the vast crowds of visitors, who were not yet there but already on their way.

A little handcart rattled along one of the gravel paths, its bucket and brooms clinking together. A plump woman was pulling it unsteadily towards the prehistoric exhibit. She passed the Palaeolithic shelter, the bronze, stone and iron age huts, and slowed down in front of what was supposed to be an exact copy of a natural excavation.

Philomène Lacarelle picked up her half-filled pail of soapy water and banged it down on the ground.

'Hmm, now that's not exactly what I'd call comfortable and clean! Poor Philomène, I must be soft in the head to put up with this sort of job. I'll get those people at the employment office! I've been working in this circus for ten days, and I'll never get used to it. Will you look at that! All those puffed-up tourists, just making the place filthy!'

Philomène Lacarelle grudgingly picked up two or three greasy papers left by picnickers and paused a moment in front of a wild boar, whose moth-eaten head stared back malevolently.

'What are you gawping at? You'd make a fine bedside rug! You're just a fat pig stuffed with horsehair,' she muttered as she got out her paraphernalia. 'They say our ancestors lived in a place like this. I'm sure that mine would have kept it in better condition! The good thing was that rent hadn't been invented then . . . Cro-Magnons they were called, what a name! What's it mean, Cro-Magnon? Sounds like a giant bird, talking of which, this old bird needs to get on with it. Come on, Philomène, it's time for some elbow grease and let's try and make the best of a bad job!'

She wrapped a coarse cloth around her broom, soaked it in the bucket, and advanced into the cave as she washed the stone vigorously, her bottom shaking. She could not see very much and now all the noise from the procession of suppliers was just a vague murmur. However, the sound of her clogs resonated gloomily in the narrow, deep cavern. A feeble light filtered through an opening in the vault. The single gaslight projected broken-up shadows on the irregular walls. What if a flesh-and-blood Cro-Magnon man, in all his nakedness, should appear in front of her? She took a deep breath and tried hard to laugh. A silly thought had just occurred to her. *There weren't any cleaning ladies in those days. I would have been a huge success!*

She carried on with her mopping and hummed:

Ma bell-mère pouss' des cris
En r'luquant les spahis.
Moi, j'faisais qu'admirer
Not' brav' général Boulanger.

'. . . ger. . . ger . . . ger,' came the echo.

Philomène stopped and pointed her broom like a bayonet. A tomb-like chill descended on her. 'Is there anybody there?' she asked.

'. . . ody there? . . . ody there . . . ?'

She lowered her broom and hit a black mass pinned against the wall. A pile of old clothes? Breathlessly, Philomène watched it collapse and froze in horror. She wanted to cry out and opened her mouth wide but all that came out was a hoarse gasp. At her feet lay the stiff body of Cro-Magnon man. His glassy-eyed face was a livid colour. She heard a piercing cry. It took Philomène several seconds to realise that the cry had come from her.

Later that morning, the only customers in the bookshop were a bourgeois couple in search of cheap bound books to decorate their sitting room.

Victor's pen flew over the paper, as he applied himself to his writing, stopping only occasionally to glance at the bust of Molière. Happy to see that Victor was working hard once again, Joseph became absorbed in scouring the morning papers, on the lookout for whatever unusual little snippet he could find. Had he looked over his boss's shoulder, he would have seen that he was obviously just pretending to work, as the bottle of purple ink was closed.

Victor had slept very little and insomnia was clouding his judgement: he could only think about Tasha. For several hours he had gone over the scene from the previous day without managing to convince himself that he had good grounds for his accusations. His fingers tightened around the inkpot. He could not bring himself to believe that she was guilty; there was surely an explanation for her attitude. He should have shown some self-control, and offered her the chance to give her version of events, but yet again he had been too impatient and angry and had spoiled everything. For God's sake! You make a mistake, you apologise, no situation is beyond repair. No, she would not forgive him. The inkpot was moist; he let go of it and rubbed his palm on his trousers. He opened his notebook, tried to concentrate on his notes. Unable to decipher his tangled scrawl, he looked up, ready to reprimand Joseph, who was irritating him by noisily turning the pages of a daily paper. Then he pushed his chair out and went over to join him.

'Do you remember if Monsieur Mori was in the bookshop on the afternoon of Friday the twenty-fourth of June? I wasn't here, and he was supposed to give a copy of the *Posthumous Works* by La Fontaine to a customer. Do you remember the twelve-part volume in red morocco leather published by—'

'Yes, yes, I know, by Guillaume de Luyne, 1696. It came from Charles Nodier's collection. It's still on the shelf.'

'The customer didn't come back for it?'

'Obviously not, Boss.'

'And Monsieur Mori, where was he?'

'Um, wait . . . just there, where you were sitting, at his desk. He came back after lunch accompanied by Monsieur Duvernois from the Champion bookshop and they worked on the wording of the essay on "Organising a Book Collection" until closing time. I remember it clearly because it was the day I finally sold the unfinished *Encyclopédie* from Rue Le Regrattier, the one that was mouldy. Why are you writing down what I'm saying?'

'Oh, my memory isn't very good these days, I'm tired,' replied Victor, quickly putting his notebook into his pocket.

So Kenji had not left the bookshop the afternoon John Cavendish died!

There was a growing hubbub in the Rue des Saints-Pères. The two customers went over to the door of the shop and Joseph eventually joined them. Lost in thought, Victor went slowly to stand in front of the desk, his back to the window.

The indistinct murmurings turned into exclamations. An eccentric pair, the one on the left in a blue boubou, the one on the right in a red uniform, hemmed in by a bevy of gossiping women, were coming down the street.

'Look at that big soldier, he's armed to the teeth! But where's he come from? It's not carnival!'

'He's what's called a spahi. Have you never seen a spahi?' shrieked Madame Ballu, the concierge from number 18.

Like a queen amongst her subjects, she stepped forward from amongst the chattering crowd, and once there was a respectful silence, she bowed to the two men.

'But how does she know that? She never leaves her lodge,' huffed Euphrosine Pignot.

'They come from North Africa,' declared Madame Ballu.

'Rubbish, in North Africa there are Arabs, not black people!' cried the fruit-seller.

'You don't know anything, Madame Pignot. Why don't you stick to selling pears?'

'How dare you say I don't know anything! I've read books, I'm not illiterate!'

'Say that again: are you calling *me* illiterate? You'll see! He's a Se-na-ga-lese spahi, do you understand? He comes from Senegal. I know about this because my cousin Alphonse went to Senegal, and Senegal, unless it's moved, is in Africa!'

'Yes, but not North Africa!' retorted Euphrosine, who wanted to have the last word.

The women surrounded the two men, who didn't know how to extricate themselves. Joseph came to the rescue.

'Move along now, there's nothing to see! Go on, clear off and be quick about it!'

He drove back the inquisitive women with his feather duster, then led his mother into the bookshop behind the strangers, whom the customers were observing warily from the safety of the counter.

'Monsieur bookseller . . . Monsieur Victor Legris,' ventured the older of the new arrivals.

Victor turned round and regarded the pair with astonishment. One of them was dressed in wide trousers and a scarlet jacket. He wore boots, a chechia, and a sabre on his belt and was a good head taller than the one who had spoken.

'Samba,' murmured Victor.

'I have very important news for you. I asked my friend Biram to come with me. He knows this town well, he fought for you during the 1870 war and he lives at the military school barracks.'

Biram nodded vigorously in agreement.

'Why don't we go upstairs – it's more private up there?' said Victor.

Samba indicated to Biram to stay downstairs, whereupon the spahi was immediately cornered by Euphrosine, who insisted on knowing if he had ever had to use his sabre.

Victor took Samba into the dining room and invited him to sit down. The old man looked furtively around him and put his hand in front of his mouth as if he was afraid of talking too loudly.

'It's about your friend, the opera singer.'

'Danilo Ducovitch?'

'Yesterday evening, I went with him as far as his cave and was waiting for him while he changed, but he didn't come back, so I went in and found him . . . dead.'

'Dead? Are you sure?'

Samba lowered his voice even further. 'I think someone killed him. I think the murderer saw me. I haven't slept all night. I hid in one of the stations of the little train, and I waited for the dawn. Then I walked to the Colonial Exhibition and went looking for Biram. You're the only one who can help me in this barbaric country.'

Incredulous, Victor stared at the old man, whose strained features attested to a real fear. 'Let's see, perhaps Monsieur Ducovitch was taken ill . . .'

'No, I've seen dead people before . . . His eyes, they were staring at something that we cannot comprehend!' shouted Samba, who had suddenly got to his feet.

'Please calm yourself. I'm going to check the newspapers. If your story is true, it will have made the front page.'

'You don't believe me,' said Samba bitterly.

'Yes, yes, I do believe you. I simply need confirmation.'

The couple seeking books by the metre had set their sights on the complete works of Monseigneur Félix Dupanloup, which Joseph was jubilantly piling up.

'This is going to free up space in the stockroom,' he murmured to Victor, out of the side of his mouth. 'Today's newspapers? They're on the counter. Not much this morning. I haven't come up with anything very interesting, except for the birth of a calf with two heads in the Allier.'

'What were you hoping for?' asked Victor drily. 'Another murder?'

He unfolded the dailies, and looked through them. There was no mention of a death. He went back up to his apartment. Samba had not moved.

'There's nothing,' said Victor.

'Perhaps the body hasn't been found yet.'

Without replying, Victor went into his study. He wanted to give Samba the snapshots that he had taken of him at the Colonial Palace. On the roll-top desk the *Dictionary of Drugs and Poisons* lay open at the entry on curare. He couldn't remember if he had closed it or not. He took the envelope containing the prints, removed the pictures, counted them, then counted them again. There were three missing: the photos of Tasha at the Colonial Exhibition. His heart stopped. Had she stolen them the day before, when he had gone down to compare the needles? Why would she do that? To destroy evidence of her presence at the crime scenes? That would be stupid of her as he had the negatives!

He came slowly back into the dining room and gave the photos to Samba, who took them without a word.

As they went downstairs, the old man murmured: 'Thank you, Monsieur Victor. Farewell.'

'Farewell?'

'I'm not staying in this country any longer. I don't want to be the next victim.'

'You won't be. Even if Monsieur Ducovitch is dead, it must have been an accident. I am certain that you are in no danger. Joseph!'

Joseph, enthralled by Biram, who was displaying his sabre, which he had just used to chop an apple on a plate into quarters, was now calming his mother. She had got rather overexcited at the sight of the spahi chopping up the contents of her basket.

'Joseph! Accompany these gentlemen to Les Invalides. Here's the money for a carriage.'

'A carriage! A trip in a four-wheeler! Straight away, Boss. Gentlemen, follow me. Are you coming too, Mama?'

'Heavens,' said Euphrosine Pignot, simpering, 'if Monsieur Legris allows it . . .'

'It won't cost any more!' cried Joseph. 'See you very soon, Boss!'

*

Victor had waited until everyone had left the bookshop to sit back down at his desk. Mechanically he turned the pages of the ledger in which the amounts and dates of purchases were recorded. Following a sudden hunch, he looked up 12 May, the day Méring had died. What was Kenji doing that day? He discovered that they had been together at the Hotel Drouot to attend two sales. The one in the morning had been a sale of rare and curious books on fencing, duelling and the history of swords, at which they had bought a work by Villamont for four hundred and fifty francs. The other, in the afternoon, had been a sale of newspapers and caricatures of events between 1848 and 1880. They had not been apart, even during lunch. Victor was relieved. Kenji was definitely innocent of the murders, at least of the rag-picker and of Cavendish. He thought again of the arrival of Buffalo Bill. What had Eudoxie said about it? She had not been definite: it was possible that Marius had decided at the last minute to replace the account of that event with an article on the birth of the baby on the Tower. In that case, Tasha would have spoken the truth: Marius really had sent her to do some sketches at Les Batignolles. He closed the ledger. He would have to find out from Gouvier: hadn't he said he had spoken to the doctor in charge of certifying Méring's death? That meant that he would have been there with Tasha.

All these hypotheses were now jumbled up in his head and he was unable to think clearly. He felt almost drunk. The door chime put an end to his reverie. He spun around in his chair and was amazed to find himself face to face with Samba, followed by a very excited Joseph, brandishing *L'Éclair*. 'Boss, it's an incredible story. Poor Monsieur Thiam is scared out of his skin. Look!'

The headline went right across the top of the page.

CRO-MAGNON MAN IS DEAD!
CRO-MAGNON MAN VICTIM OF THE BEES?

This morning, at 7.30, Madame Philomène Lacarelle, the lady in charge of cleaning the prehistoric section in Human Habitation, discovered the body of Monsieur Danilo Ducovitch of Rue Notre-Dame-de-Lorette. The police are investigating with . . .

'So do you believe me now?' gasped Samba.

Stunned, Victor read and reread the article.

'Blimey, it's the fourth one!' exclaimed Joseph. 'If this continues we'll beat the English!'

'What are you talking about?'

'I'm talking about Jack the Ripper.'

'You'd think it was a competition,' said Victor crossly.

A customer entered and Joseph went off to serve him.

'Apart from me, have you told anyone else about this?'

'No. All I told Biram was that I had a problem. I asked your assistant to read me the newspaper. He saw how frightened I was and I explained that it's because I work at the Expo.'

'Good. If I were you, I would go back to work as normal, without breathing a word of this to anyone, and wait for things to settle down.'

'But supposing the murderer saw me?'

'He wouldn't have taken this long to track you down. Go home. Here's some money to take a cab, and if you need anything at all, just let me know.'

Having seen to his customer, Joseph pricked up his ears hopefully. 'Shall I go with him, Boss?'

'No need, our friend is becoming a real Parisian. And besides, I need you here.'

Disappointed, Joseph climbed his ladder and pretended to tidy the hardback books. Samba took both Victor's hands in his and praised him for being a true humanitarian, just like his namesake, the illustrious writer.

'Oh, I nearly forgot, maybe it's not important, but . . . the man who went into the cave just before Monsieur Danilo, dropped this. I kept it, it's pretty. I said to myself that I would be able to use it as a model because I do silver filigree work, which I stick onto canes, boxes or cigar boxes.'

Victor started. He saw a flash of gold on the open palm of the old man, the band from a cigar. His heart was thumping.

'At precisely what time did you discover the body? Think carefully, it's very important.'

'I don't need to think carefully. It was seven o'clock – we were meant to have dinner as soon as he had changed.'

At seven o'clock yesterday, Tasha was here with me, thought Victor.

'See you soon,' were his parting words to Samba, as he hurried upstairs.

Cigar, Ducovitch, Tasha . . .

*

I should have known! I'm a hopeless detective! Every time I've suspected someone, they've been murdered. Ostrovski, then Ducovitch, whose turn is it now?

He pounced on *Le Figaro de la Tour* and carefully studied the series of names. Then he compared them with those recorded on the loose sheets of the Golden Book, which he had copied into his notebook. The names were in a different order; they should have read like this:

1st sheet. Rosalie Bouton. Madame de Nanteuil, alias *Eugénie Patinot*. The three children. *John Cavendish.*

2nd sheet. *Constantin Ostrovski. B. Godunov. Tasha's caricature.* Guillermo de Castro . . .

3rd sheet. A series of twenty names and *Kenji Mori.*

The first four he had highlighted had met their maker. Which left Tasha and . . . Kenji.

He hurtled down the stairs, rushing like a whirlwind past a bemused Joseph.

On the ground floor of the *Le Passe-partout* offices, in the typesetting room, the Linotypist, in long black apron, was operating the machine used to cast the blocks of type. Isidore Gouvier was pacing up and down, chewing the end of a cigar and overseeing the page-setter who was finishing off the final proof. Under the ceaselessly tapping brush, the type bit into the damp pasteboard, hollowing out the blank spaces so that the headlines stood out in relief.

Gouvier noticed Victor and nodded in greeting. The noise of the Linotype was so deafening that he did not even attempt to say hello, but instead invited him to the first floor by pointing upwards.

'Is Antonin Clusel here?' asked Victor.

'No. Can I help you?'

'It's not important, but since you ask . . . It's about that rag-and-bone man, you know, the one who died at Batignolles station last month. The other day in the café, you said—'

'Oh, yes, cardiac arrest – at least that's what they told me at the local police station. But now I wonder. You'll have seen that there's been a fourth murder at the Expo.'

'But were you there, at Batignolles station?'

'Yes, with the little Russian, to cover the arrival of the bison killer. She did some excellent drawings, but Marius decided at the eleventh hour to pull my article. Perhaps he was influenced by Beau Brummel.'

'Brummel?'

'Clusel, the king of reporters, our very own dandy. You must surely have noticed the flower in his buttonhole, his starched cravat artistically knotted on the right, his fashionable suits. He thinks a lot of himself. He must have insisted on having his article included on that unexpected birth in mid-air. Let me explain: on the twelfth of May, a woman gave birth to a little girl in one of the lifts of the Eiffel Tower. The event of the century, you would have thought! I'm of the old school, I don't give a fig for that kind of thing. I'm interested in ferreting about, uncovering unusual or disturbing events. Births, even acrobatic ones, I find dull. Each to his own. As for Clusel, sooner or later he'll become a naturalistic novelist, he loves those heart-warming stories.'

'So Mademoiselle Kherson was there with you?'

'I've just said so. She's a good girl, but the boss takes advantage of her. He made advances towards her, but she wasn't interested. You should see her pictures, she's very talented. She'll go far. Why are you so curious?'

'I'm planning to write a serial and that story could be an interesting way to start,' replied Victor, casually. 'What make is your cigar?'

'Cuban.'

'Havana?'

'Yeah, it's not just cheap rubbish. Do you want one?'

'Oh, well . . .'

Gouvier opened a door and Victor followed him.

'I may as well tell you that this little indulgence is beyond my means. Clusel gets them for me, he nicks them from the boss. Quite right, seeing as we're paid a pittance.'

They were in a spacious room, containing two desks surrounded by shelves crammed with old papers. A little nook for a bathroom – with a stand holding a shaving brush, razors, soap, and a basin – had been contrived behind a screen. A camp bed had been set up in a corner.

Gouvier carried on talking as he held out the cigar box to Victor, who helped himself. 'The large desk is Marius's, the writing desk near the window is Clusel's, but he usually prefers to write his articles in the café.'

Victor noticed the bottom of the cupboard that Gouvier had just opened, and where he now replaced the box of cigars before closing the doors.

'Where are the others?' enquired Victor.

'At the ceremony.'

'What ceremony?'

'The presentation of the endowment to the proud parents of the baby born on the Tower, by the butchers of the Gros-Caillou district,' growled Gouvier, passing the stump of his cigar from one corner of his mouth to the other. 'They have christened their little girl Augusta-Effeline.' He sniggered. 'That's a laugh. Effeline! Speeches, medals, drum rolls, all the fanfare. And large amounts of money, of course.'

'Where's this taking place? When is it?'

'At four o'clock, first platform. Afterwards everyone will go down to the garden party that's been organised in front of the fountain. If it sounds tempting, you can have my ticket because, frankly, for me, all those crowds . . . Here you are.'

As Victor pocketed the ticket, the page-maker knocked on the door. 'M'sieur Isidore, you wanted me?'

'Yes, here you are, print this for me,' replied Gouvier, giving him a crumpled paper.

'But it's already full to bursting! We'll never get it out if you keep adding copy right up to the last minute!'

'I'll sort it out. Excuse me, Monsieur Legris. I'll be back.'

Victor stood still a moment, then walked out onto the landing and listened. The Linotype had stopped rumbling and from the ground floor the echoes of an argument could be heard. He returned to the room, opened the cupboard and bent down to examine closely something that had made him wince a few moments earlier. He broke into a sweat.

He was about to leave the room when someone called his name. He stopped and waited impatiently.

'I hadn't seen you leave,' said Gouvier, out of breath, 'and I forgot to tell you something that might be important. Your colleague, the Japanese man, came by just before you arrived. He asked me exactly the same thing as you.'

'About Les Batignolles?'

'No, he wanted to know where the rest of the team were.'

Victor didn't immediately register the significance of this information. When he finally understood he was already running as fast as he could to find a cab.

A merciless sun beat down on the participants at the endowment ceremony, grouped together at the foot of the Eiffel Tower. Around them was a heaving crowd of curious onlookers who had come to witness the 'family photo'. In the first row, decked out in ill-fitting brand-new clothes, with shiny faces, stood Monsieur and Madame Moinot with their daughter Augusta-Effeline's perambulator. Already a celebrity at the age of a month and a half as a result of her entry into the world between the first and second platforms of the Tower, the baby had received testimonies of affection from all over France. These were heaped up in another perambulator: dolls, drinking bottles, lace bonnets, gingerbread and caramels. The curate of the church of Gros-Caillou was jealously guarding this treasure.

Marius Bonnet, Eudoxie Allard, Antonin Clusel and Tasha Kherson were standing a bit further on, along with other members of the press near a shiny brass ensemble.

The official photographer, his eye glued to his viewfinder, recorded the scene for posterity. There was applause and then the guests went along the gardens towards the pillars of the Tower, where they disappeared into the lifts. The presentation of the endowment by Gustave Eiffel was due to take place on the first platform. It was 3.30.

André Maheux had had enough. There was not an ounce of shade in front of the north pillar where he had been standing guard since midday. He was suffocating in his greatcoat, which was sticking to his back. His helmet, adorned with its red plume, was gripping his head so tightly that he felt as if it were about to explode, and the strap of his rifle was sawing into his shoulder. 'Damned awful job,' he murmured, watching a group of well-endowed elegant ladies, and comforted himself with the reflection that their corsets must be digging deep into their flesh. That would serve them right for having the privilege of attending the stand-up buffet by the fountain, whilst he must be on show, his throat dry and his stomach empty. He could kiss goodbye to any prospect of lunch because these kinds of festivities generally lasted hours. He thought about wiping a drop of sweat that was hanging at the end of his nose when he saw an Asian-looking man in a bowler hat. On seeing him approach with assurance, he felt sure that he was a diplomat attached to one of the various oriental delegations. So when the Chinaman held out a card covered with bizarre symbols he let him through the cordon without bothering to read the invitation.

Kenji bowed, and put the visiting card from the Maison Hanunori Watanabe, Importer of Prints and Curios from the

Far East, back in his pocket and hurried into the lift. He had slipped through with remarkable ease.

Scrambling from the cab at the Pont d'Iéna, Victor made for the Tower at a run. Owing to a combination of panic and thirst, his tongue was glued to the roof of his mouth, and his throat was on fire. He had a strong premonition that something terrible was about to happen. Ignoring any complaints, he elbowed his way through the tide of humanity held by barriers at some distance from the pillars. Amidst the noise could be heard discordant sounds of wind instruments being tuned up by a band. About thirty republican guards were perspiring in their uniforms, posted there to maintain order and facilitate the entry of officials to the proceedings. Out of breath, Victor reached the area where the guests had to present their special passes. He waved Gouvier's and found himself squeezed into one of the lifts between a tuba and a bass drum.

In a little room on the third platform of the Tower, a man of about sixty knotted his cravat in front of the mirror in his bathroom. Reluctantly he pulled on his frock coat, donned a top hat and examined himself critically, cursing the ceremony that forced him to put up with the intense heat dressed like this. Unfortunately there was nothing he could do about it. He went through into a sitting room furnished with sofas and armchairs.

From a round table covered with photographs and papers he picked up a photograph of a man in the prime of life, smiling broadly, and read the dedication.

Dear Friend,

I am very honoured to celebrate your Tower with the phonograph which we will install in mid-air, at three hundred metres, to sound the 'boom' of the cannon fired to signal the end of the Universal Exposition of 1889. In anticipation of this momentous day, I am continuing my research into the improvement of my kinetograph. As you are so well aware, the life of an inventor is 1% inspiration and 99% perspiration.

Sincerely,
Thomas Alva Edison

Well, I certainly agree with him about the perspiration, thought Gustave Eiffel, as he replaced the photograph and headed out to the platform where the lift awaited him.

Draped in red velvet, a podium had been set up at the entrance to the Flemish restaurant. The heat was so great that the guests avoided lengthy greetings to save their breath. They hurriedly made for a row of chairs, but were turned back by waiters in green livery protecting this special area, which was reserved for officials. There were protests, grumbles and stirrings in the crowd, whilst the courageous ones among them, who had not flinched from coming up on foot, were entertaining themselves by identifying the fashionable people.

'The Comtesse de Salignac and her niece Valentine, a very eligible young lady,' someone said.

'Very eligible she may be, but she's not a pretty face!' someone else replied.

'And that one who's wiping his bald head under his topper is the Duke of Frioul!'

'The tall thin one who looks like a goat, that's Blanche de Cambrésis.'

'And her friend Adalberte de Brix. They say she's buried three husbands!'

Victor had wandered as far as the podium. He scanned the crowd, despairing of finding the person he was looking for in that patchwork of faces. Suddenly he caught sight of some marguerites amongst the stove-pipe hats. Bent over her sketchpad, Tasha was urgently drawing with her charcoal. Not far from her, Marius Bonnet, Eudoxie Allard and Antonin Clusel were whispering to each other. Victor attempted to join her, but then a male figure caught his eye. The man was standing behind the *Le Passe-partout* team at the corner of the restaurant. The garlands of flags hanging over the restaurant's wood panelling cast shadows over his face. The knotted cravat on his shirt produced an incongruous flash of colour amongst the sombre frock coats. Victor recoiled as if he had been hit in the stomach. Only one person would wear such a loud pink silk cravat: Kenji Mori.

Someone shouted his name.

'Monsieur Legris! Cooee!'

Eudoxie was waving wildly at him. Marius, Antonin and Kenji all turned their heads towards him. One of the three men raised a hand, inviting him over. Victor gasped. Gloves. The man was wearing thick gloves. Who had mentioned gloves . . . ?

A cab driver. The cab driver involved in the Ostrovski affair! *Gloves in this heat . . .* Gloves to protect himself!

Victor realised the danger of the situation, but was so dazed he could do nothing. It was him!

The applause died down and the fanfare started with the opening bars of *La Marseillaise*. As Gustave Eiffel went up onto the podium, there was a sudden movement in the crowd. Taking advantage of the commotion, Victor made for Tasha, then suddenly changed course to the right, strode all along the gallery and reached the north staircase leading to the second platform. He went up a few steps without bothering to see if the man was following him. He was certain that he would. *Come on, you bastard, come on!*

He had to lead him away from Tasha at all costs. He spun round and bounded up the steps towards the souvenir shop. Glancing in the shop window, he saw that the man in the gloves had taken the bait. Now all Victor could rely on were his legs. A lift arrived from the ground floor. He threw himself into the crowd which emerged and mingled around them.

A voice sounded in his ear: 'It's a small world, isn't it, my friend?'

Victor turned. The man in gloves smiled, his hands deep in his pockets. Victor forced himself to look at him. 'Gouvier gave me his invitation. He said that—'

But he was unable to finish his sentence. The man crushed his foot with his heel, pressing down with all his weight. Victor yelled and tried to get through the people, but the pain slowed him down. He saw the man holding something in the palm of his hand. He succeeded in getting to the south pillar but stumbled against a woman and stayed still, waiting for the needle soaked in curare to sink into his flesh. He had time to remember that one day he had found on the banks of the Seine a fish rejected by the fisherman and still alive, only the whites of its eyes visible, its mouth perforated.

The man was coming closer, smiling. Victor had never felt such hatred. He wanted to express it by cursing at him but before he could, a shadow appeared. It raised its arm and with a karate chop, felled the man in gloves, who collapsed like a marionette. Victor, watching the scene, saw it as a succession of images, each momentarily suspended before being replaced by the next in muffled silence. It was like a real chronophotographic sequence: the incredulous expression of the man, features contorted in rage, the implacable force of the assailant, the hand knocked off course, the tattooing needle embedded up to the hilt in the thigh through the finely striped material of the trousers.

Marius Bonnet's face wore a final expression of surprise. As he had planned, death had come to the meeting, but he was the one who had been struck down by the velvet glove.

Gradually Victor began to hear sounds again: there was a commotion and shouting. He took a few steps, intending to pick up his Panama, but his muscles refused to obey him. He looked down at the gasping body on the floor, then back up at Kenji.

'Good timing,' he managed to say blankly.

CHAPTER FOURTEEN

Saturday 2 July

THE Comtesse de Salignac had divided up the territory. Raphaëlle de Gouveline had been assigned to the shelves on the left, Adalberte de Brix and Blanche de Cambrésis those on the right. Mathilde de Flavignol, seconded by Valentine, was raking conscientiously through the bookcases in the middle.

'Hurry up. Look, he's coming back!' the Comtesse shouted in her role as lookout. 'So did you find *Which One?*'

'No sign of it. But this one looks quite good: *The Rape of Lucrece* by William Sha— Shakes—'

The bookshop door opened and in came Joseph, waving a copy of *Le Passe-partout*.

'A special edition about the business on the Tower!'

'Let's see! Let's see!' the women cried.

With a wave of his feather duster he made them step back.

'A bit of quiet, please! Silence! The article is signed "Antonin Clusel". I know him. He came here. He's an acquaintance of Monsieur Legris's.'

'And where is Monsieur Legris?' the Comtesse asked.

'At police headquarters. Inspector Lecacheur called him in, along with Monsieur Mori. What a business!'

Joseph sat down on his stool, unfolded the newspaper and read out:

'In the last ten days, several deaths have occurred in unusual circumstances which have sent the Universal Exposition into mourning, and mystified the police. Was it a succession of accidental deaths caused by bee-stings or a series of planned murders? Antonin Clusel lifts the veil on this mystery, by revealing to the public the confession of Marius Bonnet, which he had left him. Bonnet met his end yesterday afternoon on the first platform of the Eiffel Tower.'

'When I think we were there, it sends shivers down my spine!' exclaimed the Comtesse.

Lowering the newspaper, Joseph looked at her sternly. 'Do you want to hear the murderer's posthumous confession or not?' he asked caustically.

'Certainly, my friend, do go on.'

'In that case, I want to be able to hear a pin drop, do you hear?'

He sat back on his perch and started to read Bonnet's confession:

'Have you ever felt the horrible sensation of iron claws tearing your body apart? Have you felt that you were suffocating, and that in your distress you were unable to react because you were so paralysed by pain? This is what I felt for the first time last year, when I attended the opening of the Institut Pasteur.

'My doctor informed me that I was suffering from angina, something that could kill me if I continued to burn the candle at both ends. But was I going to give up journalism and everything that makes life interesting? Of course not. As my life expectancy was seriously limited, I decided to jump a few stages and immediately realise my life-long dream of owning a newspaper that would be more popular than *Le Petit Journal*.

'I succeeded in obtaining a rich backer in Constantin Ostrovski. He financed me privately by giving me a personal loan. I signed a promissory note that I would honour the debt on 31 December 1889. Shortly after the launch of *Le Passe-partout*, in April, he reneged on the agreement and demanded that I repay both the capital and the interest, or else he would shut down the newspaper. When one's spent twenty years feeding popular taste, one has no illusions about human nature. With a little diplomacy I managed to get a few more weeks' grace. I immediately saw there was only one possible alternative to paying: ridding myself of him. I was going to commit the perfect crime, a motiveless crime, and at the same time I would send the circulation of *Le Passe-partout* sky high by giving my readers a mystery as disturbing as Jack the Ripper. Very soon my plan was ready. It consisted in eliminating a certain number of individuals with nothing in common except that they were present in the same place at the same time. Of course Constantin Ostrovski would be one of them. Utterly disorientated, the police would search in vain for the logic behind these murders.

'What weapon would I use? A revolver? Too noisy. A knife? Too gory. Then I remembered that Ostrovski had a taste for unusual objects. Amongst other things he had a collection of gourds and pots he had bought from a Venezuelan dealer. He had once shown me the contents: some brown, crumbly substance, mixed with earth, which he called "Death in a velvet glove". He said it was the sap from a plant that kills very quietly – curare, used by South American Indians. I pointed out the danger of storing something this toxic so casually, but he replied that one would still need to know how to prepare the fatal dose.

'I read a large number of works about poison, especially those by Claude Bernard. I learnt how to obtain a solution that could be administered by injection from some pure curare simply by boiling it in distilled water and then filtering it. It was easy to steal one of Ostrovski's ceramic pots. The next question was, how to inject the curare? With a Pravaz syringe? With a trocar? I wasn't sure what to do. Perhaps I could get something from a pharmacy? No, too risky. Then fortune smiled upon me. In my friend Victor Legris's bookshop, there's a display cabinet where his business associate, Kenji Mori, has on show all his travel souvenirs. When I saw the tattooing needles he had brought back from Siam, I almost cried with joy: I had the ideal weapon.'

'That's monstrous!' Joseph cried.

'What a terrible world we live in,' said Valentine.

'Indeed, Mademoiselle. It's best to escape from it when possible,' said Joseph, pleased that he worked amongst books. He went on:

'I now needed to test the strength of my curare on a human guinea pig. I refer you to a short item in *Le Figaro* of 13 May: "CURIOUS DEATH OF A RAG-AND-BONE MAN. A rag-and-bone man from Rue de la Parcheminerie has died from a bee-sting . . ." A bee? Not at all! That was me! My method had shown itself to be reliable; now I just needed to carry out my plan.

'Ostrovski had been chosen by the editorial team of *Le Figaro de la Tour* as their Man of the Day, which meant he would necessarily be signing the Golden Book. This small ceremony was to take place before lunch on 22 June. So I decided to murder the signatories whose names appeared in the book immediately before and after his.

'I concocted an alibi. On the pretext of celebrating the fiftieth edition of *Le Passe-partout*, on that day I invited my editorial team along with Messieurs Legris and Mori for a drink at the Anglo-American bar on the first floor of the Tower.

'I got there first. Mixing with the sightseers on the second platform, I watched the signatories, particularly the woman in red with the children. She was standing in the queue immediately in front of a big fellow in a pith helmet, who in turn immediately preceded Ostrovski. When she went back down to the first floor, I followed her. The gallery was teeming with people. I went up to the bench she was sitting on, pretended to trip, and pricked her on the nape of the neck. Unfortunately I had a bit of bad luck and the needle slipped through my glove and broke. I got the point back but I lost the handle. I had no time to waste and met my friend Victor at the entrance to the Anglo-American bar.

'When the body of the woman in red was discovered, I was the first to question the children and find out their names. That evening I posted two anonymous letters, addressed to *L'Éclair* and my own newspaper, which gave the impression that Eugénie Patinot had been killed because she knew too much.

'Was it cunning or caution? Inspector Lecacheur decided to favour the theory of death from natural causes. What did it matter? Their simplistic explanation meant I could fan the fires of the controversy in my articles, heightening the public appetite for the sordid or irrational side of the case. The print runs of *Le Passe-partout* increased dramatically.

'I then went to find out the names of my next victims in the Golden Book and discovered with astonishment that my illustrator, Mademoiselle Tasha Kherson, was amongst the signatories on 22 June. Had she seen me there? I had everything at stake and, in a jokey fashion, I reproached her for cheating on *Le Passe-partout* with the Golden Book. She laughed, she found the whole thing absurd: writing one's name, profession and address down just to prove that one had the hundred sous needed to go up the Tower. If her neighbour had not insisted, she would never have drawn that caricature. In any case he had used a pseudonym, Boris Godunov. I noticed that was the name that immediately followed Ostrovski's.

'I had no problem in finding out where John Cavendish, the man in the pith helmet, was staying. But before killing him I needed to steal another tattooing needle from Victor Legris's shop. I managed this quite easily the very same morning I sent a telegram signed Louis Henrique, requesting Cavendish's presence at the Colonial Palace. Everything happened without a hitch, and the American breathed his last at the very moment that Tasha Kherson appeared on the scene.'

'The little redhead,' said Joseph thoughtfully as he turned the page.

'I arranged a meeting with Ostrovski to return the sum he had lent me. We had decided to bring our arrangement to a close in a cab. I brought out a bundle of papers and demanded to see the document I had signed. He complied, and I pricked him on the throat. When I rummaged through his pockets he was already unconscious. I found a calling card in the name of Victor Legris, which annoyed me. The cab left me outside the Magasins du Louvre, then continued on its way to Quai de Passy. I returned to my apartment, changed, and lay down for a short while as I was tired. Mid-afternoon, I joined the team at the pavement tables of Le Jean Nicot. Victor Legris happened to be passing by and he sat down with us. In the course of conversation, he mentioned the death of Jean Méring the rag-picker and Henri Capus's doubts about the bees.'

'Méring? I'm the one who mentioned that to the boss. I even lent him the notebook where I'd noted it down!' Joseph exclaimed.

'You're intelligent, aren't you?' whispered Valentine in admiration.

Joseph blushed and carried on:

'I was in a panic. Victor seemed to be suggesting that there was a link between the death of the rag-picker and the deaths at the Expo. Victor, whose calling card was in Ostrovski's pocket. Victor, whose needles I had stolen. How could he know about things that the press had never mentioned? I decided to visit Capus. There was no chance that he would identify me. On the day of Buffalo Bill's arrival, I had pricked Méring before he'd joined him. Capus told me that a fellow journalist had come by the previous day to ask him some questions. He'd written his name down: Victor Legris from *Le Passe-partout*. I was frightened, I lost my self-control; this man knew too much. I grabbed a scalpel that he was using to dissect a rat and I slit his throat.'

The ladies cried out in horror. Unperturbed, Joseph went on:

'As soon as I was sure he was dead, I undressed him, laid him out on his bed and covered him with a sheet.

'The next day, I had a cab driver take a note signed "Capus" to Victor's home. In it he asked Victor to visit him. I returned to Rue de la Parcheminerie and lay in wait for my prey. I was there in the shadows, my arm raised, ready to smash his skull, when I suddenly had a turn. I missed my target, my heart was racing. I just about managed to drag myself to the newspaper.

'Even while I waited to resolve this problem, I needed to continue with my plan and rid myself of the fourth person on the list, Danilo Ducovitch, alias Boris Godunov, Tasha Kherson's next-door neighbour. Knowing about my connections in the world of the arts, she had asked me to arrange an audition for her friend at the Opera House. That's how I found out he was working at the Human Habitation exhibit where he was playing prehistoric man. Nothing was easier than surprising him in his cave.

'Thursday 30 June, ten in the evening. All I need to do now is to see off Tasha Kherson with a view to throwing suspicion on Victor Legris by leaving the tattooing needle in the young woman's body.'

'Here ends Marius Bonnet's confession. His criminal plan was foiled thanks to the courage and wisdom of Victor Legris and Kenji Mori. But his dream did come true. *Le Passe-partout*'s circulation is on track to equal that of *Le Petit Journal*. It is not for me to judge the actions of my editor-in-chief. I am simply respecting his final wishes.

'Antonin Clusel'

Joseph closed the newspaper.

'Your name isn't mentioned anywhere,' said Valentine, disappointed.

'Real heroes always remain in the shadows,' he declared in a world-weary way.

Late Afternoon, Saturday 2 July
Their return from police headquarters was inauspicious. Victor and Kenji did not exchange a single word. They crossed the bookshop, one behind the other, muttering a vague 'Hello' to Joseph as they passed.

Disconcerted by their attitude, he just called out: 'Germaine has left you something cold to eat!'

Kenji rooted around in the cupboards and took out two plates, two sets of cutlery and heated the water for his tea. Slumped in front of the bowls of crudités, Victor was rolling bread balls.

'That ham looks a bit strange,' said Kenji, sitting down.

'Like us,' Victor grumbled.

They finally dared look each other in the face and were able to see the ravages of the last few hours. With red eyelids, rough cheeks, and drawn features, Kenji really looked his age. As for Victor, deprived as he had been of proper sleep and food for several days, he was beginning to resemble a ghost.

'You're right,' Kenji agreed, 'we're not at our best. But it's not just our bodies that have been affected.'

'Oh, yes?'

Kenji drank down some tea.

'You suspected me. I would never have believed I could provoke such negative thoughts in someone that I think of as my son.'

Victor sighed in relief. Anything was better than silence. Daphne had often said to him when he was little: it's better always to talk about your troubles.

'Inspector Lecacheur didn't trust you either, Kenji. He didn't trust either of us. He had known the results of John Cavendish and Eugénie Patinot's autopsies since the twenty-ninth of June, so he knew they'd been poisoned with curare. What I've really been trying to do is show that you were innocent.'

He pushed back his chair, went into his apartment and quickly returned with an engraving.

'Why are you showing me a Rembrandt reproduction?' Kenji asked.

'The chiaroscuro. Shadow is what stimulates the imagination. I recently discovered that there are many shadowy areas in your life.'

'You do like to make up stories,' said Kenji, smiling.

'You gave me the taste for it.'

'Shadowy areas? Tell me where.'

'You claimed to be going to assess a book collection, but instead I saw you sell off some rare books to a book dealer and let Ostrovski have your Utamaros.'

'You followed me!'

'I felt sure you were going to meet a woman. You're so secretive about that part of your private life! You must admit that going into a luxury goods shop to buy some trinkets makes one think . . .'

'You're in the wrong business. You could have been a detective.'

'Put yourself in my shoes. What would you have thought if you'd seen on a newspaper belonging to me: "Meet J.C. 24–6 Grand Hotel Room 312"? J.C. being John Cavendish, who was found in circumstances that can be described at the very least as unusual.'

'You're right. One should chase the shadows away.'

Kenji got up, picked up the pot of sake, filled two little cups and sat down again.

'In 1858 I was nineteen. I had just finished my studies, and could speak Thai and English fluently. I met John Cavendish at the United States legation in Nagasaki. He was preparing an expedition to South-East Asia to classify flora and study the indigenous tribes. He took me on as an interpreter. We spent almost three years in Borneo, Java and Siam. In 1863 we stayed in London, where he introduced me to your father. I moved to Sloane Square. Cavendish went back to the United States and we regularly exchanged letters. A month ago he sent me a letter to let me know that he was coming to Paris, with an invitation to a reception that was to take place on the twenty-second of June at Gustave Eiffel's apartments. Do you remember that day I arrived late at the Anglo-American bar, you were with the *Le Passe-partout* team?'

'Yes, I remember. I gave you a watch for your birthday.'

'At that reception, I met my friend Maxence de Kermarec . . .'

'The antiques dealer from Rue de Tournon?'

'The very same. A few days earlier, I had suggested he buy the two Utamaro prints from me. He wasn't interested, but he knew an amateur collector, Constantin Ostrovski. He was one of Eiffel's guests. Maxence introduced me and we agreed to meet on the twenty-fourth of June at Café de la Paix on Boulevard des Capucines. That would work well for me as I was to have lunch with John Cavendish in the restaurant of the Grand Hotel. I noted down the meeting in the margin of the newspaper, which you found when you were rummaging in my room.'

'I tried to convince myself that I was reading too much into your meeting with Cavendish. What frightened me was that you knew Ostrovski, and that your name came after his on the *Figaro* list.'

'I was also worried by your perpetual absences from the bookshop. I went into your apartment and knocked over a notebook. I read the page at which it opened and I understood the gravity of the situation.'

'So we're quits, then.'

'Yes, except that I was the one who was right. I wasn't in possession of the massive amount of information that was weighing you down. All I had were the three photos you'd taken of the redhead at the Colonial Exhibition the day of Cavendish's death. The dates were written on the back. The solution was there but you missed it. Amongst the crowd I recognised a familiar figure. I urgently needed to take the train to London. I put the photos in my pocket with a view to studying them on the journey. In the station foyer at Gare du Nord I read in the newspaper of Ostrovski's death. I read the witness statement by the cabman who'd taken the fare and I realised I was on to something. If the cab driver corroborated my hunch, then I'd know who the murderer was. I gave up my trip to London and went to see Anselme Donadieu.'

'What did you need to know that was so important?'

'The description of the hat belonging to the man in the Inverness cape. Anselme Donadieu is no longer in the first flush of youth, but he has extraordinary powers of observation. Without hesitating he told me that the customer he had picked up on Place Maubert had a white hat, with a low dented crown and a wide black ribbon. He said, "That's what's called a Panama nowadays." Only one person I knew wore a hat like that, and that was Marius Bonnet. He was on the Tower the day that Eugénie Patinot died. He was also at the Colonial Palace at the time of Cavendish's death, as your photographs can attest. He was with Ostrovski in the cab. Why had he killed these three people? I was reminded of a conversation with Maxence de Kermarec and I went to see him to find out a little more. Ostrovski had sworn him to secrecy when he told him that he was financing *Le Passe-partout*. So I understood the motive for that murder: money. As to the two others, it was a mystery. I decided to go and have a snoop around at the newspaper, which was when I came across Isidore Gouvier, who told me the team were on the Tower. You know what happened next.'

They got up and went into the dining room, carrying their sake.

'For you it was a hat that got you on the right track, for me it was a cigar band that was found not far from Danilo Ducovitch's body,' Victor remarked. 'But then I made another mistake. I felt sure that Clusel was the culprit. I hurried to the newspaper offices and arrived shortly after your departure. In Bonnet's cupboard I saw the yellow kid ankle boots. I recalled Henri Capus's description of someone who had been offering advice at the very moment that Méring died, and who was wearing the self-same boots. When Gouvier mentioned your visit, I must admit that I began to doubt everything I thought I knew. I felt confused.'

'Well, now you know.'

'Oh, there are still shadowy areas! For example, *Los Caprichos*. Why did you make up that story about the bookbinder's?'

Kenji turned away and looked at the little Laumier painting for a moment.

'Appearance is no more reality than a sunset is a fire.'
He smiled and emptied his sake cup with one gulp.

Early Morning, Tuesday 5 July

Covered up, the dormer still let in enough light for the outlines of the furniture to be visible. Lying up against the wall, Tasha opened her eyes and slowly freed her arm, which was trapped under Victor's neck. She briefly looked at the man who lay asleep beside her. Something was missing this morning. She suddenly remembered Danilo Ducovitch. He would never wake her again with his singing exercises. She felt a pang. Poor Danilo, he was about to sing at the Opera House! Was he singing arias now in the company of Rossini and Mussorgsky?

Victor groaned. She put her fingers on his thigh and felt a muscle twitch. He was snoring. She loved the smell of him. Could this man, who only three days earlier she had sworn never to see again, make her happier than Hans? When he had knocked on her door a few hours earlier, embarrassed and bumbling, overflowing with flowers, the questions she wanted to ask him evaporated into thin air. She found herself once again in his arms, her mouth pressed up against his, her body wanting him and her hands finding their way through his clothes to his skin. What would happen now? Another worrying thought occurred to her. Would she lose her job at *Le Passe-partout*? If Clusel took over the newspaper, as seemed to be his plan, would he keep her on? That furious madman Bonnet had wanted to kill her. Now he was dead, but would that leave her unemployed?

Victor moved. She held her breath and turned to face the wall.

He gradually woke up and realised that he was about to fall out of the bed. He hung on to the narrow mattress, and twisted round so that his face ended up on Tasha's chest. He gave thanks to God or Providence – he wasn't sure which – for sparing them. Marius would have made a fine mess had he killed one or the other. What happens when lovers are separated by death? he asked himself, then he noticed the marks on her forearm and rolled over to kiss them. The mattress groaned. Tasha was clinging to his shoulder.

'I think the bed is going to collapse,' she murmured. 'Don't move.'

They remained motionless for a moment, laughing like idiots. Tasha got up carefully.

'Coffee?'

'Yes, but with sugar, please.'

'I don't think I have any left.'

'Well, we'll go out to have some.'

'You lead a life of luxury, don't you? You need the good things in life.'

'You, for example.'

She straightened up and stretched. He admired the splendour of her supple body. She began to dress.

'Up you get, lazybones!'

He sat up. He noticed the special edition of *Le Passe-partout* on the floor.

Because of this article, Joseph had spent the afternoon of the previous day sending away huge numbers of people who were curious to see Kenji's display cabinet.

'I just can't conceive of Bonnet being so insane as to come up with such a diabolical plan. I thought I knew him, but it was all a charade,' Victor said.

'According to Clusel he was not a madman but a genius. I thought I had the measure of him too. We'll never know everything that was going on in his mind. It's probably for the best. It's funny, you work closely with people, you get used to them, you think you have a sense of who they are, and then one day you discover you know them no better than a stranger.'

She held out his long johns. 'You can't go to the café like that.'

'Why not? Don't you like the way I look?' he asked, pulling her towards him. 'You know, as a result of this experience I'm very tempted to live with a stranger, to think about her day after day, year after year.'

He felt her stiffen.

'How about you?' he added.

'How about me, what?'

'Wouldn't you like to share my . . . private world?'

'I love you.'

She tried to break free, but he held on to her.

'Really?'

'Yes, really, despite your hot-headedness. Even if you did think I was a criminal.'

'So, marry me.'

She pushed him away gently. He stood there, naked, looking at her with a proprietorial air. She turned away, and looked at the unfinished painting on the easel.

'Ask me anything, but not that.'

'Why? Why?' He spoke in a tone of incomprehension and wounded pride.

'Because I need my freedom.'

'Your freedom . . . Does that mean spending time with the sort of friends that I would not choose to have?' He was thinking of Laumier.

'Freedom does not mean free and easy. I'm talking about my freedom to be creative,' she retorted.

'But you would be completely free with me. You could paint however and whenever you liked! What's more, I also value my independence. I'm very careful never to let people interfere in my life. Don't think I made my proposal lightly. I know life as a couple isn't simple.'

'Have you ever tried it? I have.'

He suddenly felt a blast of jealousy.

'Was it Laumier?'

She snorted. 'That oversized chubby baby? Are you joking? He was called Hans. I met him in Berlin. He was an artist, a skilled sculptor, he was kind, protective . . .'

'Did you love him?'

The look of pain on his face was not lost on Tasha.

'Yes, for a time. You're not a boy. You've had mistresses. I had a lover. Hans never proposed marriage to me and with good reason: he was already married. He installed me in a pretty room, bought me the materials I needed, cared for me. I could eat as much as I wanted, and paint. Everything was going well, and then he began judging my work. "You ought to put a bit more green here, a little less yellow here, and if I were you I'd make this character, not that one, the main subject of the painting . . . Don't you think you could lessen the light on these folds?" Gradually he undermined my work and my self-confidence. His advice may have been justified, but he was expressing his own personality, not mine. I left him. That was hard, very hard. But I took charge of my life and came to Paris.'

'You did the right thing,' Victor said, deciding to put on his long johns, relieved that the sculptor had been left behind in Berlin. 'But you're forgetting one detail – I'm not Hans.'

'I know, you are Victor.'

She stood on her tiptoes and dropped a kiss on the edge of his mouth.

'It's just that it's too soon. I'm not ready yet. You see those rickety chairs, the peeling wallpaper, the wobbly bed? I had to fight to have them. I am queen of all I survey.'

She struck a regal pose with a paintbrush between her teeth. He could not help laughing.

'You have to admit that an apartment would make you a slightly better-off queen. Instead of marrying me next week, you could come and live in a different neighbourhood near to the bookshop. I solemnly swear never to stick my nose in your artistic life.'

'Why can't we stay as we are? We could see each other every day.'

'I'm too jealous. Aren't you?'

'I saw the Laumier painting in your room. As long as you keep that on show on your dresser, I'll know that you still care for me enough not to go around having little affairs. That will be the measure of your love: my nakedness, on show to everyone, even your business associate who doesn't like me.'

She finished dressing. Victor went very still: Kenji! It was true, he didn't like Tasha. That would have to be sorted out. How? He could never have Tasha to stay at Rue des Saints-Pères for as long as Kenji lived there. And, of course, he would never be able to ask him to go and live elsewhere.

'You're probably right,' he said finally. 'Let's take our time. The main thing is that we love each other.'

Surprised at this, she gave him a sidelong glance. He looked anxious. What was he hiding? That woman done up in all her finery? She felt slightly disappointed. Her victory had been too quick. Should she be pleased or worried?

She picked up her only pair of ankle boots and sat down on a chair to put them on.

'Let me at least buy you some new shoes,' he said, kneeling down by her and caressing the tip of the shoe, which had completely lost its shape.

'I'd really like that. Some cakes too, please. And flowers, as many as you like.'

'And then . . .'

'Then we'll see. All in good time.'

She passed him his frock coat. Before they left she looked around happily at the untidy room: she had uncovered the dormer and sunshine was now flooding in.

A FEW HISTORICAL NOTES
ON THE UNIVERSAL EXPOSITION OF 1889

The fourth French Universal Exposition opened on 6th May 1889 to coincide with the centenary of the French Revolution.

In 1884, Charles de Freycinet, President of the Exposition Council, had announced that its centrepiece would be a monumental tower, and launched a competition for its design. Seven hundred entries were received, including fanciful ones such as the watering can tower which would have sprinkled Paris with water on very hot days. The contract was won by Gustave Eiffel, the celebrated builder of metal structures. His tower would become the tallest building in the world, a symbol of French power and industry.

In January 1887 seven thousand tons of iron and cast-iron began to be assembled on the Champ-de-Mars. Painted a reddish bronze, the Tower rose gradually, and soon came to dominate the Parisian skyline, provoking the admiration of some and the anger of others. J.-K. Huysmans called it 'a solitary suppository, riddled with holes', Guy de Maupassant 'a disgraceful skeleton'. As for the poet Verlaine, he made detours around Paris to avoid seeing it.

Inaugurated on 31 March 1889, the Tower rose to a height of 300 metres. The many pavilions making up the Exposition were laid out below. Everything was ready to receive massive crowds, which nonetheless exceeded all expectation: in six months 3,512,000 people ascended the 1,710 steps of the tower, and 33 million visited the Exposition.

In the aisles filled with rickshaws and Arab donkey-drivers, a visitor might come across the Prince of Wales, Savorgnan de Brazza, various crowned heads or perhaps Buffalo Bill or Sarah Bernhardt. English, German Spanish and Russian could be heard. As for the French visitors, they might just as easily have a southern or a

Burgundian accent as a Parisian one. There were fewer workers than petit-bourgois, because the price of entry, at five francs (equivalent to one hundred sous) including access to the first floor of the Tower was expensive for those who earned on average 4.80 francs a day.

The Exposition Pavilions were wide-ranging in their themes, but with a definite emphasis on all things French and modern innovation in general.

The immense Machinery Hall, in the shadow of the Tower, contained a major exhibit of French iron, a symbol of burgeoning capitalism: industrialists and men of influence had sealed their alliance in the blast furnaces and in the banks. Indeed, the Universal Exposition itself would prove to be an excellent investment for the capital city and for the country as a whole.

On show at the Exposition were also all the inventions of fin-de-siècle France, a period which saw the appearance of the first submarine, the airship of the Renard brothers, the bicycle, and the four-stroke internal combustion engine. Though not yet widespread in Paris, the wonder of electricity was much in evidence on the Champ-de-Mars and, at night, the Eiffel Tower was ablaze, surmounted by a tri-coloured searchlight, lighting up the hills of Chaillot.

Foreign inventions were also very much in evidence: in the Palace of Liberal Arts, the latest photography and cameras were on display, including George Eastman's Kodak box camera; in the Machinery Hall Marinoni's rotary printing-press heralded the enormous circulation that was soon to be enjoyed by newspapers, whilst the Edison exhibit allowed people to discover his many devices, from the gramophone to the kinetoscope. As for the telephone, invented in 1876 by Alexander Graham Bell, its usage was becoming more common: the first public telephone boxes appearing in Paris in 1885.

The fine arts were also well represented with their own pavilion, reflecting the continuing strength of classicism despite the challenge of the synthetist realist painters. These painters, led by Gauguin, staged an alternative exhibition of their works in the *Café Volpini*. Although some artists were concerned about the advance of photography, others saw it not as a threat, but as a complementary art form allowing reality to be captured in a new way. Others still, began to turn their back on realism and to embark in artistic directions that would radically change the history of painting, a departure already noticeable in the work of the impressionists in the 1850's. The same trends affected music and literature with naturalism and symbolism having their passionate followers.

The Exposition was also an opportunity to introduce the French to their colonies. Tunisia had been a French protectorate since 1881, Annam since 1883, and Cambodia since 1884. Bamako was occupied in 1882. People were talking about Madagascar and the Congo. They were closely following the digging of the Panama Canal and taking a great interest in China.

Curious spectators crammed into the Esplanade des Invalides to admire the full-sized reconstruction of one of the temples of Angkor. Enthralled by the Javanese dancers, the crowds passed effortlessly from New Caledonia to Cochin China and crossed the Senegalese village to relax in the Algerian café. Millions of people who had never left France, or sometimes even Paris, discovered whole new worlds. Italy, Spain, Hungary, Russia, the two Americas, Japan . . . the entire globe awaited them on the Champ-de-Mars, accessed by the little Decauville railway line.

The Paris of 1889 was made up of a series of villages, some were poorer districts, others were reserved for the more fortunate, and, following the work of Haussman, was already very much as we know it today. In that year, heralding the beginnings of the souvenir industry, one particular location began to be represented in miniature.

291

These tiny models, made from fragments of the iron used to build the Tower itself, were soon on sale in shops all over the world. The Eiffel Tower had become the undisputed symbol of Paris in 1889 and of France itself, a role it continues to fulfil with ease to the present day.

Also from Gallic Books:

THE CHÂTELET APPRENTICE
Jean-François Parot
Paperback May 2007
978-1-906040-00-0
£11.99

THE SUN KING RISES
Yves Jégo and Denis Lépée
Paperback October 2007
978-1-906040-02-4
£7.99

THE OFFICER'S PREY
Armand Cabasson
Paperback October 2007
978-1-906040-03-1
£7.99

Coming in 2008
The second in the Victor Legris series
THE PÈRE LACHAISE MYSTERY

THE CHÂTELET APPRENTICE
A Nicolas Le Floch Mystery
Jean-François Parot

Paris, February 1761. A police officer disappears and Nicolas Le Floch, a young Breton police recruit, is instructed to find him. When unidentified human remains are found it becomes a murder investigation. As Paris descends into Carnival debauchery it is Le Floch's skill, courage and integrity that will help him unravel a mystery which threatens to implicate the highest in the land.

Jean-François Parot is a diplomat and historian who lives in the Loire.

'A new Maigret is born: Nicolas Le Floch' *Madame Figaro*

'Complex and imaginative intrigues . . . revealing the workings of power in the Ancien Régime' *Le Figaro*